KRISHNA
THE GOD WHO LIVED AS MAN

Warm Regards,

From *Krishnaayan* in Gujarati by **Kaajal Oza-Vaidya**

Krishna

The God Who Lived as Man

Without Krishna, no form of art is complete,
To write about you is to worship the Divine.
Bhawana Somaaya

Published by

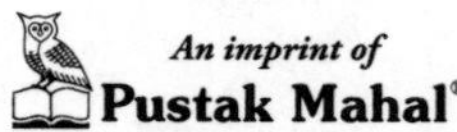

Administrative office and sale centre
J-3/16 , Daryaganj, New Delhi-110002
☎ 23276539, 23272783, 23272784 • *Fax:* 011-23260518
E-mail: info@pustakmahal.com • *Website:* www.pustakmahal.com

Branches
Bengaluru: ☎ 080-22234025 • *Telefax:* 080-22240209
E-mail: pustak@airtelmail.in • pustak@sancharnet.in
Mumbai: ☎ 022-22010941 • 022-22053387
E-mail: rapidex@bom5.vsnl.net.in
Patna: ☎ 0612-3294193 • *Telefax:* 0612-2302719
E-mail: rapidexptn@rediffmail.com

ISBN 978-81-223-1027-6

Edition 2014

Printed at : Glorious Printer, Delhi

Dedicated to

My sister Seema Thakkar
who is a constant and
strong support in my life

Acknowledgements

Rekha (*bhabhi*) Thakkar for always being there to explain the Gujarati words into English.

Shoneize Akhtar for patiently keying in several drafts of the manuscript.

And finally, Kajal and Manhar Gadhia for their undiminished support and undying spirit to facilitate this project.

Author's Note

Krishnaayan has no introduction.

People said to me, "Write something new on Krishna...Too much has been written on him already...." This included my father, Digant Oza.

And yet, ironical as it is, the Krishna I have always been looking for, I discovered in this book.

This can probably be because I have never revered Krishna as a Lord.

At best, I would describe him as an awesome personality. Born 20,000 years ago, if that really happened, he is the biggest miracle of life.

In *Mahabharata*, he is portrayed as a politician; in the *Bhagawat*, He is the Lord. In *Gita*, he is the *guru*, the fountainhead of knowledge. His association with Draupadi so many centuries ago is an ideal example of man-woman friendship. With Rukmini, his spouse, it was an equal reciprocation of love and respect; and with Radha, his attachment was so pure and intense that even today so many years later, we go beyond the society norms and revere 'Radha Krishna' as deities.

Undisputedly he was an overwhelming persona, but at the end of the day, an individual. Then why cannot we as ordinary mortals perceive and relate to him as a human being?

I have sensed Krishna reside inside and around me in my happy and sad moments. This can be because I have read that when Krishna deserted his body, his soul continued to linger over the Cosmos and that is why so many years later, his fragrance... philosophy... or rather his purity and divinity prevail in our lives guarding the entire Universe.

I have often wondered over the psyche of such an enticing man like him who encountered so many challenges in his life. I wondered what a man like him would be thinking about in his last moments.... Would he have reflected on his sojourn, and if so, would he have preferred to make a few alterations in his journey? In case, he was granted a boon to live his life again, would he live it the same way or would he live it differently...? These questions have often nagged me.

It has always intrigued me if a man perceived by the Universe as infallible ever felt the void for an ideal woman in his life? Ancient scriptures reveal that Krishna courted sixteen thousand one hundred and eight queens, but was this a reality or a fantasy? In all probabilities, the details will remain a mystery, and at the same time, one cannot overlook the fact that at least four women out of his innumerable queens played a pivotal role in Krishna's life...

His beloved (Radha), his wives (Rukmini and Satyabhama), and his friend (Draupadi).... Four intense and meaningful relationships.... I have always been curious to know what these women thought about Krishna, what did they feel for him?

Perhaps, this book is an outcome of that curiosity.... It is about his relationship with all these four women.

We inherit blood relationships from our genes and they travel with us all life long. But a beloved and to a great extent, a spouse and a friend, are relationships we gather in our journey of life. These are choices made out of our personal judgements. We sow the seeds and nurture the bonds....

It is believed that Krishna had foreseen his exit. He is also said to be the only living soul who had relived his lifespan in his last moments.... For me *Krishnaayan — The God Who Lived as Man* is his introspection during those last moments.

The book does not borrow from the scriptures nor is it an attempt to verify the various researches on the subject. I have deliberately refrained from chronological events and references of who preceded or succeeded him....

This is a story out of my imagination, my attachment for Krishna. It is my perception of his final moments!

In moments of conflict, I have preferred to look inside my heart for answers; so in a way, I'm Draupadi, Rukmini, Radha or Satyabhama of this story. Perhaps it is my undying passion to make Krishna a part of my life that has made this book possible. It is my offering to the Lord that I share with his innumerable devotees.

So here's presenting a contemporary Krishna, somebody you can meet over a cup of coffee or bump into your daily routine. He is neither a *yogi*, nor a *guru*, and definitely not a miracle worker. He could be somebody who would stroll beside you at your morning walk and casually relieve you of your self-doubts. He is a friend you can use as a sounding board without fear of being judgemental of you.

It is my assurance that if you invest faith in him, he will safeguard you and you will never seek another friend, companion or guide....

He is the supreme example of acceptance.... Offer him anything sincerely, and he accepts it without questions! In any case, isn't what we offer him all that he has granted us in the first place?

I would like to repeat what Draupadi said in her last meeting with Krishna:

Twadiyam Vastu Govind Tubhyamev Samarpyate ।

– Kaajal Oza-Vaidya

Translator's Note

For years he was just an idol in our temple at home whom mother woke up every morning with a flame and a clanging bell.

Sometimes when she was occupied in her domestic chores, one of us sisters was instructed to follow the ritual which we did but we could somehow never match her fervour or her devotion for him.

The first time I struck an independent equation with Krishna was as a teenager when I was enrolled in *Bharat Natyam* dance lessons. In the five-year-long course of learning the art form, my colleagues and I were trained to sing paeans to the Lord and enact all the *naayikas* in his life — his mother, beloved, *sakhi* so much so that all of us unknowingly fell in love with him.

As I grew older, I learnt to decipher fact from fiction but the fragrance of the first crush lingered....

The reason I was attracted to translating *Krishnaayan* from Gujarati into English was because it explores Krishna as a man rather than as a God.

Lord Krishna is the most charismatic God of Hindu pantheon who was blessed with a boon to recreate his life in his last moments. After the torturous Yadava *yatra* to Somnath where Krishna witnesses the devastation of his entire lineage, he arrives with a bleeding foot to Prabhas Kshetra.

It is here resting beneath a *peepal* tree before the river Trivenisangam that Krishna reflects on the four most important relationships in his life — his wives (Rukmini and Satyabhama), beloved (Radha) and friend (Draupadi). Four contrasting personalities but bonded in a magnificent obsession, Krishna.

Borrowing from the fable but original in structure and content, the book is fictional and a chronicle of man-woman equations.

Did Krishna love these women as much as they loved him? Did he desire and yearn for them as much as they yearned for him? Who out of these four women was closest to his heart? Whom did he feel most secure with? Did he sometimes, unknowingly discriminate one against the other or was he able to grant all of them equal justice always? Did the four women ever fantasise trading places with one another, only to scrutinise what went on in their beloved's mind?

Was Krishna attracted to Rukmini, Satyabhama, Radha and Draupadi because they were extraordinary women or was it his halo that made them so special...? Would Krishna have been drawn to these women had he encountered them in different circumstances and surroundings?

Born in Mathura, reared in Gokul, ruled in Dwarika, was he content with the flow of his life or did he secretly desire another life and a destiny for himself?

This book is not the love story of Krishna or any one God. It is the story of every charismatic individual in contemporary times who dared to love many and was in return clamoured by several. It is the story of any arresting and sensitive person, intensely involved with his life.

A wholesome relationship comes with requisite baggage of pathos and pain. But beneath the suffering are layers of happiness emanating from attachment. Love brings enrichment and enlightenment. It is our involvement with our dear ones that adds hues to our life.... And that includes both the Supreme Entity and us ordinary mortals.

Krishna — The God Who Lived as Man is one such story of passion and pain.

– Bhawana Somaaya

[1]

Sitting beneath the *peepal* tree, Krishna closed his eyes but the images replayed in his mind. Dwarika Palace... Kurukshetra battle... Draupadi's *swayamvar mandap*... Rukmini's abduction... and glistening eyes of Satyabhama while leaving for Prabhas Kshetra.

The images conjured in sometimes flashbacks and sometimes in flash forwards. People... places... and memories!

The *peepal* tree above him spread its foliage providing a shade that resembled the Shesh*naag* (serpent) with its multiple heads opened out. Krishna looked over the three rivers — Hiranya-Kapila and Saraswati flowing before him in three different directions. This was the holy Trivenisangam located close to Somnath Temple recognised as Prabhas Kshetra and revered for literature and fine arts.

Krishna recalled that it was only some time ago that he had renovated the Somnath Temple and enhanced it with gold and silver. It was only some time ago, that the Yadavas conducted elaborate prayers and offerings here....

Today, sitting beneath the *peepal* tree, with his eyes closed, Krishna tried to relive all those moments.

He was in deep agony and conscious of a shooting pain passing through his entire body like a current.... It felt as if a thousand poisonous snakes were biting into his skin....

Before him was Jara, hands folded, seated on the ground.

Krishna's foot pierced with an arrow had formed a pool of blood on the ground.

It wasn't easy for him in his present condition to walk from the forest of Prabhas, all the way to the river shore.

It was all the result of the curse of *Mata* Gandhari...

...The curse of Durvasa...

...They had not gone futile!

One by one, all his brothers, uncles, nephews, children, grandchildren, friends and well-wishers were to be sacrificed into the flames to be finally joined by him.

It's true that Krishna had foreseen the future, but it's also true that he was just a helpless spectator to the events that unfolded before his eyes.

Krishna wondered why he had to endure the torture of watching the devastation of his own people.... Was it necessary for him to witness the tragic scenario where the Yadavas degraded themselves...?

It's true that Krishna did not actively participate on the battleground, but the violence and the bloodshed he witnessed continued to hound him even today. Was Arjuna right when he said that an empire created on the deathbed of loved ones was worthless...? Was that the reason the Pandavas could never sleep peacefully after the Kurukshetra battle...? Considering that they were the ones to initiate the battle for justice, had they in true sense conquered injustice...? Thoughts gushed into his mind and flooded him like the innumerable waves rising into the sea.

Krishna was hounded by questions and felt increasingly distraught.

He wondered if everyone felt the same way in their last moments. Innumerable memories... innumerable images... innumerable questions and innumerable expressions awakened a gamut of emotions in Krishna that didn't allow him peace even for a moment.

He tried to distract himself but could not. He was restless. He would have preferred to meditate and enter into a *samadhi* where his *aatma* (soul) could be united with *brahma* (the ultimate truth), but that was not to be. Krishna found himself embroiled in a whirlpool of emotions....

Strange... a man who lived his entire life by his principles and infinite knowledge... how could the soul of a man as enlightened as him feel so restless...?

How could somebody as clairvoyant, revered as a deity feel so out of control...? Could this be because he had conquered his future but remained distressed with his past...?

Or was this an indicator that there was no way out whereby even Krishna could save himself today?

And if this is what a deity incarnated as a human goes through, what about us poor mortals...?

The battle amongst the Yadavas had just ended.

So many dead bodies of brothers, kinsmen, children and grandchildren were all scattered over the dark, dense forest of Prabhas.

At a little distance, Krishna looked up at the skyline changing colours. The trio-rivers were getting ready to embrace the morning. There was a nip in the air and the *peepal* tree beneath which Krishna took refuge, dropped withered leaves that were strewn away in different directions, as if carrying tales of Krishna's woes.... The first streak of sunrise piercing through the dark sky formed an orange blaze resembling a *yajna* flame. Though invisible by their presence, it felt as if the ambience echoed with a team of *Brahmins* chanting religious *mantras...*

Mamaivansho Jivloke Jivbhootah Sanatanah ।
Manah Shashthanindriyani Prakrutisthani Karshte ॥

Krishna had said that after his lifetime we shall find him existing in the five ingredients of Nature, and the sixth would be the hearts of people where he would always reside.

Seated beneath the dense tree he asked himself if his was a death haunted by life or a life haunted by death, or was truth somewhere between the two...? The divine force who narrated his philosophy of life on the battlefield was restless today... and in his turbulent moment Krishna was reminiscent of his debut meeting with Draupadi.

Krishna slowly turned over the pages of his past. He was unable to fathom why Draupadi said that to him.

It was the day she was to return from Dwarika to Hastinapur and she had broached the topic unexpectedly...

...Feeling choked but voice full of force, her large expressive eyes as yet unshed with tears... Krishna had sensed her vulnerability.

"Didn't you say that...?" Draupadi repeated her query, "Didn't you say *sanshayatam vinashayti*...? You were right, my friend, awareness leads to questions. I should know this, I have lived my entire life as a question mark and every question I encountered added to my woes and tortured my dear ones like piercing arrows.... My questions, my doubts have damaged my self-esteem, bruised my loved ones! Now at least relieve me of this anxiety... pain... and questions."

More memories sprang up like waves in Krishna's mind adding to his torment.

Krishna wondered why he should be reflecting on all these episodes now, at this juncture when it was time for farewell.... Why did memories chase him like a mirage...?

Draupadi had come to him seeking freedom, but was Krishna free himself to grant her that privilege...?

So many questions still unanswered... so many people to be accountable to...! One by one they would all come seeking their rights.... All of them were to bind him and he had to seek salvation from all.

Or was it that it was only after liberating everyone that Krishna could find salvation, and knowing this he had begun the process...

◆

[2]

"You will die like a beast, alone and in anguish!" *Mata* Gandhari had cursed Krishna, when he had gone to meet her after the battle of Kurukshetra.

He could never forget her heart-wrenching voice.

It was reminiscent of mother Yashoda's outcry when many years ago, Krishna departed from Gokul.

"Probably it was the universal anguish of a mother parting with her son.... Perhaps, they all sounded the same in every century, in any *avatar*!"

Gandhari had said, "I have lost ninety-nine sons. My feet are still soiled from the blood that spurted out of Duryodhan's injured thigh... I'm exhausted of cleansing my feet again and again... the sight of Dushasan's hacked arms fallen apart from his body wake me up startled at midnight even now... Krishna, you did not do justice!"

Even Kunti, fully aware of the truth had held him solely responsible for the devastation. "Undoubtedly my sons have emerged triumphant, but what about the many mothers of Hastinapur who lost their sons? With so many families around me orphaned, how can you expect me to rejoice our victory? You will never understand the pain of Gandhari, Krishna, because you are not a mother..."

It wasn't as if Krishna did not understand Gandhari's distress. He did, but how could he explain that it was all predestined?

He was destined to endure all he did.... Destined to witness the bloodshed and the devastation.... He was destined to count their last breath himself. There was just no way out for him without fulfilling his mission and it was to Krishna's credit that through all this he remained focused, dispassionate and courageously faced the circumstances to fulfil his duties.

...*Abhyuthanama Adharmasya Tadatmanam Srujamyaham*.... The promise had to be fulfilled.

When a deity comes in the *avatar* of a human, he has to live like one. So he gets attached to his body and all the emotions emanating from it, like love, attachment or compassion. There is no escape from the anxieties associated with matters related to the mind and heart...

That is why, today, watching the suffering of his brethren, his friends and his family, Krishna felt anguished...

Once again the image of Draupadi conversing with him reoccurred before his eyes.

Twadiyam Vastu Govind Tubhyamev Samarpyate ।

✦

[3]

That day while returning to Hastinapur, Draupadi had out of the blue, broached the topic.

"I can no longer carry this burden of awareness... I don't know where I'm headed to but I know I want to be free of the baggage of your debts!"

What freedom was she referring to?

Both Krishna and Draupadi were aware of the baggage. The baggage of bonding... the longing for freedom...

They realised that their relationship was drawing to an end. Uncertain about how, where and why but both recognised their last moments together and unwittingly, prepared one another for the final parting...

Draupadi invariably always sensed Krishna's innermost thoughts and feelings. Krishna acknowledged an indescribable feeling rising within him for her. Usually it was his privilege and expertise to read everyone's thoughts and therefore it was out of turn for Krishna to feel transparent in front of Draupadi...

"Was I so deeply connected with Draupadi for her to have gauged my darkest secrets...?" Krishna asked himself, "Or was it that she had determined to free me and in the process free herself...?"

Krishna could foresee a larger message in all this, but could Draupadi? Was Draupadi aware that the only way she could liberate herself was by detaching herself from Krishna?

Draupadi had often said, "We women are better acquainted with our feelings than you men can ever be.... You get into recurring conflicts because you are unable to choose between the mind and the heart while we willingly let our hearts rule over our minds..." She had been in an argumentative mood and went about it relentlessly....

"...Tell me *sakha*, does something called mind really exist and if so, does it have any colour or shape? Also isn't it peculiar that this one specific part of the anatomy should rule our entire life, our past and also our future? It's not as if we women don't befriend our minds... we store many secrets in there but it's up to us whether we dance to its tunes or make it dance to ours.... But not men, you get possessed by your mind. You gauge every situation clinically and then take a call.... That is why men and women never think alike!"

"But thoughts don't follow any specific direction, so how do you control them?" Krishna asked Draupadi.

"*Sakha*, a mother bears five sons of different temperaments, but does that deter her from relating to all...? They exhibit different behaviour patterns and emotional quotients but they stand equal in the eyes of the mother. In that same way, I'm able to synchronise my varied thought processes. All women are not able to do it with same facility, for thoughts often get entangled like the threads in a spinning loom, but just as the loom clears the weft and warp and moves on, so do we..."

"Yes, I have always found you focused and can vouch for you conducting with clarity, not always composed though, for I have often witnessed you provoked. But you are consistently articulate in thought, word and action. How do you accomplish this so effortlessly, *sakhi*?"

"That I'm unaware of but I'm conscious of doing things the right way, whenever you have been watching me."

"It is unusual, but observing you with your different husbands has been like watching five different women..."

"Today these five women assembled as one surrenders in admiration of a complete man. A man who I place on the highest pedestal, for he's a friend... a companion... a confidant... and..."

"And what, *sakhi*...?"

"And..." Draupadi continued self-consciously, "To whom I offer all of myself... my identity, my femininity... I'm at a loss of words to express my feelings, so I surrender to you everything endowed by you and also what is not endowed by you..."

Draupadi's eyes appeared vacant. The beautiful eyes that forever danced with joy today appeared lifeless. Detached, almost disconnected with life, she stared blankly at Krishna. This was the final moment of parting. As Draupadi turned to leave, she felt something crumbling inside her.

"Is that why she had come to meet me... to seek freedom...? Or had she visited me to grant me my freedom...?" Krishna wondered. Is that the reason she said:

Twadiyam Vastu Govind Tubhyamev Samarpyate ।

✦

[4]

When Draupadi and the five brothers last visited Dwarika, little were they aware that on their next visit it would be a Dwarika without Krishna....

Before her return, Draupadi had visited Krishna in his bedchamber at dawn. This was an hour when usually nobody dared to disturb Krishna. Neither his queens, nor his brother Balram, for it was the time that Krishna devoted to prayers and meditation. He preferred isolation in the morning but Draupadi had no choice but to trespass his privacy today. What she had to communicate to him could only be expressed in private and she could not wait. If she did not visit him now, soon after his meditation, Krishna would be engrossed in the Rajyasabha.

Draupadi comprehended his routine and sought the opportune moment to have access to his private chamber.

Krishna had just concluded his prayers and looked radiant. The *chandan tilak* emblazoned on his forehead, his bare body without the armour resembled a well-sculpted marble. The image was beautiful and flawless. His waist slender like a lion, his broad shoulders and a bare chest devoid of the jewels except his *janeu* (sacred thread), his dark curly hair combed behind without the crown and a few grey strands behind his ears added to his magnificence. But most important, his large expressive eyes ever filled with eternal compassion...

Draupadi stared at him for a long time. "Probably this is how a deity born as a human should look!"

Krishna was not surprised to see Draupadi in his chamber. Still holding the *aarti thali* (plate used in prayer) in his hand, Krishna smiled at Draupadi, "Welcome *Yajnaseni*, to set my eyes on a *Devi* like you soon after my *puja* is an auspicious omen."

"*Sakha...*" Draupadi started hesitantly but could not complete her sentence. Krishna offered her a seat.

For a long while, Draupadi continued to sit demurely and stare at Krishna.

Draupadi had arrived fresh out of a shower, simple yet distractingly attractive. Her face and arms glowed and her long lustrous hair left loose was still damp and fragrant.

Though past her prime, but still curvaceous, she looked exceedingly sensual dressed in a fawn coloured bustier over which was draped a silk saree. She appeared distraught, the dark circles under her eyes revealed the story of her anguish.

Time and again Draupadi attempted to speak but could not...

Her eyes wandered all over from her palms to the ceiling and to the sky outside.... It was as if she was arranging and re-arranging her thoughts before articulating into words...! Unable to form her thoughts, she played with the edge of her saree.

"Do you want to say something, *sakhi*?" Krishna asked, "Is something bothering you?"

"Yes... but I don't know how to say it..."

"Just attempt to begin and you will find the words on your own," Krishna encouraged.

"That's true, *sakha...* I've never had to search my words with you... You've always understood what's in my mind without me having to express myself..."

"Then what prevents you today, speak without hesitation."

"No hesitation with you but today, I somehow sense fear. I fear that after expressing myself I may not be left with anything to call my own and that terrifies me..."

"How can you ever fear losing me when I'm forever with you and beside you?"

"That's it! That's what I wanted to tell you, *sakha...*" Draupadi replied looking deep into his eyes.

For the first time Krishna sensed something unfamiliar in Draupadi's eyes as if something was about to explode. It was the first time he sensed her eyes turn moist.

She tried hard to fight back tears but couldn't and slowly the dam burst. Draupadi felt a lump in her throat and without turning back, exited Krishna's chamber.

Draupadi had stomped out of the room, but so many things she had told Krishna haunted him…

Twadiyam Vastu Govind Tubhyamev Samarpyate ।

✦

[5]

It wasn't just Draupadi but everyone associated with Krishna who believed that the purpose of life was to surrender to Govind what he had bestowed on them.

"If you accept him wholeheartedly, there is no way he is going to reject you."

Udhav, Arjuna, brother Balram had acknowledged that acceptance was a part of Krishna's temperament!

He was completely devoid of contempt or rejection and when he detected it among others, he was quick to reprimand them. "It's in our capacity to conquer the inauspicious as well as the insincere for they are all extensions of originally positive emotions.... You cannot accept one side of the coin and reject another.... Sunset is inevitable after sunrise..." Krishna would say, "It's only when we accept people, things and ideas wholeheartedly that we transform into complete identities. Our fulfilment is dependent on their reciprocation, for it is only completeness that can lead to accomplishment..."

Somehow the most unattractive and the negative transformed into aesthetic and positive after coming into contact with Krishna...

For someone who lived his entire life to the fullest, Krishna cheerfully awaited his end. He was composed and conscious of something deep churning within him.

That's why probably Draupadi's words kept ringing into his ears.

"It's not in your nature to reject, Madhav, and therefore you have accepted me wholeheartedly... my happiness, unhappiness, my honour, my self-respect, my rage and my annoyance… I'm aware there are no half-baked measures about you. You leave no scope for suspicion or incompletion around you…. And still, today I desire to ask you a question, Govind. In accepting me, have you not safeguarded your own acceptance? All of us have reciprocated your trust and affection and in accepting you, have accepted your beliefs, your passion…. We have embraced your sorrows and joys without discrimination. I have relished every blessing showered by you, and today I return those innumerable moments to you. In doing so, I surrender my life time to you… I have faith that you will not reject my offering…"

She wasn't wrong. Krishna had never discriminated between his ecstasy and gloom. He lent as much importance to questions as to the answers…. He paid respect to all and received it from everyone…. He professed and practised righteousness…. No living soul, before or after him, has so profoundly internalised human behaviour. Krishna accepted all….

He had a way of addressing conflicts, of unravelling mysteries. Somehow, doors opened up wherever he walked…. His charisma was overpowering and perhaps that is why he was referred to as the All-Knowing in his time.

Though the fountainhead, he was never imposing, he was never desolate and never dejected.... On the contrary he viewed life like a panorama… filled with dance, music and love. Krishna lived life not as an amusement, indulgence or display but like a celebration! Unlike many others who watched from the periphery, he plunged into it headlong, participated in it like a like a festival.

The journey from self to Cosmos was spontaneous…. To discover self and surrender in service of others was the goal of Krishna's life. If one is fixated to one's soul then life becomes a celebration. To remain duty bound, detached and to retain balance was the quintessential Krishna….

He was for everyone… forever accepting everyone…

✦

[6]

And yet he was alone today.

Krishna's foot hurt him acutely. He sensed his end was near but strangely felt all the more peaceful and accepting...

All this while Draupadi's words splashed his heart and mind like the wet and salty waves crashing into the river.... Or were these waves an extension of Draupadi's tears...?

Tears, she had swallowed all her life...

Tears, she carried with herself while emerging from the flames...

Tears that travelled with her to her *swayamvar mandap*, to the Rajyasabha, to the Kurukshetra battlefield and much later continued to drench her, yet she stubbornly kept them away from her eyes.

The same tears today threatened to spill over, but Draupadi blocked them with her outcry.

"Govind... I offer to you all that you have bestowed on me but still don't comprehend the meaning of surrender. In my association with you, a question that has long worried me is that if I submit to you all my joys and sorrows, what remains within me to call my own...? I believe that for the welfare of others, I must preserve my joys and submit just my sorrows. I have discovered that life is not a weighing scale and we cannot wish away our misfortunes.... Every individual and situation we encounter in our life is predetermined and has a purpose. By not accepting it or escaping them we cannot alter our destiny..."

✦

[7]

In the wake of dawn, when the rejoicing Yadavas departed from Dwarika, little were they aware that they would never return home again. Riding their golden chariots right up to the shore of Dwarika, they boarded on to the ferries. When they arrived on the shore of Somnath and anchored their ferries in a row, none of them had any inclination what destiny laid in store for them. They bathed in the river and offered prayers to the Lord.

The Somnath Temple is revered as the most powerful amongst the twelve *jyotirling* temples. It is said that Lord Chandra had meditated here to be relieved of the curse of demon Prajapati. And Lord Shiva overwhelmed by Lord Chandra's devotion had set him free of the curse…

To get them to worship at the holy shrine and to relieve them of ancestral bondage requisite for a journey to heaven was all a part of Krishna's master plan.

When Krishna arrived at Prabhas with brother Balram and the Yadavas, he was aware that none of them would return alive. All of them dipped in the holy water and later strolled into the forest. There, over free flow of food and drinks, they got into a heated argument. Some of them turned violent and resorted to their weapons. Most of them were not equipped with their arms and therefore just plucked out the poisonous plant (*erka*) growing in the forest and attacked each other. It was a dangerous plant with sharp thorns that poked into their skin and most of them died instantaneously! Krishna watched on sorrowfully. Those surviving were consumed with rage. They picked up their soiled vessels to hammer onto each other's heads. Some went to the extent of even biting each other.... The powerful Yadava lineage documented as the golden period of Indian history was on the road to ravage!

Krishna had pledged not to access weapon in the battlefield but to ensure that his kith and kin did not endure further bloodshed and suffering, he took a decision...

The more violent they turned the more macabre it became and the more Krishna suffered.... Finally, unable to bear it any longer, Krishna plucked a fistful of the same *erka* plant, separated every leaf and flung it all over the grieving Yadavas. Every leaf of *erka* transformed into a torch lighting pyres of the dead bodies, while chanting farewell *mantra* to all.

It was the end of Yadava lineage.

The curse of Durvasa had come true.

The Yadavas had perished...

✦

[8]

It was now time for Gandhari's curse to be fulfilled.

Slowly and steadily, Krishna walked to the bank of river Hiranya and seated himself beneath a *peepal* tree. The clear water reflected the pristine moonlight.

He continued to watch the waves till his eyes could fathom no living creature in the surrounding area. The sun was about to rise.

Krishna watched the three rivers – Kapila, Hiranya and Saraswati – entwine into each other. This was where his elder brother had entered into his *samadhi*. When the Yadavas embarked on their exodus, Balram had sought leave from Krishna and he had granted him departure with a heavy heart.

Balram arrived at Trivenisangam and sat in meditation. And as he did so, he overheard one shepherd tell another, "Do you know that one man transformed into a seven-headed snake and dived into this deep sea…?"

✦

[9]

Tormented at watching his lineage breathe their last, Krishna did all in his capacity to bid them a dignified farewell. He ensured that they were not deprived of their last rites and only after that, Krishna limped on his bleeding foot from the forest towards Prabhas. Without his crown and without his characteristic ornaments, he appeared forlorn…

…though still alluring, his eyes full of anguish as if awaiting the inevitable…

Dragging his foot, he somehow managed to arrive in Prabhas and took shelter beneath a *peepal* tree…

Seated in an awkward position, his left foot upon his right thigh, Krishna had slipped into meditation with his eyes open. It was almost as if he had transformed into a statue. The eyes that once sparkled with mischief today appeared vacant, staring into space as if watching and awaiting the inevitable. It was the dawn of Durvasa's victory… his curse to vanquish the Yadava bloodline and with them, their leader Krishna. In anticipation of his end, Krishna awaited beneath the tree at Prabhas. He felt tormented…. Was this the agony of the moments gone by or was it the fear of the approaching moments…? Perhaps that is why the morning sun emerged pale without the halo, as if pre-mourning the farewell of a divine presence on earth. It was in this twilight time, when a hunter, far away on a prowl pointedly parked himself. In the darkness, Krishna resembled a dormant deer.

◆

[10]

"You will die like a beast… alone, helpless and in agony…. The way I lost my children, you too will witness the devastation of your ancestors, your children…. Your kith and kin also will suffer and die in front of your eyes like mine..."

Gandhari's voice echoed all through the palace corridors as if determined to engrave it on every stone.

And yet, Krishna had bowed and folded his hands in acceptance of the curse!

Who else but *Mata* Gandhari could have the power to curse Krishna? Besides, hadn't Krishna provoked the situation where she could inflict the curse on him?

Destiny had not been fair to Gandhari who lived her entire life as a sacrifice…. Was it because she overlooked the limitations of her children and held Krishna responsible for their failure...? Or was it because she was the chosen one to curse Krishna and free his spirit like only a mother can?

Krishna was never in favour of the battle or the bloodshed. He professed acceptance and his entire life was a prime example of reconciliation…. It is believed that *samadhi* is the final stage of detachment, but Krishna lived his entire life in detachment; he never wavered in his focus and yet it was his destiny to witness this tragedy.

It was the only way to end injustice.

Or was it that Krishna was looking for reasons to renounce his body…? He owed it to the Universe…

…and therefore created circumstances where *Mata* Gandhari would curse him. When she did, he raised his hand to utter "*Tathastu!*" He accepted his end…

Calm, dispassionate… who else besides Krishna could be so?

✦

[11]

...And death was fast approaching!

It was Krishna's desire that when he renounced the Universe, the entire Yadava lineage departed with him. They were blessed to not live in the times of *kalyug* and therefore cursed by Durvasa.

In Pindaratirath on a moonlit night, *rishi* Durvasa was in meditation. The young and power-obsessed Yadavas were notorious for wine, women and gambling. They were arrogant and offensive and often intoxicated beyond all limits of decency. One day, the youngsters got together and decided to play a prank on the sage. They disguised Saamb, who was Jambuvanti's and Krishna's son as a woman and presented him before Durvasa...

They arrived in his chamber and without greeting him said, "She is the consort of Babhru Yadava.... She desires a child... what will she conceive?"

Just out his meditation, Durvasa was affronted by their misconduct. "She will conceive *mashal* (torch)... and it will destroy the entire Yadava bloodline..." he cursed Saamb.

Terrified by Durvasa's outburst, the Yadavas deliberately held back the information from Krishna but true to the *rishi*'s prophecy, Saamb conceived *mashal*. The young Yadavas conspired and crushed the *mashal* into powder, which they immersed into the ocean. That same powder, in Prabhas Kshetra sprouted into a plant called *erka*.... Every time the plant was destroyed it rose higher and stronger, upright and sharp as an iron...! While these plants were mushrooming into a lethal weapon for a battle that the Yadavas were ignorant about, many miles away, Dwarika, was all set for a turning point!

A stray iron piece of the *mashal* that could not be dismantled by the young Yadavas floated across the ocean and was swallowed by a shark caught by a fisherman. He extracted the piece out of the shark's gullet and handed it over to a hunter named Jara...

Jara picked the piece and pasted it on his arrow...

Only Krishna was in the knowing of what was transpiring.... Only he knew that the arrow that was to end his human *avatar* was in the process of getting ready...

Jara scrutinised the attached piece on his arrow and aimed his shot at the dormant deer...

There was a whistle in the air...

The divine thumb that had frequently brushed away Udhav's tears... that had stroked hair locks of Rukmini and dipped into *chandan* (sandalwood) to adorn his forehead, suddenly turned lifeless. It was as if a flame had pierced through the thumb and ignited his entire body like a current...

Jara's arrow hit the sole of Krishna's foot and slit it all the way like a lethal weapon. It was time to realise the curse of *Mata* Gandhari which Krishna had blessed with "*Tathastu*"...

Assuming that the deer was injured and writhing in pain, Jara swam across the waist-deep water and arrived at the opposite shore. On landing, he was alarmed to discover instead of a beast, the Lord himself!

Jara was unprepared to discover a human life injured.... He made unsuccessful attempts to pluck out the arrow from Krishna's bleeding foot...

"Let it be, my friend!" said a sinking voice almost inaudible. This was the voice that once echoed on the battlefield.

Niyat Kurum Karma Tva Karma Jayayo Hyakarmanah |
Shariryatrapi Cha Te Na Prasidhyedkarmanah ||

Our scriptures define *niyati* (fortune) as predestined. It means that we follow what is in store for us. Unless we do so, we cannot forsake our body when the time comes...

Jara had lived by his *karma,* done his duty as was predestined. He could sense insurmountable pain in Krishna's voice…

A few grey strands, half-shut eyes and a face that sparkled devoid of the crown and the peacock feather, he was still as alluring and his face radiated with immense compassion.

As blood splattered from his arrow-pierced foot and his pain increased… Krishna was getting ready to renounce his body…. The divine *avatar* was getting ready to renounce his human bondages and unite with *brahma*…. Once again, Krishna remembered Draupadi…

Twadiyam Vastu Govind Tubhyamev Samarpyate ।

Why? Why did that one sentence continue to torment Krishna? What were those attachments that still bound him and refused to set him free? What were these echoes that hounded him and prevented his sojourn when his soul was fluttering to set itself free from the cage? Were they reminders of some duties unfulfilled? And what were these duties?

Jara was sobbing loudly… Krishna was startled from his reverie.

A dusky man attired in a loincloth, his hair band stuck with feathers… hands folded… head bowed… weeping… pleading… stood before him. Intimidated by Krishna's awesome presence, Jara trembled with nervousness…

After a long time, something brought a smile to Krishna's face even if it was a sad, weak smile soaked in pain. He said to Jara, "Who are you, my friend?"

Jara trembled, "I'm Ja…Ja…Ja…Jara."

Krishna continued to smile, "Jara…! I was waiting for you…. What took you so long, my friend?"

Jara was confused. He folded his hands and said, "O Lord, this arrow…"

"Belongs to you…" Krishna completed the sentence for him. "I'm aware of it. I recognise the piece of iron attached to it…. Since early morning, I have been remembering Durvasa and *Mata* Gandhari."

Jara stared blankly.

"You are the messenger of my freedom," said Krishna.

"Please forgive me, O Lord," Jara sobbed bitterly.

"You have done nothing to fear.... You have relieved me of my human incarnation. You will go to heaven. I'm indebted to you."

Krishna folded his hands and shut his eyes. His face brimmed with pain and relief.... Pain, that resulted from his bleeding foot, and relief from feeling attachment. He felt dispassionate.... He seemed to be getting ready for his final journey...

Jara looked intently at Krishna. His face, his quietude, his half-shut lotus eyes covered with eyelids and his bleeding toe! Only he could smile thus in the prevailing circumstances despite so much of suffering...

Jara wondered what kind of a life was this where he had to injure Krishna to find a place for himself in the heaven...

It was beyond his comprehension...

Krishna compressed his eyes... in pain and in solace!

He who had cured so many from their sufferings was today in excruciating pain as he set to renounce his body. It was Krishna's destiny to witness an action replay of his entire life cast before his eyes.

✦

[12]

That dawn when his journey with the Yadavas came to an end, Krishna pleaded with his *saarthi* Daruk to flee the venue. But Daruk was unwilling to leave Krishna's side even for a minute. The golden chariot that had won Krishna his various battles, his *sudarshan chakra, kaumudi* weapon, *sharang* arrow and the two baskets strapped onto his shoulder, the five-ingredient conch and the *nandak* sword... Daruk was a witness to all these taking a *pradakshina* of the Lord before moving in the direction of sun! Daruk stared at Krishna.... It was time for farewell. He knew it and so did Krishna...

Krishna was aware that he would not sustain till the time Arjuna reached him. It would be Arjuna's responsibility to break the unfortunate news to the kingdom of Ugrasen, to Devaki and Vasudev, his parents.... They would all have to bear the pain of his loss.... For the first time, Krishna understood the pain of losing a loved one.... He understood how human beings felt when they lost their beloveds....

Krishna requested Daruk to escort Arjuna to the shore of rivers Hiranya and Kapila. Perhaps, it was his desire to breathe his last and renounce the world at a holy place.

It was not easy for Krishna to break away from human bondage.... Love, sorrow and affection had embroiled Krishna like every other human being. They obstructed him, his final journey. Engulfed in the overwhelming pain, Krishna meditated, appeared frozen like a statuette beneath the *peepal* tree. For reasons beyond his control, Draupadi's outcry continued to reverberate in his mind.

Today, when he was all set for his final journey, what was it that was making him so restless...? What had he left incomplete that was troubling the divine Lord...?

✦

[13]

It was here that brother Balram entered into his *samadhi*. Perhaps it was Krishna's desire to breathe his last in the very same spot and therefore despite agonising pain struggled towards Trivenisangam…

…It was almost as if brother Balram was beckoning to him, "Come, come Kaanha, it's time for us to leave. How long are you going to keep resting here? I have been waiting for a long time. Wake up, and come along…"

With great difficulty, Krishna rose and strode towards the shore. One step at a time, coiling in pain…. With every step he leapt forward, the pain worsened but Krishna was determined to reach the shore.

Hesitantly, he looked back one last time, folded his hands to bid farewell to Jara. "It's time for you to go your way too…. How long will you continue to follow me?"

"But you are all alone…" Jara replied with tear-stained eyes.

Krishna chuckled, "This is the final sojourn, my friend. Nobody can accompany anyone. Everyone has to travel alone…. So farewell, my friend..."

Jara stood dumbstruck.

The shooting pain obstructed Krishna's every step but he was determined to reach the spot.

Seated beneath the tree with enormous foliage, Krishna had prolonged his last breaths. He looked over the three rivers entwine into each other and float lyrically. The slightly muddy water of Hiranya, the pale green of Kapila and the pristine white of Saraswati combined before his eyes and united into the ocean, their final destination.

Just in the way the ocean is the destination of all the rivers, heaven is the destination of all souls.... Krishna closed his eyes. In pain and in solace!

Echoes of *Aham Brahmasmi*... resounded in all directions. As dust got ready to mingle with dust, the soul was restless to enter the gates of paradise.

Resting beneath the *peepal* tree, it was as if Krishna was in a trance. It was time to sacrifice acceptance... identity... time to sacrifice everything.

Jara tried to wake up Krishna, "Lord, O Lord! Your foot bleeds profusely.... Let me apply some ointment...You will feel better..."

Krishna smiled weakly, "You are right... Everything will be alright soon... for everyone..."

He could hear echoes of chorus of *shanti mantra* recited at his Guru Sandeepan's *ashram*...

> *"Om Shanti Antarikshagunda... Shanti Prithvi... Shanti Vanaspataya... Shanti Brahma... Shanti Shanti Reva... Om Shanti Shanti Shanti..."*

Finally, there was quietude inside and outside...within and surrounding him.... Finally, his mind and body will be at peace...!

✦

[14]

The flute... and the music emanating from it echoed into Krishna's ears.... The waves hit the shores in a rhythm and resembled the high tide in river Yamuna.... The *kadamb* tree almost drooped over Krishna's eyelids. A cold breeze blew from the tiny shrubs growing along the riverbank. A cluster of peacock feathers sprinkled over and slipped past Krishna's body. It felt as if the cows of Gokul had personally come clanging their bells to awaken him... and every lane, every street was stretching out its arms to embrace him saying...

"Come... come along..."

The rising sun combined with the chirping of the birds brought back many familiar sounds... the cows returning home after grazing... the humming domesticity as families got ready to start their day... Krishna heard all this! He could hear his mother singing *prabhatya* (morning prayers)... it was that hour of the day... Krishna tried to open his eyes but could not. He felt as if someone had placed heavy weight over his eyelids. In his hallucinatory state, he visualised Draupadi's face swimming over the sparkling water of Hiranya... it seemed to say, "*Sakha*, you bestowed on me happiness, sorrow, respect, affront, life and death. I accepted all and now return it back to you..."

Krishna recalled Draupadi's torment, her struggle, her spirit to fight life and her courage to not give up after losing... Krishna admired her strength. Her virtuousness was her identity and when a woman of her calibre surrendered so completely, Krishna anticipated what to expect...

For the first time he speculated what could transpire when a woman like Draupadi surrendered.... Was it in his capacity to accept her? He asked himself if he was deserving of such generosity and enormous sacrifice... "Am I deserving of such honour... and what do I offer her for all this in return? That too now when I'm in the process of exiting... where do I find time for total acceptance? It's too much of a baggage. The burden weighs on my shoulders.... Why do you bind me in such responsibility at sunset hour, O *sakhi*?" Krishna could not help asking.

The fiery eyes before him filled up and spilled over with tears.

[15]

"Have I lived up to the title of an ideal wife?" A kind face stared at Krishna. Looking over the zigzag flow of river Kapila, Krishna pondered over the intense question. He had no answer. He could visualise Rukmini's face floating over the waves, staring at him with moist eyes…

It had been so many years ago but the question still aroused heartburns in Krishna. "Why must you *Aryaputra* carry so much baggage all alone? You prevented me from accompanying you on your last journey…. You didn't even momentarily stop for me…." There was more suffering and less anger in Rukmini's eyes. "I would have never obstructed you… if at all I would have aided you in clearing all the thorns on your way and spread your path with flowers. Like a flame I would have absorbed all the darkness around you…. So why did you determine to undertake such a painstaking journey on your own? Didn't I as your consort deserve to be a part of your misfortune, my Lord?" Krishna had never sensed her eyes so vacant and felt increasingly restless. He couldn't ride over her feeling of desolation….

"I held your hand through duty, through commitment and attachment. And now, when it is time for *moksha* (salvation), you will travel alone?" Rukmini repeated her question while Krishna remained silent.

He felt weighed down. It was true that Rukmini had surrendered all of herself to him… her integrity… her beauty… her identity. In fact not just her but all women who had lived their lives dissolved into Krishna appeared so forlorn today… their eyes were sad. What were they yearning for? Had he failed them somewhere, not lived up to their expectations? Krishna felt saddened by the thought.

◆

[16]

"Whenever you feel sad, lonely or confused, think of me.... Close your eyes, take a deep breath and you will sense me beside you... I never let you out of my sight but you've determined to leave without me.... But I'll follow you to your isolation... become a part of your reflection, your seclusion.... Just remember there is no escape from me because I'm your subconscious and it's not possible for you to ever distance yourself from your memories. I'm a part of you residing inside you, all you have to do is to inhale and call out to me.... See, I'm already beside you...."

On the quiet waters of river Saraswati, Krishna sensed two anguished eyes of Radha, part complaining and part longing, as if to say "How can you determine to take this journey while I plead you so much...? Let me accompany you, for your pursuit cannot be accomplished without me. I'm not just your extension... but also your muse, your shadow... how can anyone travel without his shadow, Krishna?"

✦

[17]

Krishna was lost in his innumerable memories of Gokul.

Eyes still closed, his mind wandered in the by lanes of Gokul. It was morning time and the milkmaids were getting ready for the day. They filled their milk pots and departed for sale to Mathura.... On their way they stopped by to greet Yashoda. Krishna heard distinct sound of his mother's bangles as she swayed her arms to and fro to churn buttermilk in the pot. It was a familiar sound that felt like music to his ears and filled the entire house with fragrance....

Outside, the cows pegged in the courtyard woke up their calves gently and they tugged at their mother's breasts untiringly. Their froth trickling mouths and the aroma of fresh milk mingled with the sound of churning butter evoked a distinct memory and rendered a distinct melody in Krishna.... The tiny bells attached to the churning strings, the jangle from mother Yashoda's bangles, her anklets, the early morning prayers combined with flute strains played like symphony. And amidst all this was a voice calling out to him...

"Kaanha... O Kaanha... Kaanhaa... O Kaanhaa..."

The three rivers entwined as if playing hide-and-seek with memory. It was as if the friend, the wife and the beloved combined into one complete woman, the ultimate of sensuality! They were all soaked in Krishna's fragrance as if all three had pledged to raise him to supremacy. The three rivers eventually ended into the ocean. The vast ocean embraced them all but it had its own limitations. The rivers drenched itself in the ocean's salty waters.

A stray thought crossed Krishna's mind. The four women in his life also had come into him with high expectations but like the ocean, Krishna had his limitations and had unwittingly transferred his bitterness to all of them.

A human being arrives into the world with predestined relationships. He cannot choose his parents or siblings but he is at liberty to choose his spouse, his beloved and his friend. These are the only relationships he determines, treasures them, nurtures them and sometimes even destroys them. Krishna wondered if he had done justice to his relationships. Had he offered himself adequately to his wives, beloved and friend?

Krishna's mind was a rewind and once again the four faces frazzled him.

While leaving Gokul, Radha said, "Don't make empty promises, Kaanha. I'm never going to leave Gokul and you know you are never going to return again. The river Yamuna, the *kadamb* flower branches and the streets of Gokul will never forget you and I will make sure that I never remember you…."

Krishna remembered his response. He had said, "One remembers those who one forgets… you will never forget me and if I forget you I will cease to breathe?"

✦

[18]

One day, Draupadi had out of the blue announced, "I shudder at the thought of how you would have responded had I ever asked you if you love me…! Had I questioned you what is my significance in your life…! Have you ever, even for a moment, yearned for me…? Don't respond immediately *sakha* for I have not yet asked you these questions. I'm not sure if I want to or for that matter if I'm even ready for the response…!"

That time Krishna had responded, "If you desire an answer, you may question me but I don't think you need to seek an answer that resides in your heart. Our relationship survives on trust and if this trust has to be questioned, I don't deserve to be called your friend. Still, you are at liberty to question whenever you desire… to me… or to your heart… it's the same thing…"

✦

[19]

After many nights of patient waiting, an exhausted Rukmini had in a comparatively happy moment asked her husband, "Lord, am I married to the king of Dwarika or to the beloved I eloped with? Are you the same person to whom I wrote a love letter and surrendered my life to? Will you forever only worry about others and never think about your wife? Have you ever stopped to ponder what I desire or what are my expectations of you...?"

Krishna had smiled in response, "The day I stop to ponder about myself, I will automatically start to worry about my better half. My beloved, the one who sits on the throne, wears a crown full of thorns. For the outsiders, this crown may appear like a beautiful ornament but only the one who wears it knows where it hurts...."

Rukmini looked at Krishna with surprise.

There was weariness in her eyes. What was troubling Rukmini? Why did she appear so pained...?

"Only the one who can bear the thorns has the right to wear the crown..." elaborated Krishna, "For beneath the throne lies buried the happiness of an entire kingdom. The throne remains stable only and as long as the king remains responsible towards his subjects...."

Saying this he enveloped Rukmini in a warm embrace and Rukmini fell in love with Krishna all over again.

◆

[20]

When he was leaving Gokul, mother Yashoda had pleaded with Krishna, "Don't embark on this journey. I will bail you out from Akrur*ji*… I'm not yet satiated spending time with you Kaanha. It was only a few days ago I cuddled you in my lap and now you've grown so big to take on challenges and fight with Kansa. Shouldn't you first worry about your mother….What will happen to me when I get aged, when my eyes turn feeble? Who will lead me holding my hand? Who will remember to walk me to the Yamuna bank? Who will provide me my medicines? Who will light my pyre? Why do you need to depart on this journey…? Please don't go Kaanha…"

Krishna had clasped his mother in a tight embrace and she had sobbed bitterly….

As he gently stroked his mother's back, he seemed to remind himself today, "I'm nobody's son, nobody's beloved, nobody's husband…I'm here to fulfil my *karma* and there's no escaping that."

✦

[21]

Fleeting images of Yashoda during different phases haunted Krishna. He remembered an angry Yashoda reprimanding him, the indulgent one serving him mound of butter. Her pleading him at the shore of river Kalindi... her eyes seemed to blur with the yearnings of mother Devaki. Their collective suffering churned multiple emotions in Krishna resulting in a tear at the corner of his eye that finally trickled down his face.

He remembered the fear-ridden eyes of father Vasudev as he bid him farewell on the bank of river Yamuna when he left for Mathura. More images floated on his consciousness... Krishna was troubled by the questioning eyes of Sudama, of Rukmini, of Subhadra, of Draupadi, of Arjuna and Bhishma *Pitamah* (patriarch) lying incapacitated on a bed of arrows. He recalled his own dissembling eyes and the defeated eyes of Duryodhan after being injured....

Eyes of mother Gandhari that nobody had seen before but had stared fixedly at Krishna as if reminding him of the pending curse!

It was as if all these eyes had jointly come to haunt Krishna.... He recalled the streaming eyes of Udhav that even today filled his eyes with tears. Krishna tried to contain his sorrow, to assimilate himself. He watched the setting sun and hoped that his suffering would abate soon...

It was as if the child Krishna was tied up in the loft and was pleading for freedom...

✦

[22]

...Krishna watched the events of his life unfold before him with his eyes closed.... He remembered the fateful night when Udhav and he waited below Rukmini's window, outside the palace. Krishna felt that dark night dissolving inside his heart.

He had made up his mind.

The journey of the Yadavas was determined. Now all that was left was to confirm the time.

And one day even the time was confirmed.

Standing in his chamber verandah, Krishna was looking at the sun setting into the sea. The evening had spread its orange splendour all over the sky.

Watching the sunset, a thought crossed Krishna's mind. He decided that the time had come for Durvasa's prophecy to come true...

Just in the way the sun rises and sets at an allotted time, the human body also must renounce the world when time beckons...! Krishna could hear his own echoes:

Kaloasmi Lokshyakrut Pravrudho ।
Lokonsamaharturmih Pravrut ॥
Rutedpi Tva Na Bhavishyanit Sarve ।
Yedavasthitah Pratyanikeshu Yodhah ॥

It was just a few days ago when the messenger of God visited Krishna in disguise carrying greetings from Lord Vasu, Aditya, Ashwini Kumar, Maarut, Rudra and other deities. He said, "Almighty, you have fulfilled your duty but if you are relishing being on the planet you may stay longer. I'm but your slave and visit you only to remind you of time."

And Krishna had replied, "The Universe cannot be free of the burden unless the Yadavas are totally destroyed. Whenever there is injustice, inequality, I will be reborn to absolve human suffering. Until I travel everyone with me to their rightful destinations, my duty remains unfulfilled. Until I witness the Yadava devastation, until I meet Jara, until I destroy unhappiness all around me, I cannot leave this Universe... I cannot return to heaven..."

The messenger dutifully carried back Krishna's message to the deities in heaven.

It was time for breaking through the bondages.

It was time for preparing for the ominous... and time for bidding farewell.

And it was neither day... nor night... nor dusk... nor dawn...!

✦

[23]

That night there was high tide in the river. The waves roared and lashed at the shores. It was a still, dark night at Dwarika…. Seated in the queen's chamber, Krishna stared at the setting sun from the window.

It was not unusual for Krishna to sit in solitude. Ever since she was married to him, Rukmini was accustomed to him devoting a lot of time in meditation and now sensed little difference between solitude and loneliness. It was the destiny of the queen of Dwarika to forever wait for her Lord…

Everyone accepted that Rukmini was extraordinarily intelligent. She was well versed in both, the art of weapons and in palace politics. Her father, king of Kundinpur did not discriminate in the rearing of his son Rukim and daughter Rukmini who were trained by experts to shoulder royal responsibilities.

And yet sometimes Rukmini wondered if it was indeed an advantage to be so gifted. She often felt that she would have been happier had she been ordinary like other women… had she not been so scholarly, so sharp witted…. She frequently felt weighed down by her own knowledge.

Krishna seldom spent any time with her…. And when he did, he was more inclined to discussing royal affairs with her than personal matters. On many occasions, Rukmini complained, "After pining for so long I get to see your face. I don't want to spend my precious time discussing the politics of Dwarika… I don't want to discuss Duryodhan or Hastinapur... I'm your wife not your minister, why can't you just love me?" she would express uninhibitedly.

✦

[24]

It was only yesterday she had spent the entire night awake, all alone in her bedchamber. Every window, every corridor, every door and the doorman of the palace, was a witness of her yearning for Krishna. They were accustomed to it for so many years that they were no longer surprised by the all night burning lamps.

They empathised with her insecurities, her recurring disappointments.

Every street of Dwarika, every resident, every devotee at the temple and every deity inside it knew of Rukmini's tragedy.

Many summers ago, when she left the lush Kundinpur, a narrow triangular region based on the shores of the rivers Veena and Bhadra, and arrived for the first time in Dwarika, Rukmini was not yet the queen of Krishna. She was only sixteen, a virgin and besotted! She was drawn to everything about Krishna – his eyes, his smile, his voice!

Set on the shores of river Payoshini, the kingdom of Kundinpur was based on the south of Hastinapur.

When Krishna came riding his chariot to the boundary of Kundinpur and stretched his hand, Rukmini for a moment closed her eyes to recall her *isht devata* (ancestral God) and… gave her hand into Krishna's hand…

Krishna lifted her like a flower and raced the chariot with a lightning speed.

For Rukmini, that moment transformed into her wedding vows of trust and surrender. From that moment onward, Krishna was her husband and also her Lord.

Rukmini's brother Rukim had vowed to free his sister from the clutches of Krishna and bring her home. He had followed them with a full army of Vidarbha but was unsuccessful. Krishna defeated Rukim in the battle but granted his life.

The mere thought that the man who defeated an entire army of Vidarbha, who defeated her warrior brother, who was more beautiful than a dream, ferocious like a lion and held her like a flower was the magnificent man she was wedded to made Rukmini feel precious...!

She had heard a lot about the golden city Dwarika, and when she descended on it the first time accompanied by Krishna she was awestruck. The vast stretch of sand sparkled like silver. Rukmini stepped down from the chariot and held the silver sand in her fist but it trickled out blowing in all directions.

Krishna turned back to look at her and smiled seductively!

At that time, little did she know that it wasn't sand, but time that Rukmini was holding in her fist which was gradually slipping by...!

She could not recall how many years ago it was when Krishna married her by rituals and brought her to the palace.

There was hardly any difference between that first night spent in the chamber and today...

That time too, Krishna stayed out all night and today, even though present in the chamber, Krishna was preoccupied. Rukmini remembered her first night vividly.

It was a night meant for festivities. The chamber was adorned with flowers and mud lamps, *rangoli* (drawing) made out of flower petals mixed in perfume was painted all over the room and the wide bed covered with silk bedspread and cushions.

She had waited for this night all her life. The cold breeze coming from the river rattled every door and window of the chamber, tore apart the flower festoons and scattered the *rangoli* as if to announce her Lord's entry. Could she be hallucinating for she heard Krishna's flute in the breeze swaying brass bells attached to the curtains.... The waiting was not over.

Her alluring beloved who adorned the *Vyjayanthi* necklace and the peacock crown did not return!

Some boats were held up on the shores of Dwarika and Krishna needed to be there....

It didn't matter to him that it was the premiere night of his personal journey and he had left his consort to weather the storms all alone, all night.

That was her wedding night.

Rukmini accepted that day that her intensity for her beloved did not guarantee attention. Krishna did not solely belong to her.

Her Lord – her beloved – her husband was not exclusively hers. His time and he were for everyone.

He belonged first to others and if something remained, he belonged to her.

He was her husband and she was the queen of Dwarika, but is this what she had wanted out of life?

She was neither the first one, nor the last!

She loved him, yearned for him, surrendered to him, but she was not the only one who was consumed by him. The entire Gokul, all of Dwarika, all of Hastinapur, all of Indraprasth, all the Yadavas, *Mata* Kunti, all the Pandavas, elder brother Balram, mother Devaki, sister Subhadra, Udhav, Akrur, Vidur, Narad and... and...

With her heart missing a beat, and with great difficulty, came the name...

Radha...

How many names to remember? All of them Krishna besotted-Krishna obsessed-Krishna possessed...

And this was not one-sided, for Krishna reciprocated to the love of them all.

The way she had sought him in distress to save her from her liaison with King Shishupal and Krishna had obliged, so had the others sought him in their moment of sorrow and Krishna had stood the test of time. He was always there for everyone.

✦

[25]

Rukmini always complained, "You never devote sufficient time to me, my feelings, my desires, my dreams.... So many years later it is Radha-Krishna who are worshipped everywhere. Nobody ever talks of Rukmini-Krishna.... Is this fair?"

She was the wife of Krishna and the queen of Dwarika and yet Rukmini nursed a perennial sinking feeling.... She wondered why.

✦

[26]

Fragmented moments from the past sprang up in her memory… Rukmini recalled that Krishna had once promised to celebrate *Janmashtami* at the palace.

After participating in the festivities in the adjoining palaces, Krishna lived up to his promise and arrived in their bedchamber.

When dusk fell, Rukmini presented him a flute. It was a beautiful work of art embossed with a peacock and a parrot studded with diamonds, rubies and emeralds. The edge of the flute held silk strings attached with thread balls.

Krishna surveyed the flute, then stared at Rukmini for a long time and finally looked away...

He appeared forlorn… he quietly placed the flute aside and picked up the five-ingredient-conch. One didn't know what was in his mind but when he blew it, it delivered the most mournful sound…

…Even today whenever Rukmini recalled that wail she shut her ears in fear! She could never get over the haunting image of tears streaming down Krishna's eyes as the sound of his conch reverberated in the Universe.

✦

[27]

Seated beneath the *peepal* tree, Krishna recalled his anguish while blowing the conch.

He recalled the fleeting expressions of rejection and betrayal in Rukmini's eyes. Today, the same eyes had come to haunt him.

Undoubtedly, the flute had evoked turbulent memories within Krishna but his suffering was not restricted just to his pining for Radha.

It was the gloom of the tragedy to follow... the gloom of the forthcoming battle.

But how was he to explain all this to his beloved wife?

On the eve of the *ashtami* in the month of *Shravan*, Krishna could hear the drums of the ominous to occur on the *karthiki purnima* day.

In the festivities of *Janmashtami*, Krishna foresaw the shadows of the storm to come...

Invisible figures of dancing spirits, of trumpeting elephants and galloping horses...

In the midst of all this chaos, his innocent wife had thought of gifting him a flute... presenting him a new *raga* (tune) of life.

✦

[28]

Rukmini was aware that music could be revived with the same fervour in Krishna's life again. The flute was a testimony of his lost childhood, a reminder of his euphoric days and its memories were not restricted to only Radha as Rukmini assumed but included a host of related images like his mother Yashoda, father Nand, brother Balram and his innumerable cowherd friends.... The flute was associated to the bank of river Yamuna and the various foliage-laden trees.... It was associated with his various adventures and celebrations.

It was his yearning for the cherished sepia memories that compelled Krishna to blow the conch. He was announcing the fatal moment to come. The echo spread in all directions. Krishna was preparing for the wailing to follow... preparing for the many sleepless nights to come...

So many women were to get widowed... so many children were to be orphaned...

And he was to witness all this... just witness! That was his *karma* and it was unavoidable.

And at a time like this, his wife had thought of presenting him with a golden flute...

He felt helpless... Rukmini's yearning and passion for him after all these years filled Krishna's eyes with tears.

✦

[29]

The memory of the incident consumed Rukmini with envy for Radha even today.

"I'm the fortune of the Yadavas, the empress of Dwarika, but am I the beloved of Krishna? That privilege belongs to Radha! Am I his friend? That privilege belongs to Draupadi! Satyabhama often gets upset with the Lord, complains and even sulks for days, but Krishna always cajoles and pampers her.... The one who blossomed with his touch is Kubja and the one he transformed into a timeless beauty is Trivakra...

"...I'm neither the daughter of Charuhasini Shaibya, nor am I the daughter of Jambuvanti or Rohini, who sacrificed their lives for Krishna. So who am I, what's my significance in his life...?

"...He is the Almighty.... He narrated the *Gita* to Arjuna, donned different *avatars* in different centuries. He screened the Universe in his mouth for his mother Yashoda; he is the Govardhandhari, the Kurukshetra guide, while I'm but an ordinary woman with ordinary dreams... I dreamed of my beloved in the role of my husband... but did I find him...?

"...A husband who would love me, admonish me and fight with me, reprimand me when I made mistakes and pamper me when I was annoyed... somebody who would come home every sunset... and when night fell, he would envelop me in his arms... someone whom I would wake up every morning.... This wasn't asking for too much, was it...? And still..."

✦

[30]

Rukmini turned to look at Krishna standing in the verandah. He appeared preoccupied. Rukmini wondered what worried him.

The wedding vows described the wife as an equal partner. "A deceptive description," thought Rukmini who was of the opinion that an equal partner was the one who matched her consort's every step...

In the circumstances, she wondered what her duty as an equal partner entailed. To forever wait for her Lord... or to wait for the time Krishna determined his path and then to oppose him?

Rukmini looked at Krishna staring blankly into the skyline from his window.... It perplexed her. What he could be thinking about?

Ever since the battle of Kurukshetra, Krishna spent long hours in quietude staring at the setting sun.... He had isolated himself from everybody and Rukmini had got accustomed to his growing silence. But today, she was ill-at-ease with his non-communication. There was something ominous about his silence, as if warning about a predicament. His weary eyes seemed to say something but his lips didn't grant permission. At midnight, when Rukmini could bear his silence no longer, she sent her messenger to summon Udhav to her room...

On receiving her message, Udhav didn't waste a moment to arrive in her chamber.

Together, they stared at the lonely shadow of Krishna melting in the darkness of the night... watching his silhouette in the dark, Udhav had a premonition of the events to unfold.... Krishna's shoulders held back like a gallant warrior, his broad chest and his marble-like torso… his narrow waist like that of a lion clasped into an ornamental band… and below it, his characteristic *pitamber* (yellow *dhoti*).

Udhav's heart missed a beat. A stray thought crossed his mind… something within him told him that this was the last time he was watching his dear friend and Lord….

Usually Udhav refrained from disturbing Krishna while in meditation. But today, he could not hold back and charged towards the window to join Krishna. Eyes filled with tears… Udhav fell at Krishna's feet…

"Oh Lord, what are you up to? Why have you turned me so restless?"

Just then a fierce wind passed them and blew away Krishna's stole. It fell on Udhav's face. Very gently, Krishna pulled back his stole and bend down to affectionately raise Udhav from his feet…. He embraced him and Udhav burst into tears, sobbing uncontrollably as if pre-mourning some forthcoming event…

"What is happening to you, my Lord… and why is it happening…?" Udhav choked over his words.

Krishna caressed Udhav's head gently…. The experience for Udhav was akin to being seized by a cold breeze from the Himalayas. Udhav looked into Krishna's eyes and sensed them slightly moist!

"What is it?" Krishna asked smiling at him.

Udhav looked at Krishna with complaining eyes. He had several questions in his mind but they rushed past his mind like the angry waves jumping in the ocean. He felt he was losing his bearings and wondered if he had been hallucinating a while ago.... Was he in a heightened state of consciousness or was he delirious...? Udhav was unable to decipher his own condition. He wiped his tear-smothered face to look at Krishna again. His Lord was a picture of serenity. His eyes resembled the flowing Yamuna.

Krishna held Udhav's hand. Then as if determining something, he shut his eyes, compressed his lips and stood motionless for a moment all the while gently stroking Udhav's hand…

Suddenly, it felt as if a resonating voice emerging from the deepest cave was echoing all over the palace. The voice seemed to say, "The time has come for you to depart to Badrikaashram…. It is time for the extinction of the Yadava lineage! When the golden urn of the highest temple of Dwarika is engulfed by the waves of Yamuna, it's my wish that you find peace at the foot of the Himalayas…."

Udhav felt as if this was the final moment of his life! Why was his friend, his Lord, saying all this to him at this moment? Was it possible to have any life without Krishna? He didn't need to travel to Badrikaashram or to the Himalayas because without Krishna it was in any case futile to live in this Universe…

Udhav fell at Krishna's feet once again…

Rukmini watched all this standing far away…. She watched Krishna's moist eyes sparkle in the darkness…. For a moment, she felt tempted to run and embrace him…. She felt tempted to ask him what troubled him…!

She knew that unless she fathomed the cause of his worry, she was going to spend many sleepless nights…. So many years… days and nights had been spent devoted to him…! She was familiar with his every nerve and fibre… his likes and dislikes, his happiness and sorrow, his worries and his desires were her own. Yet today, he seemed so unfamiliar, almost like a stranger!

Rukmini felt so pained that she could hear her heartbeats. What was it that her husband did not want to share with her, but confided in Udhav…? The thought depressed her.

She hadn't felt as defeated even while sharing Krishna with the seven queens of his palace as she felt just now. Today, for the first time, Rukmini seemed to have lost her right as a spouse…

Udhav continued to weep and plead at Krishna's feet… "No, my Lord! I will not go anywhere. Without you there is no peace for me."

"Udhav…! Have your forgotten my words, my friend? Do I have to repeat the entire message I narrated to Arjuna at the Kurukshetra? All of us who are born have to die…."

By now Udhav was furious, "So if I'm born why shouldn't I…?" He left his sentence incomplete.

Krishna smiled and in his smile Udhav discovered answers to many of his disturbing questions…. The chariot parked in the middle of the Kurukshetra battlefield, the *sarathi* narrating the *Gita*…

"Accept your circumstances... accept your sorrow the way you accept happiness.... You've accepted birth, now be ready to accept death, for that is your duty, your *dharma*, Udhav.... Nothing is possible before time and without Lord's calling...

"...It's time that is all-powerful and it makes no discriminations.... Today, time is spreading its arms and beckoning me, I will have to go..." stated Krishna.

"...And me, my Lord, when will time beckon me?"

"Time is under no one's spell..." Krishna continued poignantly.

"One who does not discriminate between happiness and sorrow and surrenders, is my true devotee.... It's because he trusts me and therefore accepts my judgement as my showering."

Rukmini continued to be a silent spectator. She was curious what the two could be discussing for Krishna to demonstrate such tenderness towards Udhav.

Slowly, Udhav rose from the floor and dispersed out of the chamber as if carrying a body without a soul. Never before had Udhav ever entered or exited Rukmini's chamber without greeting her. She looked dazed as Udhav walked past her without even a glance.

There was a halo around his head, his mouth partly open as if unable to contain a smile while his eyes streamed down with tears.

He appeared in a trance and Rukmini slightly worried, ran behind him but it was difficult to keep pace. Udhav strolled past the doorman and the innumerable maids, as if walking over the clouds. He registered none of them, just walked ahead staring into the skyline until he left the palace, as if waiting some unknown moment...

✦

[31]

When Rukmini got back, Krishna was still staring at the ocean.

It was almost dawn.... The waves had returned to the shores and the ocean had gradually turned calm. The skyline had turned crimson and the sun was all set to rise....

The changing hues of skyline reflected in Krishna's eyes. They told stories of his sleepless, restless night....

Rukmini hesitantly approached Krishna, stood beside him at the window. Some moments passed by in silence... then Rukmini gently placed her arm on Krishna's shoulder.

Krishna turned to look at Rukmini beside him.

She stared at his fatigued, moist eyes.... There was something unfamiliar about his expression. This was not Vasudev, her husband. She felt as if she was staring at a complete stranger.

...This was not the cowherd who had dared to abduct her in his chariot at Kundinpur.... He was not the beloved with whom she had shared many intimate nights...

Nor was he the king of Dwarika recognised as her husband.... Then who was he?

Rukmini stared at him confused.

So who was this man whose expression she could not fathom and looked visibly distressed? It was as if Krishna had read her thoughts.

"Yes, do you wish to say something to me?" Krishna asked her in a deep, mournful voice.

"I'm waiting to hear it from you," Rukmini responded hesitantly.

"From me...? What can I say to you?"

"Whatever you said to Udhav?"

"So you want to know all that I told him!"

"If it's intimate, you may refrain, there is no pressure."

"Nevertheless you are curious, aren't you?" Krishna smiled mysteriously.

"Shouldn't I be, after all I'm your *ardhangini* (wife) in happiness as well as in sorrow..."

...Krishna spread both his arms around Rukmini and turned her to face to him holding her by her waist.... He drew her closer and lowered his head into her ears to gently whisper...

"My beloved, these precious, intimate moments are about to end... I was destined to enjoy your commitment and companionship only until now.... Time has once again beckoned me and we will have to submit to time... I will always cherish your presence... always miss your tender touch..."

Rukmini was speechless.

It was beyond her how Krishna could remain so calm in the wake of a storm! She held him by his shoulders and shook him vigorously.

"What do you mean? Are you suggesting that your *avatar* as a human has come to an end?"

"*Devi*, we are all committed to fulfil our duties, for completion is truth and Krishna has never run away from truth."

"Is this the only way out, my Lord?" Rukmini asked unconvinced. She could not believe that the man she trusted implicitly and holding on to whose hand she had dared to leave her maiden kingdom, had today become a suspect. She could not believe that she doubted his intentions...

"...Are you aware of what you speak, my Lord?"

Krishna continued to smile.

"As my better half you ought to know that I've never expressed anything to you without meaning?"

Rukmini's eyes brimmed with tears. "Does it mean that you will now…?" She could not complete her sentence.

"Yes, my duty as a human has come to an end!"

"And me?" Rukmini was unable to contain her sorrow, "What happens to me? You are a part of my body and my soul…. Is it ever possible for the other half to survive without the first?"

"But…" Rukmini stopped mid-sentence. There was so much she wanted to tell Krishna… so much she wanted to ask him but watching him, she felt she was staring at some outsider. She felt helpless and alienated….

Krishna enveloped her in his arms and as he did so, Rukmini who had been trying to be brave all along, broke down…! That day she let out a wail that nobody could ever forget... Rukmini sobbed like a child and the entire Dwarika palace drenched in her grief. Krishna was no exception. It was difficult for him to tear her apart from him but staring at the heavenly abode, Krishna seemed to be sending a signal to his companions. "I've had enough and I'm homebound!"

◆

[32]

The battle of Kurukshetra was all set to take off on the banks of rivers Hiranya and Kapila. On one side was the army of the Pandavas and on the other side were the Kauravas… in between stood the solitary chariot of Arjuna. Suddenly Arjuna developed cold feet to oppose the elders in the family and expressed to opt out of the battleground…. It was not until Krishna presented himself in his formidable *avatar* to Arjuna that he changed his mind….

Blowing the conch to a mournful note, Krishna said, "Only the one who is devoid of anger or attachment is the one who is truly aware. The one who conquers his mind is the one who conquers the Universe…"

The message was not directed towards just Arjuna but the entire Universe and echoed in all directions. "The one who is devoid of desires, devoid of expectations from anyone, is the one who is free from worldly attachments…. One, who is positive, focused and victorious… who is egoless, selfless and feels compassion for all is the one who attains salvation…"

Krishna felt his body sinking. He wondered why it was so difficult to desert the human incarnation…. Did every human being deserting his body endure similar suffering and anguish?

Krishna was in excruciating pain. His eyes still shut, he recalled the engulfing darkness while inside mother Devaki's womb…. He remembered Devaki's labour pangs on the *ashtami* day of *Shravan* month before his arrival into the world…. Perhaps, his pain today was similar to that of Devaki that dark night…

Is this the destiny of mankind to be born to pain and to die in pain...? Is the human life meant to be just a journey of suffering...? He recalled his own words.

"For every living being, death is inevitable and after death there is rebirth.... Dust thou art and to dust thou shall return."

Yet today, his own words sounded futile to Krishna. Was he able to detach himself from love and relationships? Had he in all fairness fulfilled his role and duty in the Cosmos? Was he in the true sense disconnected from everyone and everything? Had he really set himself free?

Had mother Devaki and father Vasudev, his various cowherd friends and the innumerable lanes of Gokul and the bank of river Yamuna succeeded in bidding him goodbye?

Why had he entwined himself into these bondages and increased his own suffering?

Krishna's toe wounded with Jara's arrow bled profusely and succinctly his entire body turned pale.

Jara stared helplessly at Krishna's foot and the surrounding pool of blood. Krishna had not yet opened his eyes.

"O Lord, what can I do to reduce your suffering?" said Jara.

Krishna stirred from his position. "It was your duty, Jara, to cause me pain not to reduce my suffering.... It was your role to bring me dismay so even if you attempt to offer me solace, you can only cause me sorrow, my friend.... That is your destiny...!" Krishna said with a faint smile.

A cluster of peacock feathers fell into cohesive heaps around him and strains from his flute reverberated in the atmosphere....

It was as if the flute was beckoned by a familiar melody from the other end of the shore. The melody of a caressing, full of yearning lullaby calling out to him...

✦

[33]

"Kaanha... O Kaanha... Kaanhaa... O Kaanhaa...!" mother Yashoda was getting restless and calling out to him.

It was an everyday exercise for little Krishna to hide behind the tree in their courtyard and watch his mother turn furious.

Mother Yashoda had got used to looking for him everywhere before lunch time and finally dragging him into the kitchen, twisting his ear. Today, for a change, Kaanha was inside the house but he could not resist playing pranks on his mother.

Yashoda emerged from the house looking for Krishna. She caught a glimpse of his yellow *dhoti* while hiding behind a tree. She ran after him and holding him by the ear dragged him inside the house.

"Open your mouth, let me scrutinise what you have been eating..." she demanded.

"*Umhu...*" Kaanha compressed his lips and shook his head. He was determined to harass his mother.

"Are you going to open your mouth or not?" Yashoda sounded exasperated.

"*Umhu...*"

By now mother Yashoda was livid, "So you don't want to eat?"

"*Umhu...*"

"Make up your mind, if you don't have your meal now, I will not serve you food for the entire day."

"*Umhu...*" Kaanha shrugged his shoulders.

"Fine, now if you come asking for food I will hit you," Yashoda concluded knowing fully well that this was not true.

"It's okay," Kaanha announced and fled out of the room.

"Kaanha... O Kaanha... Kaanhaa... O Kaanhaa..." Yashoda went screaming after him but he had disappeared out of sight.

✦

[34]

"Kaanha… O Kaanha… Kaanhaa… O Kaanhaa…!" A melodious voice soaked in the cool breeze of river Yamuna had been calling out to him for a long time… Kaanha heard the cries but chose to ignore them. He was angry. Sitting at the bank of the river, throwing pebbles into the water and watching them swim across, Krishna was sulking…. The subtle waves mingled with the singing birds in the sky and created an unusual melody. It was as if the sun was indicating to the clouds to get ready for sunset…

Kaanha had been sitting all day at the shore, ankles dipped into the water, throwing pebbles. He had not eaten anything the entire day and was repentant about it.

"Kaanha… O Kaanha… Kaanhaa… O Kaanhaa…!" Now the sweet voice seemed to come from close quarters and in a little while stood before him. Radha had arrived on the river bank of Yamuna looking out for him and on spotting him said, "What are you doing here? I have been looking for you everywhere, all day."

"Why?" There was no trace of Kaanha's anger reducing. On the contrary, on an empty stomach he sounded more sarcastic. Clearly his prank had cost him dearly.

"Why!" Radha asked sitting beside him at the riverside. He was about to fling more pebbles into the water but Radha snatched them away from him.

"Why do I look for you every day, Kaanha?"

"Yes, why do you? I have been meaning to ask you that. Go away and don't chew my brains."

"Chew your brains!" Radha got up and held Krishna's hair and ripped them apart. "So you appear to be angry?"

"Yes," Kaanha snapped. Then snatching the pebbles from her hand he threw them into the water.

"And hungry too...?" Radha smiled, "Then why didn't you eat when mother called you for food, what prevented you at that time?"

"Because," replied Krishna, "I had not consulted you then."

"Oh... but you have now, so why don't you run and grab a meal quickly," Radha replied soaking her ankles into the water.

Getting irritated Kaanha interrupted, "Will you leave now?"

"Most certainly, but not without taking you with me... Mother has ordered me to bring you along with me."

"Then why didn't you say so all this while?"

"But you didn't ask me?" Radha was enjoying teasing him.

Kaanha rose to his feet instantly and grabbing Radha's hand said, "Let's leave soon!"

"Why, let's sit for a while, what's the hurry?" Radha ragged him.

"Are you coming or should I leave without you?" Kaanha said without letting go off her hand.

"But if I go without you then what do I tell mother? Do I tell her that I have returned home because I'm hungry?" Kaanha was in conflict while Radha continued to dabble her feet into the water. She showed no signs of getting up....

Kaanha thought for a while and then pushed her hard. Not expecting this and sitting on the edge of the rock, Radha fell into the river with a splash. She got up drenched to her feet in the cold water while Kaanha, without turning back ran with all his might towards home....

"Kaanha... O Kaanha... Kaanhaa... O Kaanhaa...!"

The melodious voice so many years later trailed after him...

✦

[35]

Those were days of the gushing Yamuna River. Today, he sat by the gently flowing Hiranya and Kapila Rivers.

Then he was an arrogant, temperamental, young boy. Today, he was the worldly wise, meditating Krishna.

Everything seemed so close and yet it felt as if somebody was calling out to him from very far away...

"...Kaanha... O Kaanha... Kaanhaa... O Kaanhaa."

Krishna woke up startled and looked around him dazed.

There was no one around him except Jara sitting on his knees and hands folded. But the echo persisted... Krishna clearly heard someone calling out to him. He strained his eyes to look around him but spotted no one...

"Lord, what can I do for you? Should I serve you some water?" Jara pleaded to him.

Krishna felt restless. He looked around with searching eyes.... He could hear the voice echo in his ears but felt fatigued and shut his eyes again.

"Kaanha... O Kaanha... Kaanhaa... O Kaanhaa...!"

Somebody was obstructing his final journey. Somebody he had failed in his responsibilities towards. Who could that be? What was that task he had left incomplete that prevented Krishna from detaching himself with the Cosmos...

✦

[36]

The journey to Mathura was determined. Akrur*ji* had arrived to collect Krishna at Nand *baba*'s home and was waiting in the courtyard.

Krishna's uncle, *mama* Kansa had invited him to participate in the *yajna*. Yashoda was not in favour of letting Krishna leave for Mathura and had relentlessly argued over it with her husband, but Nand *baba* had left the final decision to his son. He had always treated Kaanha as an adult and had intrinsic faith in his intelligence and prowess. He believed that whatever Krishna did was right and somehow for the betterment of everyone...

✦

[37]

Standing below a dense tree beside the Yamuna, Radha wept bitterly. Her long tresses uncombed and her saree carelessly draped.... It was evident that she had not devoted any attention to her dressing in her hurry to meet up Krishna at the river bank. It took a long time for Krishna to accomplish his pending tasks and arrive at the river bank. On spotting Radha with her long hair loose, he moved forward to tie them into a bun. Radha pushed him away.

"Go away," she said unable to control her tears. Kaanha tried to explain himself but she was not willing to be pacified.

"Do not undertake this journey, Kaanha.... What will I do without you?" she had asked the same question umpteenth time to him since morning...

"You can go to sell the milk... fill the grains... and... take care of Ayan," Krishna chided her even though he felt deeply affected by her tears.

"Is that so?" Radha retorted looking at him sternly, "It appears you have made up your mind, haven't you? You don't seem to care about us any longer..."

"Radha, you know very well that Gokul is just a beginning for me. I have many more journeys to undertake. If you will prevent me thus with your tear-filled eyes, how will I continue my voyage?"

"Then don't go.... What can be so important awaiting you in Mathura?"

"Don't you know that, my dear?"

"I don't... I don't know anything.... Go away."

"That's it... every time you get angry and sulk with me I love you even more..."

"Love me...?" Radha chided him, "Is that the reason you choose to leave me and go away."

"Yes, that's the reason I have to leave you. If you continue to love me so dearly, I will not be able to go anywhere, and if that happens, I'm not sure how long I will have to remain shackled in these bondages."

"I don't comprehend anything of what you say..." Radha said looking perplexed.

"It does not matter," Kaanha smiled. "Akrur*ji* should be here any moment, so can I take your leave now? I still have to pacify my grieving mother."

"You want to forsake so many relationships only to fulfil your commitment to uncle Kansa.... He is a wicked man, so why do you need to go to him?"

"I have to... because everyone has a right to freedom..."

"I have never been able to follow your mysterious talks..."

"Nor have I, Radha; and that is why it's imperative that I take on this journey."

"Go, go away... and don't ever come back again," Radha said turning her back on him.

Kaanha stepped closer to her, was about to place his hand on her shoulder, but changed his mind. He stood still for a moment and said, "Say that again...."

"I will.... Go away and don't ever come back again..."

Kaanha's eyes filled with tears. He looked soulfully at Radha, inserted his flute into his waistband and raising both his arms said...

"*Tathastu...*"

He turned his back and began walking. Radha heard his retracting footsteps but had made up her mind not to stop him this time.... But just a few minutes later, as if struck by a lightning she charged behind Kaanha...

"Kaanha... O Kaanha... Kaanhaa... O Kaanhaa...!"

The melodious voice trailed after him and continued to ring in his ears after all these years.

The echo reverberated in the surroundings even now, as he sat all by himself at the river bank.

The glorious rays of the sun had spread its splendour on the shores of rivers Hiranya and Kapila. The pristine water of Hiranya shimmered like golden waves. Jara was still waiting beside Krishna on bended knees and hands folded.

The amber sunrays fell onto Krishna's face from time to time.... Seated beneath the *peepal* tree, he could hear the rumbling breeze.... The sunrays combined with the rustling of *peepal* leaves conjured a vision of what was to unfold in near future....

It was evident that Krishna was in agony but he continued to smile through it with his eyes closed. He could still visualise a cluster of peacock feathers falling into heaps around him.... He could hear the melody of the flute.... This was no ordinary melody.

The voyager had embarked on his journey but something held him back.... Eyes still shut, Krishna spoke in a painful voice. "Why do you entangle me in your love, Radha...? I have to go... let me go... my sojourn is still incomplete!"

✦

[38]

Fresh after his bath, there was the usual glow on Krishna's face as he entered into Rukmini's private chamber. He appeared normal but there were tell-tale clues of the previous night trauma…

Rukmini stood before him holding the *aarti thali.* She looked at the flickering lamp and was unsure if it was a result of the breeze or her trembling hands.

She raised her hand to place a *tilak* on Krishna's forehead. To do so, she had to stretch herself extensively…. Her hands still trembling, she stuck raw rice on his forehead and performed the *aarti* after which she stood for a while looking at Krishna, unable to control her tears...

"*Devi*... this was inevitable… didn't you know it? So why this tremor and so much fear?"

"It's not fear… it's attachment, my Lord."

"And how come you have fallen prey to it?"

"This human incarnation is not only about duty but also about bonding…. This body is tempted by desires."

"I'm surprised that you should be saying all this," said Krishna.

"Why surprised? Nobody knows us women better than you," replied Rukmini.

"Are you being sarcastic?"

"Am I not permitted to?"

"This is not the time for it…" Krishna said, cupping Rukmini's face in both his palms, "We're running short of time."

Rukmini's eyes brimmed over with tears, "Are you going to abandon all our love, affection and attachment...? Are you going to desert so many relationships...?"

"It's inevitable that the one who is born has to die..."

"But you are..."

"I'm Krishna... born from the womb of mother Devaki, reared by mother Yashoda, your husband and the emperor of Dwarika, that's all...!"

"I understand but I'm not able to accept it."

"If there is self-realisation, then acceptance should come automatically..." Krishna placed his hand on Rukmini's head. She closed her eyes. Tears that had been threatening to overflow for a long time, now dropped from her eyelashes. Krishna closed his eyes as well and stood motionless, his hand resting on Rukmini's head.

Suddenly all the despair, anger and protest suffocating Rukmini evaporated in that one magical moment with Krishna's touch. It was as if Rukmini had along with the *aarti thali* submitted her body, mind and soul to Krishna.

Rukmini said in a voice almost inaudible, "*Twadiyam Vastu Govind Tubhyamev Samarpyate...*"

Krishna was startled, "You too, Rukmini!"

"Why... why is everyone submitting themselves to me completely? If I decline them, it would be unfair and if I accept them, where do I take them from here...? It's up to me to resolve these obligations, to free myself from human bondages..."

Krishna was bewildered. These were women he had known intimately yet never fully comprehended them. Still they had recognised his quest for salvation and what's more accepted it.... But had he succeded in understanding his wife, her desires and her expectations...? She, who lived her entire life aspiring for his happiness, had he made adequate efforts to fulfil her dreams...?

Krishna looked at Rukmini. Her eyes shut and head bowed, Rukmini kneeled at Krishna's feet weeping....

Krishna felt mesmerised by the visual, obsessed by the human incarnation and bondage.... Fragrant memories of several magical moments of his lifetime overpowered him.

He recalled Rukmini and Draupadi. Two contrasting identities... they had nothing in common with each other and yet were so similar in their devotion and surrender to him. Krishna wondered how strange that Nature should create two diverse personalities with identical emotions.

They had recognised his need for salvation even before he could express it. His two favourite people had travelled inside his heart and articulated his thoughts for him.

"It was as if they were leading me through my maze and helping me to find my way.... Probably something only women can accomplish," thought Krishna.

"Only they have the expertise... only women are able to conquer both their mind and heart and fulfil their duties.... They have the virtues of forgiveness, acceptance, endurance and affection! Only they are able to endure pain to create life. That is the reason she leads the fourth round of death during the wedding rounds by fire and lives up to the title of, '*sahadharmacharini*'."

Krishna broke from his reverie and after great effort asked, "*Devi*, will you grant me leave now...?"

"Grant you leave! It is your right to order me, *Yajnaputra*, I'm merely your slave bound to obey you."

Her eyes still shut, Rukmini was kneeling at Krishna's feet... Krishna bent to gently pick her up and tenderly held her by her back. Eyes streaming down with tears, Rukmini raised her lashes and threw back her head.

Krishna held her eyelashes between his fingers as if holding a flower petal and then bent over her tear-stained mouth to drop a passionate, lingering kiss.

It was a farewell kiss.... Perhaps, the final!

◆

[39]

It was as if the river was overflowing with peacock feathers. They grew in heaps and added in numbers. Its texture and its innumerable colours drew unusual patterns in Krishna's mind and the patterns entwined innumerable motifs from innumerable relationships…

Krishna who never knew leisure in his lifetime, today waited for time to take him across. And time deliberately moved slowly as if testing Krishna's patience.

Krishna lingered on the heaps of peacock feathers. He wondered how many colours were imbibed in the feather… three… four… five… or were they innumerable…?

Colours of passion… of deprivation… of anxiety… of longing... of separation... of affection... of indecision.... of acceptance... of compassion... of surrender... of faith... of retreat... and of resignation…. It was as if all the colours had intermingled…. They conjured and erased different images in his mind….

So much can unfold before closed eyes… and so much was unfolding!

Krishna rolled his tongue over his dry mouth and was surprised to taste it salty. In a way unknown to him, his lips had drenched in his own tears.

◆

[40]

The parting with Rukmini was perhaps the most painful moment for both of them!

This must be true for all companions. After spending a lifetime together, they are frightened at the thought of parting from each other.

Most of them live in the illusion that the moment will never come or lack the mental capacity to accept it.

It is futile to destroy the present by worrying about the future but by blanking it out or hoping that it will never occur or get postponed is being ignorant too.

Separation is inevitable. What has commenced has to at some stage end. Those who understand this and accept it are able to relish the present better than others. They don't live under illusions of permanence and accept the present as a step towards future.

"So *Devi...*" Krishna turned to Rukmini. She was still trembling after the passionate kiss and her eyes were overflowing with agony and tears. Krishna broke her trance to complete his plea, "I seek your approval to leave now, *Devi*."

"Will you get approval by asking?" Rukmini responded with complaining eyes.

"If I don't, I get into further trouble..."

"Lord, can I ask for something?"

"I have surrendered to you my soul and my body.... Is there anything more important?" Krishna asked placing his hand on her shoulder.

"I'm aware and I'm fortunate to be your consort.... But my Lord, in all these years you have not submitted to me your heart," Rukmini whined tearfully.

"Do you really believe that?"

"Isn't that true? Have you shared your thoughts, your sorrows, your worries and your fears with me?"

"But *Devi...* "

Rukmini interrupted him mid-sentence, "Now don't tell me that you have never felt the desire because these anxieties are part of human bondage...."

"What makes you bring up this topic today, at this moment...?"

"If not now, then when...?" pleaded Rukmini.

They were quiet for long moments, eyes locked and comfortable in each other's silence... Rukmini refused to shift her gaze as if looking for answers in Krishna's eyes.

In so many years for the first time, Krishna was discomforted looking Rukmini in the eye.... She had not looked so pained even when he brought Satyabhama home.... She had accepted Jambuvanti and his other queens and showered them with affection, but when he wedded Satyabhama, her disapproval was evident in her streaming eyes....

Those tear-filled eyes were sad and helpless. There was betrayal in them but her agony was not as intense or penetrating as they appeared now...

It was as if she was shooting arrows from her eyes that pierced deep into Krishna's heart.

Unable to meet her gaze any longer, Krishna said...

"It's time for me to depart *Devi*; may I take your leave?"

Rukmini's face blazed like a flame.

"Depart...? You still need to depart? Or is this your final departure?"

"You know better about my departures and also the results of it..." Krishna folded his hands, "If I have hurt you intentionally or unintentionally, I plead forgiveness..."

Rukmini held on to both his hands for a while.

Their eyes closed, it was as if they were building barriers for the flowing tears...

"Beloved..." Krishna had to search words... "Don't stop me even for a moment now. If you do, the moment will once again transform into a century.... You understand what I mean, so please grant me leave..."

"And me?"

"Time conquers all. What has to happen will happen and no one can change that *Devi...*"

"As you desire, my Lord.... It seems there is no way out except salvation."

"Salvation also is not a solution, it's a mere direction. There is no escape from following a path that is predetermined..."

Without waiting for another moment, Krishna stepped out of Rukmini's private chamber as she stared after his sculpted back without blinking...

She was aware that his journey was predetermined.

She was aware that everyone who had emerged with Krishna had to return to the roots... including Goddess Lakshmi!

And even the Shesh*naag*...

✦

[41]

Writhing in pain a mournful Krishna waited for his dear friend. Daruk had departed from Prabhas Kshetra to go and fetch Arjuna.

Krishna was aware that Arjuna would be heartbroken with the news. Falguni, as he lovingly called him had not been able to love anyone more than Krishna in his life. It was solely on Krishna's conviction that he had dared to fight the Kurukshetra battle and won!

Krishna sensed his entire body burning with pain…

Head resting on the *peepal* trunk, Krishna was able to see clairvoyantly with his eyes shut. The peacock feathers had by now grown in heaps on river Yamuna and floated far and wide with the fluctuating waves of high and low tides.

Somebody was hiding amidst the *kadamb* tree and playing the flute as a result of which the entire tree was swaying.... Who was swaying the tree?

Was it Balram standing beneath the tree?

Or was it the hissing of Kalia*naag?*

The deity revered as Parambramhan and endowed with conch, *chakra* (discus), *gada* (mace) and a lotus flower, heard echoes of "*Aham Brahmasmi*" in his ears. The deity who said "Among the trees I'm *peepal*" today rested against it. Fretful, holding on to his every breath…

Was he really awaiting Arjuna or was it something else?

✦

[42]

At the Prabhas Kshetra when the Yadavas were turning violent, Balram turned to look at Krishna seated calmly. It was difficult to gauge what was going on in Krishna's mind but Balram was trembling with fear…

He walked towards Krishna and tried to shake him.

"What are you doing Kaanha…? What is this…? The Yadava bloodline will be destroyed in this manner…"

"I'm aware…" Krishna appeared fearfully calm. Balram looked into his eyes. His usually sparkling, cheerful, mesmeric eyes today were expressionless like the carved eyes of a statue.

"Kaanha…!"

"*Dau* (elder brother), don't you remember the curse of *Maharishi* Durvasa?"

"I…d…do…" Balram stumbled over his words…the stuttering was partly due to intoxication and partly out of fear… "Does it mean that we too…?"

"Why, are we different from the rest?" Krishna responded icily, his eyes reflecting the fragrance of water, air, earth, fire and ether…

He fixed his gaze on Balram…

> *Dehinoasmin Yatha Dehe Kaumaram Yauvanam Jara* ।
> *Tatha Dehantarpraptridhirrastatra Na Muhyati* ॥

"*Dau* there is no mourning of adolescence, youth, old age and transmigration of soul…"

"I don't want to hear any of this..." Balram was quaking. Krishna placed his arm over Balram's shoulder and gently drew him close to him. He embraced him tightly and held on to him for a while...

When they parted all doubts had subsided inside Balram's heart. He had no more questions. No sorrow and no regret could touch him now...

It was a strange experience where life seemed to sustain on breaths without the involvement of body or mind. Balram closed his eyes, folded his hands and bent to bow to Krishna... as he did so his tears fell on Krishna's feet as an offering...

Krishna, eyes closed, stroked Balram's hair while a deep and dense voice resounded in all directions...

Yathakashsthito Nitya Vayuh Sarvatrago Mahan ।
Tatha Sarvani Bhutani Matsthanityupadharya ॥

'Just as the sky is rigid in its position and air even though fickle does not let go off its place, in the end all living planets have to reside within me. Do understand this...'

Balram was still crying. In the cacophony around them caused by the battling Yadavas, Krishna's soothing voice echoed like a prayer in the surroundings.

This was the brother who would soon be transformed into dust.... This was the brother with whom he had shared so many beautiful moments during his childhood. This was the brother who Krishna loved more than his own life...

"You may leave now..." Krishna said.

Balram was visibly affected by the battling Yadavas. "And you?" he asked.

"Me?" Krishna looked and sounded unruffled. His eyes were trifle moist.

"Me?" he repeated "I have to be here until all this ends and after that..." he didn't complete his words.

"Why? Why Kaanha? Why should you endure all this, be responsible for it?" Balram was getting worked up. "Why should you...?"

"Why should I bring this on myself…?" Krishna completed his sentence.

"*Sanshayatam vinashayti….*" The one who had forever enlightened everyone was today filled with doubts…

He could see the Yadavas transform into demons before him. Krishna witnessed the visual through misty eyes layered with tears…

"You must leave now," he repeated his request to Balram and brushed away a solitary tear before it could trickle down his cheek.

Balram clasped Krishna in a tight embrace as if transporting him into his own body…

He held his brother in his strong arms for a long while and then briskly walked away… in the direction of Trivenisangam…

Far away, the sun was setting behind the Somnath Temple.

As he moved farther and farther away, his fading shadow resembled a golden sculpture brewed in the pale, amber sunrays. He could still hear the mournful cries of the dying Yadavas behind his back... Balram quickened his strides as if to escape the wails. He felt as if the tormented Yadavas were beckoning him and he did not want to turn back…

Deep down, he held himself guilty...

The root cause of all this was alcohol…

And if alcohol was freely accessible in Dwarika, it was under the patronage of Balram.

Even Krishna was aware of this.

And it's because he felt embarrassed questioning Balram on this matter that the Yadavas had exploited the situation.

✦

[43]

"May I come in, please?" Krishna sought permission before entering Balram's room…

It was late evening. The salty breeze from across the river blew away the curtains over the doors. The orange sunlight spreading from the setting sun filled the room like flames…. The entire room and everything within it appeared orange…. The flickering sunlight on Balram's fair body spread out like a pinch of saffron sprinkled in milk….

"You, at this hour, Kaanha…?"

"Why? Is it an inappropriate time?" There was a hint of sarcasm in Krishna's tone, which was unusual.

"No, it's not that… tell me…?"

"If I really speak my mind, you may not like it, *dau…*" Krishna said looking directly into Balram's eyes.

Balram matched his gaze, "I know… I'm aware of what you are about to tell me is going to hurt me… I'm also aware that you've been pained getting to know things about me…. The truth is even after hearing you out I may still…" Balram looked away to stare at the setting sun from his window.

"Kaanha, some things are better left unsaid…"

"That's a lame excuse, *dau*…. The biggest drawback is submitting to your weakness…"

"Kaanha, if you have come to advise me, please go away but if you have come to join me you are more than welcome," Balram pulled out various silver vessels and began placing them over a small stool nearby.

"*Dau*, you are responsible for the prosperity and protection of the Yadava race and you…?"

"Protection… responsibility…!" There was cynicism and a nagging pain in Balram's voice. It had the melancholy of a man startled by his own voice when echoed in empty corridors…

"Kaanha, you are the king of Dwarika, you are the provider, the protector and the caretaker of this land, so why do you torment me with these elaborate words?"

Balram pulled out an ornate bottle, poured some liquid into it and relished a sip.

"*Dau*…" there was betrayal in Krishna's voice and eyes. He could not believe what he was witnessing, "What are you doing, *dau*…?"

Balram stopped Krishna before he could complete his sentence.

"I'm your elder brother, yet everything in this land transpires according to your dictates."

"What can I do, do I have a choice?" Krishna sounded like a fatigued, dejected lieutenant, "I don't even have a say about where I wish to dine…. The option is never mine. I'm a mere prisoner of time who has no right to express himself…"

"Is that so?" There was nastiness in Balram's tone…"So you indulge in word play with me as well… wonderful!"

"*Dau*… have I hurt you unknowingly…? Have I erred somewhere?"

"You…?" Balram's tone was sharp and hurting, "Can you ever err? You are infallible. Everyone bows to you."

Krishna looked at Balram. His eyes reflected the pain of a dejected king.

"You know very well that they don't bow to me. They bow to my strength, my power and my strength is you, Balram…"

"Do you realise that today…?"

"There are things in life one understands but find it difficult to accept…. I empathise with your bitterness… your pain, but…"

"Is this the narrator of *Gita* at the Kurukshetra battle talking to me...? The infinitely knowledgeable supporter of Pandavas and the guide of Arjuna...? I'm surprised..." Balram was intoxicated. He was slurring on his words, speaking dramatically...

Yato Yato Nischarati Manaschanchalamasthiram I
Tatasta To Niyamyetadatmanyev Vasham Nayet II

"If your mind wanders, you need to track your mind and restore it inside your soul.... Isn't that true? You know everything, you are impeccable! We are *shudras*... poor and deprived.... You saved us from the Kurukshetra battle and we are at your mercy..."

"*Dau*... I'm your slave... I will do as you say but I cannot bear this despair..."

"Ah... the king of Dwarika cannot bear sorrow...?"

"I'm your younger brother..." pleaded Krishna.

"But you are the king, the leader of the affluent, aristocrat Yadavas... the emperor of Dwarika... the Lord of *Bharatvarsh*... the most popular man of this era and the narrator of Kurukshetra..."

Krishna sat at Balram's feet and held them with both his hands, "How could you fester so much sorrow... so much pain...? You have harboured so many grievances in your heart without ever sharing them with me..."

Krishna sounded heartbroken and watching him in this state filled Balram's eyes with tears as well. He placed his hand over Krishna's head and shut his eyes.

For a while both continued to sit silently...

They recalled their childhood adventures, their frequent quarrels and truce, their conflicts and anxieties, their revenge and trust.... All these moments passed by like a watershed.

It was difficult to determine how long they had been sitting thus, but to Balram it felt like a century.

Then very quietly, Krishna rose, without disrupting the quietude or the mood of the moment.

"May I take your leave, *dau*?"

Balram continued to sit looking dazed.

"Please forgive me, Kaanha," Balram folded the hands...

"*Dau*, you put me in sin..." Kaanha held his hands and Balram began to cry.

"I have let you down... I have wronged you..." Krishna helped Balram rise and then embraced him...

The brothers clasped in an embrace. Balram was still weeping on Krishna's shoulder.

Krishna was in a trance. He had foreseen the footsteps of future.... He made a decision. Never again would he reprimand his elder brother on his habit of drinking.

✦

[44]

He was the brother who had several times saved him from his mother's wrath. They had played *gilli danda* together and were partners in ragging the milkmaids...

They would contest to check who would be the first to swim across the river Yamuna, and so that a defeated young Kaanha would not cry, elder brother Balram had on so many occasions deliberately swum leisurely.

Together they would harass the cowherd women on their way to Mathura. They would climb the trees at the Yamuna bank and break the water pots of the village belles passing by.

For Balram, Krishna was dearer to him than his own life.

He couldn't bear tears in Kaanha's eyes and would punish the cowherd boys for troubling Kaanha by chaining them to a tree.... Later he would climb the same tree and shake it vigorously until the little boys screamed out of fear and frustration. He sought vindictive pleasure in their torment and wouldn't set them free until they apologised to Kaanha....

But when mother Rohini took Krishna's side, it made Balram uncomfortable for some mysterious reason.

It wasn't as if mother Yashoda did not love Balram but there were two things he wasn't willing to share with anyone. His *gada* (mace) and mother Rohini...

Since morning Balram had been looking out for Kaanha.... He wondered where Kaanha could be hiding.... It was almost noon but there was no sign of him.

Balram had searched all his regular places of hiding....

At the bank of river Yamuna... amidst the bushes of *kadamb* tree... on way to Mathura... beneath the *peepal* tree... the cowshed... behind Radha's home... but Kaanha was nowhere....

How could Balram have found him when Kaanha was hiding in the courtyard of their home since morning?

"Kaanha... O Kaanha... Kaanhaa... O Kaanhaa...!" Balram called out to him.

"*Sssh... sssh...*" There was a sound. Who could this be except Kaanha...? Balram looked around him frantically.

Little Kaanha was hiding in the courtyard behind the house.... Time and again he would peep inside through the window waiting anxiously for a hand to emerge... a hand that was to bring him food...

Today, once again, he was punished by his mother.

His friends and he had invaded Kokila's home and polished off all the butter in her pot.... That was not all... they had also thrown pebbles and raided her home...!

When Kokila carried her complaint to mother Yashoda, she was already upset with Kaanha over something and Kokila's protest triggered her to rage....

"Balram... O Balram..."

Balram had been eavesdropping their conversation and awaited summons.

He dropped his *gada* and rushed inside the room....

"Yes, *badimaa,*" Balram responded fully prepared about what to expect next.

"Go and fetch Kaanha right away."

"But mother..."

"Didn't you hear me, bring him immediately.... Today I will not spare him... I will teach him a lesson.... Just bring him here right away..."

Rohini overheard this while returning from the cowshed carrying manure. She went and stood beside mother Yashoda...

"Let it be, *didi* (elder sister)... what difference does it make? He is a child after all, won't he create mischief?"

"Rohini, don't you dare come between us." Balram was pleased to hear mother Yashoda's rejoinder...

"But..." Rohini made another futile attempt in defence of Kaanha...

Usually when the village belles of Gokul carried tales of her Kaanha, Yashoda was the one to defend him. Today however she was not willing to be indulged....

"Balram, bring him at once... I will tie him in the loft and won't give him any food all day..."

Balram was gleeful, "Today there is no escape for Kaanha."

In normal circumstances, Balram would have protected Kaanha and if necessary would even lie to save him but by intervening, mother Rohini had needlessly ruined it all...

Balram had searched for Kaanha at all his regular hiding places.

At the bank of river Yamuna... amidst the bushes of *kadamb* tree... on road to Mathura... beneath the *peepal* tree... the cowshed... behind Radha's home... but Kaanha was nowhere.

How could he have found him when Kaanha was hiding in the courtyard behind their home since morning?

Mother Rohini had spotted him while returning from the cowshed and taken pity on the small, mischievous boy.... In any case Rohini was always soft on Kaanha when mother Yashoda penalised him and deprived him of food...

It was she who had drawn his attention and gestured him to wait for her.

She had, in fact, gone inside the house to fetch food for him.

"*Sssh...sssh...*"

Balram spotted Krishna and came closer.

"What are you doing here...?" Balram asked innocently.

"*Sshshh*..." little Kaanha placed his finger over his lips. His wide innocent eyes shared a secret with his brother, "I'm hiding.... That Kokila has gone and told everything to mother..."

"Is that right?" Balram feigned ignorance.

"So mother is looking for me... today she will not spare me... I will be either tied up in the loft or locked inside the cowshed..." Kaanha felt sorry for himself, "I haven't eaten a morsel since morning..."

"Why? What about that pot full of butter?"

"I didn't eat that alone.... There were so many of us... and that was in the morning... I'm ravenous..."

"Then what will you do now...?"

"Mother Rohini has gone inside to fetch some food. She will pass it to me through this window... I will grab it and run away to return only late in the evening.... By then Nand *baba* would have returned.... Once he is home, I need not fear...." Kaanha communicated his master plan....

"I see..." Balram nodded sagaciously and then got up to leave.

"Where are you going?" Kaanha asked him...

"To check out what mother is doing... what is taking her so long...?" Balram moved towards the house portico.

Kaanha stared after him with anxious eyes.

After a while, a hand stretched out from the window...

It held a delicious *roti* (grain bread) over which was placed a big lump of butter.

Kaanha felt his mouth watering....

He stretched his hand and was about to snatch it from the opposite hand...

...when another hand pushed out of the window and grabbed Kaanha's hand...

She held both his hands and tightly chained them to the window.

"Mother... Rohini...!" Kaanha was not ready to believe that mother Rohini could do this to him.

"Mother..." Kaanha began to plead and called out to her in a sorrowful voice.

"Shut up... I don't want to hear a word... You are going to spend the rest of the day here..." scolded mother Yashoda.

And who was this standing behind his mother...? Elder brother Balram...? How could his own brother do this to him? How could he carry tales to his mother?

Kaanha could not believe his eyes.

"My own brother...?"

He still could not believe it.

✦

[45]

'My brother Balram, can he really do this?' Krishna still could not believe it.

Krishna felt deeply wounded and shut his eyes.

Udhav stood before him.

"I don't intend to cause you distress but it's my duty to report to you about all that goes on in Dwarika..." began Udhav.

"I suspected but not in my wildest imagination did I envision that *dau*... my *dau* can do something like this..." Krishna felt heavy hearted, "If *dau* drinks alcohol openly in Dwarika, how can I prevent the other Yadavas?"

"My Lord, *dau* has been encouraging everyone to drink freely. When Duryodhan visited him, the two of them sat on the river bank and drank together in public view..." Udhav informed and Krishna closed his eyes in sadness.

"Now the Yadavas will follow his example and it will be difficult to control them.... Their children have in any case turned power drunk and obsessed with money.... If they get addicted to alcohol then nobody can save them...."

Krishna looked at Udhav sorrowfully and once again shut his eyes in distress...

"Who can alter the path of destiny, Udhav? Despite my several attempts I have not been able to change the dictate of time.... What is meant to be will be, and there is no escape from that. I have understood that..."

"What is meant to be, my Lord…? What do you refer to…?

Krishna smiled weakly, unable to disguise his torment.

"That is future, Udhav…. It has already been conceived…. Now we have to wait for it to unfold… a frightening future… that will become a reality…"

"*Prabhu…*" Udhav could not comprehend all of what Krishna said but this much he understood that something ominous was to occur to the Yadava lineage…

◆

[46]

Having decided to undertake the journey to Prabhas Kshetra, Krishna felt it was imperative to first intimate Balram about his plans...

...In all of Dwarika, Balram was his only childhood companion.

Krishna believed that embracing his brother, he would be able to get rid of all his sorrows... his discomfort...

He put on his wooden sandals and began walking towards Balram's palace.

Udhav walked beside him but as Krishna's strides became faster. Udhav found it difficult to keep pace. Normally Krishna was always considerate towards people walking along with him but that day was different.

Today, he walked ahead without looking back...

He did not realise that Udhav had stopped midway.

Udhav sensed something seriously amiss... Krishna was unusually restless...! Sensing his feeling of extreme lowliness, Udhav held back.... He turned away without asking a single question or expressing himself...

Krishna realised that Udhav was not beside him only when he reached the staircase of Balram's palace.

"May I come in?" Krishna sought permission to enter his brother's room.

Balram had been addicted to alcohol for some time and always made excuses to avoid meeting up with Krishna after sunset. Krishna was his younger brother but he felt inferior to him… Balram accepted that alcohol was destructive for him but was not able to give it up…

Krishna had tried to reprimand him several times…. But rather than discuss the topic further, Balram preferred to never come before Krishna after dusk…. Whether it was a political matter or personal conflicts, Balram made sure to accomplish all tasks before evening.

Krishna was aware of his brother's weakness and as far as possible refrained from visiting his brother's room before dawn…

"May I come in…?" Krishna sought permission to enter Balram's private chamber.

Balram had just woken up. His room was filtered with the golden rays of the sunlight, his silken bedspread crumpled and his eyes still heavy with intoxication…

Once upon a time an extremely handsome man, Balram had started looking haggard due to regular drinking. His face appeared swollen early in the morning and his eyes looked strained and red…. His day began leisurely, for it took him considerable time to stir out of his stupor…

Krishna stepped into Balram's room and occupied a seat…. Balram was taken aback by his surprise visit. He had to still get into his morning motions and Krishna had landed at his doorstep.

"Kaanha… so early in the morning…?"

"Is it early morning? We are on the third phase of the day, *dau*… the trellis everywhere has turned golden…"

"The trellises in Dwarika are in any case golden, Krishna. They don't need the sunshine to sparkle… over here both the sun and time move according to your command…"

"*Dau*… time listens to no one…"

"Kaanha, you are saying this? You, the emperor of the golden Dwarika… the provider of fifty-six provinces… the creator of the land devoid of death, sorrow or disease… on whose command time travels… directions change course and seasons blossom…" Balram sounded not just intoxicated but extremely arrogant.

"Don't live under any illusion, *dau.* Lord of time is all powerful. Whenever things are moving according to our wishes, it's usually the beginning of something ominous... always remember that."

"Must you sermonise such profundities early in the morning...?" snapped Balram.

Krishna smiled weakly, "Of course not, such profundities should be reserved after sunset, am I right?"

Balram was startled, "Krishna, we will not discuss my drawback..."

Krishna responded, "*Dau,* is there anything left for discussion?"

"Don't trap me in your maze of words, Krishna.... You have kept aside all other work to visit my chamber in your Rajyasabha hour the matter has to be important..."

Krishna smiled knowingly, "You are very clever, *dau*... you do know me very well..."

Balram staggered out of his bed... his bare sculpted chest... strong arms... broad shoulders and a cluster of pearl necklaces around his neck... his uncombed black hair... and intoxicated eyes... Krishna stared at him for some time with affection, with compassion.

"I desire that we accompany the Yadavas to Prabhas Kshetra...!"

Balram standing beside the window was aghast. He watched the sunrays dancing on the flowing water in the river. The golden waves rumbled all the way to the shore and quietly scattered amidst the sand. It was low tide and there were many hours to go before the tide changed. Still, one could hear the angry, crashing waves inside Balram's chamber...

A shell-shocked Balram turned to Krishna and stared at him unblinkingly. He was searching for answers.

Krishna closed his eyes as if preventing Balram from letting into a secret.

For some time, there was no sound in the room except the sound of the waves...

"Prabhas...? Why Kaanha...?" There was tremor in Balram's voice and fear of the unknown.

Krishna opened his eyes.... He looked at Balram and continued to stare at him wordlessly.

"Are you trying to tell me that the time has come, Krishna?" Balram finally found his words.

"What can I say, *dau*...? The time has come for the spoken words to transform into reality..."

"Cannot we postpone this time?" Balram pleaded with Krishna exactly the way he had pleaded to *ma* Yashoda to save Krishna from her wrath in childhood...

"Postpone time?" Krishna had a smile on his face. He locked his eyes with Balram.... Balram's eyes were moist....

Balram signalled Krishna to come closer and spread both his arms. Krishna rose from his seat and clasped his elder brother in an embrace....

The brothers hugged each other tightly, their eyes shut as time passed by.... The waves in the river Yamuna resounded in the luxurious chamber of the magnificent palace situated on the river bank.

And amidst all this chaos, were two worried souls....

Both aware of what was to entail the following morning... one, fear ridden, the other hankering for everyone's salvation...

✦

[47]

It was midsummer afternoon in Dwarika and the entire town was in a celebratory mood.... There was festivity on the streets.... It was a beautiful visual to pass through a row of elevated golden chariots owned by the Yadavas. All these chariots were glorious and elaborately decorated with jewels, accompanied by distinguished *sarathis* (charioteers). The entire scenery was reflective of a hugely prosperous town.

Today Krishna had invited all the Yadavas for a carnival at the Prabhas Kshetra...

And they were all looking forward to the festivities...

There was a time when this town was eternally in a celebratory mood. After the devastation at the Kurukshetra battle, however, everything had turned desolate. There was not a single home in all of Dwarika that had not lost a life in the battle... and ever since, the once happy town had been in mourning....

Even Krishna had turned unusually quiet after the Kurukshetra... almost disconnected.

He who nurtured everyone around him... whose entire existence was a symbol of celebration... to watch someone so effervescent and vibrant just wither away... the hangover was bound to reflect in his surroundings....

The Yadavas had been in the shadow of death for so long that they had forgotten the meaning of joy or festivity.

For many years now Dwarika had not witnessed the buzz and the fanfare associated with the celebration of *Janmashtami.*

That is why today, Krishna personally went from door to door, to invite the Yadavas – all the men – old and young for celebration at Prabhas Kshetra. Clearly, Yadavas were euphoric.

Their women were so excited that they decked up in jewels. The children were dancing on the streets in ecstasy.

And the men could not wait to relish the euphoria that had come to them after a prolonged eclipse...

◆

[48]

Krishna looked at the carnival around him from his window.

He heaved a deep sigh.

Had he taken an appropriate decision, he wondered.

Someone as enlightened as him, who had lived his entire life on the path of truth and justice, for the first time experienced self doubt. Was his decision right? Was he taking the right step?

So many people were ready to embark on a journey solely on his honour.... They had implicit faith in his word. And to think that none of them were going to return home alive....

What had they achieved out of Kurukshetra?

Was the victory of Kurukshetra in the true sense a conquest?

Had they relished their success? Was it in all honesty a triumph of duty?

Had he fulfilled his duty?

For that matter, what did even the victorious Pandavas accomplish from the battle... corpses of their sons?

Or those last few breaths of loved ones lurking in the shadows of death...?

And for that matter, wasn't this a journey towards another Kurukshetra as well...? Would they eventually succeed in destroying injustice?

Before he could set off on the early evening journey, there were many questions and doubts in Krishna's mind.

He had been introspecting on these issues for a long time.

He was unafraid as long as he had not encountered the moment.

But now, when he was face-to-face with the moment and questioned himself about consciousness and credibility, even Krishna who was Arjuna's *sarathi,* for a brief spell felt gripped with fear.

✦

[49]

"Let's go, I'm ready," it was Satyabhama's voice.

She emerged from the inside room and addressing Krishna said, "Let's go, I'm ready to leave."

Beautiful and fragile as porcelain, wheat-complexioned Satyabhama was extremely sensual and characteristically well-groomed...

Krishna stared at her.... Her long thick hair tied up in a bun decorated with a variety of fragrant flowers... her earlobes strung with beautiful *karan* flowers and a similar necklace strung in gold chain with flower shaped rubies and pearls, strung around her swan-like neck... and beneath her smooth, shining skin that resembled vigorously stirred butter mixed with a dash of kohl... tanned, smooth and sparkling.

Her curvaceous body dressed in a white bustier covered with a white saree, Satyabhama always looked stunning in white apparel – like a blossoming lotus in the blue waters of Yamuna.

Krishna's eyes filled with tenderness...

When Satyabhama laughed, her smile resembled the long string of identical pearls around Krishna's neck...

"Will I never be able to see this beautiful smile again...?" For a moment Krishna was mesmerised by her.

He pulled Satyabhama close to him.

"What are you doing, my Lord?" Satyabhama blushed but submitted to him without the slightest protest.

Satyabhama always basked in Krishna's attention. She relished and blossomed in Krishna's overtures.

Her constant endeavour was to forever captivate Krishna in to her beauty in a manner that he could never be distracted by anyone else.

Rukmini was too generous and mature to pay heed to these childish gestures and most of the time laughed off her pranks. Not Satyabhama! She detested every other queen of Krishna.

She never expressed so to Krishna because she knew him so well, but the night he did not visit her chamber, she lay awake all night...

Sleepless on her large velvet bed, she spent the entire night thinking about Krishna... thinking about what he was doing... and getting worked up.

In the days to come, she would on some excuse or the other fight and sulk with Krishna...

He would indulge her, cajole and pamper her and she would eventually drop her defences.

It had become a pattern of their relationship that Krishna was familiar with. Since Satyabhama was years younger than all the other queens, everyone treated her like a child.

✦

[50]

Krishna was surprised to find Satyabhama all dressed up.

"You?" he asked her.

"Of course, would you enjoy yourself anywhere without me? The festival will be lack lustre without me beside you, am I wrong, my Lord?" Satya flashed her pearly smile once again.

There was a childlike glee… wonderment in her eyes…!

Once again Krishna pulled her towards him. This time Satyabhama protested mildly but was happy to be clasped in his embrace. She placed one hand over Krishna's chest and the other played with his armlet, her eyes locked into his all the time…. He was much taller than her and she could comfortably rest her head over his chest.

Krishna began to gently stroke her back…. Fresh as a rose petal and tanned in complexion, Satyabhama sensed a different yearning in Krishna's touch today…

This was not the touch of a lover…

It was the touch of a provider… of a patriarch…

Krishna inhaled her fragrance.

He took a whiff of the fresh jasmine flowers in her hair… and the familiar aroma of tresses rinsed and steamed in sandalwood and camphor… the perfume captured his mind and heart… Krishna took a deep breath and without saying a word pushed Satya away from him.

Satya was taken aback and looked at Krishna a bit startled.

What was different about his touch today…? What did it indicate…? Pain… renouncement… sorrow…? The thought disturbed Satya. Her Lord, for whom she had taken such effort in dressing up, had not given her adequate attention…

Krishna had been in a different mind frame for quite some time… ever since the Kurukshetra…

He was frequently in a meditative mood and preferred isolation…. Sometimes out of not wanting to be left alone, he would wake up Satya from her sleep…

Sometimes, he would lie wide awake besides her staring all night at the stars without exchanging a single word….

And sometimes, he would merely look into the waves and spend the entire night in the verandah of the palace…

Sometimes his beautiful eyes would be overflowing with tears and sometimes he spent days without speaking a single word.

It wasn't as if Satya was not familiar with all this. She had made several attempts to get him out of his distress…

She did so at times with sensuality, at other times with sensitivity…

It was difficult for Satya to understand and accept the changing Krishna. Satya had always envisioned Krishna as a lover… a passionate lover who only thought of her pleasures….

Her happiness was his priority.

Krishna always fulfilled all her desires even before she could express them!

Satya was consumed in her love for Krishna and was unable to come to terms with his changing personality….

Interestingly she exhibited rare courage during such moments. The more Krishna went inwards, the more efforts she made to draw him out of it.

When his conflicts turned severe, Krishna visited Rukmini's palace to resolve them. This was unacceptable to Satyabhama….

In the olden days, when Satyabhama got affronted and sulked with him, Krishna spent hours pampering and pandering to her…. But not any longer…. Now when Krishna returned from Rukmini's palace, a sulking Satyabhama could spend the entire night weeping on her side of the bed, hiding her face but it did not deter Krishna from spending the rest of the night standing in the verandah waiting for daybreak to take a stroll at the river bank.

This occurred frequently and for Satyabhama to be rejected by Krishna was more humiliating than death.

◆

[51]

"*Maharani*, there is a celebration at Prabhas Kshetra," Manorama spilled the news. Manorama was Satyabhama's favourite maid and her messenger of all that occurred at Rukmini's palace or the Rajyasabha.... She narrated first hand account of all happenings and had to this date never been wrong on her news. Yet today for some reasons... Satya could not believe her information....

"Are you sure?" Satya asked her again.

"I swear by your feet... Lord Krishna has personally delivered invites at every home.... They are to depart tomorrow late evening.... Everyone will assemble here... in the palace lobby..." Manorama filled in details.

Satyabhama held her by her shoulder and excitedly twirled her around. She felt as if the entire palace – all thirty-two chambers had lit up with Manorama's good news... she felt as if every fibre of her being was singing.

"Manu... Manu... I will fill your palms with pearls... drape you in silk sarees... gift you my golden bracelet... you have no idea what wonderful news you bring me today! It seems as if the good days are back....

"...My Lord, my anchor, my lifeline, my beloved's heart is finally breaking free from the shadow of mourning.... He will come out of it Manu, he will definitely return to me..."

Satyabhama was so energised that she did not pause for Manorama to complete her message.

Manorama wanted to notify that the celebrations were exclusively for the Yadava men folk… but Satyabhama was so ecstatic that Manorama couldn't furnish details, and watching her *maharani* so jubilant even Manorama saw wisdom in keeping momentarily quiet.

◆

[52]

On the bank of river Trivenisangam...

Krishna was quiet.

His eyes still shut...

Satyabhama watched over him, her eyes full of rage and rebuke. There were complaints... sorrow and tears that refused to subside.... When Krishna tried explaining to her that the celebration was restricted for Yadava men, Satya was unwilling to accept his argument.

Satyabhama's only passion in life was to live as Krishna's beloved. He was the purpose of her existence and she was forever absorbed in her fantasies. She built dream castles that had nothing to do with reality and therefore remained unconvinced by Krishna's explanation.

It was unacceptable to Satyabhama that Krishna could seek any entertainment independent of her... or find any pleasure in her absence.

This was understandable because happiness for Satyabhama commenced and ended with Krishna.... To be forever engaged in the loved one's fantasies is perhaps what others describe as love!

To view your beloved as a reflection is natural in love... the heart only listens to him and accepts what is acceptable to him or what is desirable to him....

Had Krishna incurred the mistake of confiding the truth into Satyabhama, there were all possibilities that Satyabhama would have collapsed on the spot....

Satyabhama was consumed by Krishna and it was unimaginable for her to exist without him, in fact it was akin to ending her life....

For Krishna his final goal was *karma*.... There was still time for Satyabhama to pursue salvation....

Her *karma* bound her to Dwarika. There was still time before she could severe all bondages and follow her Lord.

✦

[53]

Krishna pulled her to him… and took a whiff of the fragrant hair…

"Beloved, Charusheela, only the men folk are going for the celebration…"

"Why, where have the women flawed?" Satyabhama sulked.

"They haven't and that is the reason they cannot accompany us in the festivity…" emphasised Krishna.

"I cannot understand, *swami*…"

"Beloved… even when you are not beside me you're always inside me… I'm always carrying you with me…"

"*Swami*…"

"You are my life… my better half… and a part of you will always reside in my heart… don't you agree?"

"Words… you always trap everyone in your word play…"

"My dear, if I could take you with me I would have never left you behind…"

"So who is preventing you…?" Satyabhama taunted.

"Who can prevent me…? But it is not time as yet…!"

"Time…?" Satyabhama was perplexed, "Time for what…?"

"Appropriate time, my beloved…. There is a time for everything…. And today is not the time to accompany me…. You are meant to be here…"

Strangely Satyabhama did not get into any further arguments with him after that and it was out of character for Satya to not sulk either. She seemed to recall what Krishna had told her in one conversation…

Yo Maam Pashyati Sarvatra Sarva Cha Mayi Pashyati ।
Tasyaham Na Pranashyami Sa Cha Me Na Pranashyati ॥

One who turns to me and searches for everything inside me, I'm never far away from them and they from me.

"Devi, you are forever and always within me…" there was gloom in Krishna's eyes… it was perhaps the pain of parting with such an extraordinary woman!

✦

[54]

Krishna sensed a shooting pain in his heart.... He felt helpless about not revealing the truth to Satya even at the last moment.... There was a possibility that had he done so, he would have prepared her on her path to renouncement....

In his absence, will she be able to cope with his betrayal and the subsequent sorrow...? She was bound to feel tormented.

The philosopher who sermonised the mystery of death to Arjuna in the battle of Kurukshetra with two simple words – Everything is predestined – today, sat writhing in pain with his eyes closed. He was caught in an acute dilemma.

He sensed Satyabhama's taunting eyes looking at him with rage. He recalled the several erotic nights spent at her palace.... Somehow her searing, tanned body had a way of calming his nerves...

She had surrendered her body and soul to her Lord! And despite it he had betrayed her.

Yam Yam Vapi Smaranbhavam Tyajatyante Kalevaram ।
Tam Tamevaiti Kaunteya Sada Tadbhava Bhavitah ॥

"...All that we remember and desire during our last few breaths, we obtain in our next life... I have said this and yet today I..."

Krishna was in conflict.... "Who will inform Satya that her beloved who indulged her... pampered her... had betrayed her? Also why should someone need to inform her...? If Satya's soul was really connected to his, she would sense it on her own.... The void inside her heart will indicate his absence to her. Will Satya be able to survive without him...?"

Just the thought brought a smile on Krishna's face.

Maybe not.... She would feel tormented... hallucinate death every moment, but would that compel him to return? And if not, of what purpose was this introspection? Was this not attachment?

Somewhere deep in his heart Krishna yearned that after he was gone the women in his life suffer an aching vacuum and hanker for him every moment...

Did this indicate that he was no different from other ordinary mortals?

The human bond is so strong that even God is unable to free himself from it.

And Krishna understood this clearly resting beneath the *peepal* tree...

✦

[55]

These were the twelve months Draupadi had to spend with Arjuna....

It was late night and all of Indraprasth was plunged into darkness. The fading lamps of the palace flickered in the breeze....

Arjuna woke up startled from his sleep to discover that Draupadi was standing in the verandah.... Though middle-aged now, she was still as arresting as she was in her youth, and this was evident in her erect posture and glowing complexion....

Arjuna felt as attracted to her today as he did the first time when he set eyes on her at the *swayamvar*....

He rose from the bed to come and stand beside her.... She sensed his footsteps and looked back surprised....

Her usually fiery eyes were moist today.... It had the dampness of clouds when soaked in rain....

"Not getting sleep, Yajnaseni?"

"Sleep has deserted my eyes for many years.... How I crave to get into a deep slumber...!"

"So do all of us..." Arjuna responded with a deep sigh.

"Parth, I don't know why but I have a sinking feeling.... Something is not alright.... My hands and feet tremble... I feel parched and anxious..."

Draupadi looked at Arjuna with her large expressive eyes.

Arjuna very gently pulled Draupadi close to him.

"It has been a recurring feeling for all of us.... I have been frightened of the sunset ever since the battle of Kurukshetra... I'm startled by the sound of the blowing conch... Frightened of the screeching, rushing crowds... Frightened of the hungry vultures on the prowl for prey...

"...I'm frightened of the ogling wolves shrieking in the darkness of nights... I'm terrified too, Draupadi... terrified that it will soon be dawn and I will have to adorn the arrow in my hand again... I will have to once again kill my loved ones... and once again be deafened by their wails.... My heart sinks too, just at the thought of all this... I'm hounded by those nightmares again and again... I feel alarmed as well... my heart feels gloomy..."

"My fear is different, Parth!"

"What is it, Yajnaseni?"

"Parth ..." Draupadi began hesitantly then as if making up her mind said...

"Parth, I need to visit *sakha*.... Now, this very minute..."

Arjuna looked into Draupadi's eyes.... Those sparkling eyes that forever resembled a flame pulled out of fire, today appeared wilted....

Something was amiss... some unknown fear, some sorrow... a premonition of something ominous to occur that only Draupadi seemed to have an indication about.

Arjuna placed his hand over her shoulder.

"What's the matter, my love? Why this decision all of a sudden?"

"I don't know...! I have no logical explanation but I know that at this moment, I want to visit him.... My mind is restless and my heart is in despair.... I just know that it's a warning of something untoward to unfold.... Falguni, I know this sounds strange but I feel again and again that *sakha* is calling out to me... I can hear his voice resounding in this room.... I can hear the echoes..."

Draupadi clenched her fist as if trying to grab something in the air surrounding them... "See..." she opened her fist before Arjuna.

Her hand was empty. Arjuna looked into her eyes. She appeared paranoid... almost unstable with trepidation or something else. "Here it is... *sakha's* voice... I have been trying to capture it since morning but have been unable to.... Now I've clasped it in my fist... I cannot comprehend what he has been trying to say... but I know he needs me.... He has been calling out to me.... Please order the chariot for me, I have to leave for Dwarika right away...

"But my dear, how do we know whether he is in Dwarika at this moment or somewhere else...?"

Draupadi interrupted his sentence midway...

"He is in Dwarika... I can visualise him standing in the verandah of his palace... I can envisage his moist eyes... I can hear the gushing waves of river Yamuna... I have to leave Parth; I must leave before it gets too late..."

"My dear, I cannot comprehend your agony but I can feel your pain... I will do the needful at sunrise..."

"Sunrise... by then it may be..."

"Why do you harbour such negative thoughts, Yajnaseni? He is the Almighty.... Millions survive on his faith.... How can anything go wrong with him?"

"Almighty...? I have never regarded him as a deity.... For me he is a human being... much superior and on a higher pedestal, but a man...! I have seen in his eyes all that you see in a living being... I have sensed his emotions, his experiences.... It's the people around him who have given him the manifestation of a God but in reality he is..."

Arjuna stared at Draupadi in disbelief. "Are you saying this, Yajnaseni? You, who have been the recipient of his maximum miracles... you, who have most frequently experienced his divinity... you, who have existed in such close proximity and interacted with him on several occasions...?"

"Yes... I'm saying this and nobody better qualified than me to make this confession. What you describe as miracle is for me his supremacy... a great power originating from a fervent desire to connect with other people... an unbelievable force that transforms him from the ordinary to the extraordinary..."

"And how do you explain the phenomena of the nine hundred and ninety-nine apparrels he wrapped you around with...?"

"That was his love..." she said in a matter-of-fact tone.

Watching how earnestly she revealed herself, Parth felt tempted to believe her.

"Just think about it, Parth..." Draupadi continued, "If he was God and capable of miracles, would he have allowed me to be dragged from my private chamber to the Rajyasabha? Would he have permitted Dushasan to touch my body? Dushasan's hand should have burnt before touching my apparel had *sakha* been capable of miracles.... And why go so far, if he was God would he have allowed you to lose in the gamble?"

Draupadi was speaking breathlessly and Arjuna heard her in rapt attention, almost mesmerised by her flawless word flow.

"He is the beholder of an extremely pious heart, a heart superior to all of us and as pristine as the water of Mansoravar... a heart so transparent that you can watch the sky reflect in it... a sky that appears auburn.... What you call miracles is his transparency... sheer lucidity of his heart..."

"Yajnaseni, you analyse circumstances and personalities so clairvoyantly and articulate your thoughts just as efficiently..."

"It's the influence of *sakha*... whatever I am is the result of his infinite affection..."

"Only him?" there was a twinge of envy in Arjuna's sharp tone... "A result of only his infinite affection...? So what about us? Who are we, Yajnaseni? The husbands who failed to protect you at the Rajyasabha, who sent you on a twelve-year exile...?" Arjuna cast his eyes down!

"You are also the one to present me with Indraprasth?" There was tenderness in Draupadi's voice. Very affectionately, she placed both her arms on Arjuna's bare chest.

"Are you envious of *sakha*?" she asked looking him directly in the eye.... There was so much warmth... compassion in her voice that Arjuna did not repent his query. But when Draupadi very gently, without causing the slightest hurt posed a counter question to Arjuna, his expression gave him away.

"Me? Can I ever be envious of *sakha*...? How can you even suggest so, Yajnaseni? He is my life... I breathe because he exists.... If I eat it's because he is there... I'm alive because he lives... I'm his reflection, a part of his being..." Draupadi looked into Arjuna's eyes. He was speaking the truth...

"Then what made you ask this question? Don't you know that all of us are what we are because of *sakha*...?"

"Yajnaseni, my beloved, I'm aware that all of us are alive today because of *sakha*... If he wasn't with us in the battle of Kurukshetra then perhaps.... Of course I'm aware of it all and I understand you... him... but sometimes, when I witness your intense love for him I turn restless.... It's as it is difficult to share you with my four brothers and now this..."

"If you cannot decipher between love and devotion, Parth, then who can...? To tell you the truth, Parth, love has ceased to exist for me in everything....This body and its various passions... this lifetime and the luxuries, the enjoyment and the entertainment. Do you believe that I'm really relishing all these emotions? No Parth no... all these are virtues inculcated into me by *sakha*...

"...It's his emphasis on the duty of – *samastama sweekar* – whole-hearted acceptance under all circumstances, acceptance of all of humanity. He taught me how to stay bonded in relationships and yet remain detached... how to be in the midst of blooming prosperity but reside like a hermit. He enlightened us that co-existence of all these virtues, like wrath, love, sacrifice, fortune or goal is possible provided we submit to our circumstances. He has taught us to endure and survive, not to abjure and renounce. *Ten Vyakten Bhunjithah* has been *sakha*'s prime lesson to all of us and I learned them when I attempted to sacrifice..." Draupadi laughed, "Or maybe endured and attempted to abjure!"

"Krishna.... It feels as if Krishna is personally saying all this.... It's so convincing..."

"It's the marvel of time.... You feel so because my relationship with *sakha* is not different from a child attached to his mother's umbilical chord... a mother's heartbeats, her body movements, her various thought processes and expressions may be her own but a part of it travels to the child inside her.... That's why the child reflects her temperament, her choices. It's the same way with me, Parth."

Draupadi's eyes brimmed over with tears. "Take me to *sakha*, Parth.... Take me before it gets late..."

Arjuna held Draupadi's hand, stroked it gently as if consoling her. It was an intimate moment between the two. Then abruptly Arjuna went out of the room.

Draupadi attributed his quick strides to his discomfiture.

✦

[56]

It was daybreak and the sun was gradually spreading its rays all around. The sand covering the shores of rivers Hiranya and Kapila had turned warm. Krishna was in a meditative mood resting against the *peepal* tree taking brief breaths.... He was watching the changing activities of time. A pale smile soaked in pain lingered on his face. His eyes were open and full of sorrow. Watching the marvel of the constantly moving time, a thought crossed Krishna's mind...

"...Wasn't life in many ways like a trapeze artiste balancing his walk on a tight rope...? The performer walks to and fro but returns to the same spot.... Though all the time on the move he reaches nowhere... strange..." pondered Krishna with a smile.

Jara was seated at his feet on bended knees. He folded his hands.

"O Lord... if you are uncomfortable, please stretch your legs.... You have been leaning against the *peepal* trunk for so long.... Your back must be hurting..."

Krishna gave a broad smile.

"Jara, my brother, why do you spare me so much thought? You have not eaten a morsel since yesterday? And today you shot me instead of a deer.... Think about what you are going to eat... your next meal..."

"*Prabhu,* how can I when you are in this condition? Until you find peace I cannot think of anything else... I have lost all appetite..."

"How can you feel so much for me, Jara?" Krishna looked at him fondly and shut his eyes. For a while, he stayed in that condition. Jara was confused. He stared at Krishna.

...Suddenly he heard a splash in the river.... He turned back to find a deer drinking water at the bank. Jara looked at the deer and looked away. The deer finished drinking water and slowly strutted away...

Krishna opened his eyes. He could spot the deer far away.

"Jara, did you not see that deer?"

"I did, my Lord, it was right here."

"Then...?"

"Then what, my Lord...?" Jara asked with childlike candour.

"You have not eaten a morsel since yesterday..."

"*Prabhu*..." Jara looked at Krishna feeling extremely emotional...

"My brother, it's time for me to depart now.... Don't worry about me.... But you have to live and hunger is an essential part of human existence. It's time now to think about yourself, my friend..."

"I will, my Lord, but not until I have fulfilled my incomplete task.... Hunting is my livelihood, if I don't hunt what I will eat.... I understand that my Lord but just now, at this moment, I cannot think of anything except your welfare. Not about myself, my hunger or my living..."

Krishna shut his eyes again. He recalled what he had said to Arjuna.

"...One who worships me without doubt, without obligation and out of his free will, one who is selfless and strives for the wellbeing of mankind, is in the true sense deserving of liberation.... One who in his quest for devotion renounces his duties and is willing to erase all doubts for love is enlightened even if he is not a seer..."

✦

[57]

Arjuna returned back faster than he had gone...

"Yajnaseni, the chariot is ready. How long do you think you will stay away?"

Draupadi looked at the skyline. It was deep red even though the sun had yet to rise. In a little while it would be dawn... what they described as *Brahma mahurat*.... Draupadi lingered her gaze on the sky as if asking it...

"How long will it take?"

✦

[58]

The mighty force who had all along controlled time… who had every moment under his spell, today, observed himself play along for time… Lord Suryadev watched Krishna's bleeding foot and turned dismal…. He had been anticipating Almighty's final journey but until that happened, he preferred to stay behind the veil of clouds…

A bright light fell onto Krishna's face and pierced his closed eyes.

The sharp rays emanated from the pristine, pious eyes of *Mata* Gandhari that Krishna visualised floating before his eyes. Her eyes were not blindfolded today… instead, they were streaming with tears.

What was this…? Tears in mother Gandhari's eyes?

It was as if *Mata* Gandhari was asking Krishna… "Does it hurt you too much, my son?" Krishna could sense mother Gandhari's hand on his head.

"*Ma*… this is your blessing…. Blessing of salvation that will enable me to embark on my final journey."

"Krishna, why did you accept my curse?"

"*Ma*… this is not a curse, it's a blessing. Who else but you could grant me liberation? It's the heartfelt blessing of a mother to her son. Finally, all my duties have been fulfilled…. My time to depart was determined long ago. I was just waiting for your intimation and you have given that to me now! Who else but a mother can so easily understand the earnest communication of her son?"

"Krishna," Gandhari continued to stare at him and weep incessantly, "I have sinned..."

"How can you say that, mother? You have sought my freedom and one who grants that is blessed, not punished..."

"Stay back Krishna, please don't go away.... How will all of us survive without you?"

Was this the voice of Gandhari or the voice of a mourning Yashoda on the banks of Yamuna?

"My son, I have been deeply pained or I wouldn't have cursed you thus.... Don't I understand that my curse was inadvertently the freedom of Duryodhan...? How could I curse the one who freed my child from the vicious cycle of life and death...?"

"Why do you grieve so deeply, mother, and add to your anguish? I have no complaints, for I wholeheartedly accept your prediction."

"That's the tragedy, my son.... Had you rejected my curse I wouldn't have to witness this day. How am I going to face Devaki, Kunti and Yashoda? What will I tell them?"

"Mother, one thing is certain that you are not responsible for all this.... You are flawless.... Somebody who is revered and worshipped every morning... who is as pious as you can do no wrong... you are the prestige of the entire Kaurava lineage...."

"And what about the responsibility of one mother towards another...? What about the Kaurava bloodline, on the path of destruction...? It has produced Duryodhan and Dushasan... what purpose does it serve to be recognised as the prestige of such a bloodline... Krishna...? If it's possible for you, please forgive me..." *Mata* Gandhari lowered her eyes...

"Duryodhan and Dushasan are not the only ones, Vidur and Sanjay herald from the same Kauravas, don't they, mother? The water that creates muck... is the same water that comes of use to cleanse our soiled feet... our heart is like that water...."

"My son, can I ask you for something?"

"What can I proffer you, mother? What do I have in my possession to present you...?"

"That's true… whatever you possessed you have distributed in the Universe…. You have absorbed our grievances… accepted all complaints…. You have imparted purity, righteousness, affection…. Everything we have today is your showering and permeated by you…. Still, I have a desire, my son…"

"Speak up, mother… only the privileged have the opportunity to serve you…"

"Will you grant me what I ask…?"

"How can I promise…? I have nothing to offer… even my breaths are no longer my own… and yet…" Krishna took a long, deep breath…

Gandhari's eyes sparkled with some divine light…

"I want you to be born from my womb in your next life…"

"You are once again chaining me in human bondage… won't you free me, mother?" Krishna saw images of Devaki and Yashoda in Gandhari's eyes…

"*Tathastu*…" Gandhari raised her hand… Krishna fixed his gaze on her open palm and noticed that she had a long life line. There was a long way to go for Gandhari.

✦

[59]

Gandhari was sobbing irrepressibly and her wails echoed in the domes of Hastinapur palace. Kunti was stroking her back and consoling her, but Gandhari was inconsolable.

"I have committed a grave sin, *maharani* Kunti.... Even God will not forgive me."

"What are you referring to, Gandhari?"

"Krishna... I'm referring to Krishna..." Gandhari could barely speak amidst her sobs.... No matter how hard she tried, she could not stop crying.

"What about Krishna?"

"I grieve in regret.... My conscience does not permit me peace.... Time and again I'm haunted by the echoes of my own curse.... Why did I do it, how could I dare to curse the infallible... the magnificent Krishna...?"

"He accepted your curse, didn't he?"

Kunti continued to stroke her back, "...With grace and dignity!"

Gandhari's eyes streamed with tears that drenched her blindfold... "That's his greatness and to think that I cursed such a great man... the narrator of *Gita*... I cursed him to die like a demon... I will never be free from *karma*.... What more can there be to endure after witnessing the demise of my hundred sons...? I don't understand what binds me to this earth, on this desolate land of Hastinapur..."

Kunti smiled weakly.... It was a smile mingled with sorrow... "But you have not seen anything, Gandhari, how could you when you lived your entire life blindfolded...?"

"The blindfold does not prevent one from what you need to see, Kunti. On the contrary, it's even more painful because what you watch in your imagination is always more frightening than what happens in reality.... It brings you greater sorrow.... The blindfold cannot protect you from your suffering... if at all, it adds to your anguish..."

"Maybe what you say is true, Gandhari, but now don't cause yourself more heartache by grieving any further. Whatever has happened has happened and it cannot be undone.... There is no point in repenting. Words that cannot be retrieved.... The curse has come true.... The arrow has hit the mark.... All voices resound in the Universe and return to the root. Its acceptance is inevitable."

"Perhaps this is what they call *karma.* If Krishna desired he could have freed me of the sin by rejecting my curse..." Gandhari sobbed.

"Krishna believes in acceptance.... He has never rejected anything..."

"I'm deeply pained by my action..." Gandhari once again began to wail... "Krishna, please try to forgive me... liberate me... I don't wish to breathe on this earth any longer.... With my eyes bandaged I don't wish to be tormented any further in my imagination.... Free me, my Lord.... Free me, my Lord..."

✦

[60]

Jara poured some water carried in a mud pot into Krishna's mouth.... Very slowly he swallowed down the tiny drops of water.... One could sense relief on Krishna's face after a long time.... There was a feeling of satisfaction....

"One values water only when one is thirsty.... Without thirst we have no regard for water..." Krishna recalled his own words!

Watching him smile Jara asked, "Are you feeling better, my Lord?"

"Yes Jara, to drink water from your hands has given me immense peace. Parth will be here as soon as he receives my message... without wasting a single moment..."

"*Prabhu*, Arjuna is your very dear friend, isn't he?"

"Yes Jara, he is very close to my heart..."

"What if he takes too long to arrive here my Lord...? In which case you...?"

"Then me...?" Krishna smiled... "Then I may not be able to wait for him.... Time and circumstances wait for no one.... Today my time forbids me too... forbids me from waiting longer than my due..."

"*Prabhu*," Jara stared at him unblinkingly.... He wondered what kind of a man was this who talked of his death so calmly and naturally....

Here he was in the face of death, but he was so composed.... This was no ordinary man.... He had to be the Almighty.

Unknowingly, Jara folded his hands again.

✦

[61]

Arjuna was pacing his chariot.

In normal circumstances, he was always accompanied by his *sarathi*.... But today he was in a hurry to fulfil Draupadi's wish and decided not to wait for his charioteer. In respecting Draupadi's instinct, he was participating in her anguish and inadvertently following the call of his destiny....

Arjuna's mind galloped in multiple directions and the racing chariot was unable to keep pace with his rushing mind....

What could it be that had turned Panchali so restless? Could it just be her hallucination or was Krishna really beckoning to her...?

How come only she heard his echoes...? Why was he unable to hear his cries...?

Did it signify that Panchali was more intimate with Krishna...? Why did he not possess the same level of intimacy with his Lord as her...?

Krishna had always treated Arjuna like his protégé. He loved him to the extent that he was partial towards him, but at the end of the day Arjuna remained just his student. The protégé who wanted to flee from the Kurukshetra battlefield... a weak... demoralised... and a diffident individual.

On the other hand, Draupadi was the daughter of fire...! On the battlefield when Bheem pulled out Dushasan's arm from the rest of his body and invited Draupadi to soak her hair in his flowing blood, she didn't hesitate for a moment...! She stretched out her palms and dampened her tresses with his gushing blood… emblazoned her forehead, cheeks, face and lips… right down to her breast into it…. Her saree… her bustier was drenched in Dushasan's blood as Draupadi dabbed some more into her scalp as if dabbing oil…

During the battle when Duryodhan injured his thigh, Draupadi had stood before him and laughed loudly…. There was madness in her eyes that day and her expression was demented…. It was evident that she was relishing her quest for revenge….

What a ruthless image that was!

To watch a beautiful, sensual woman transform into a horrific image extolled with blood marks all over her face tormented Arjuna even now when he sometimes held her face in between his hands and watched her closely.

Arjuna had confided his deep fear to Krishna and Krishna had smiled contemplatively. Immensely disturbed by his silence, Arjuna had turned agitated and barraged him… "Someone like you, who recurrently talks about forgiveness... professes acceptance… explain to me Krishna, what kind of duty is this…? Does it entail justice for anyone?"

"You cannot equate duty with justice, Parth," Krishna smiled solemnly.

"Even if Draupadi had not referred to Duryodhan as blind man's son and addressed him as something else, their communication would have been equally ugly…. There is a remote possibility that she would have been pleasant; and truth is seldom pleasant…."

Arjuna was still unconvinced, "I'm not discussing truth or counterfeit, this is not about courtesy or unpleasantness. My argument is about duty, about justice… Panchali accused and cursed Dushasan but we were equal participants in the crime. She held Duryodhan and Dushasan guilty, so how come we were forgiven and they were penalised…? In the present scale of justice, there is no difference between Dhritrashtra and Panchali. Dhritrashtra discriminated between his children and the Pandavas, and so did Panchali…. So what out of this is justice Krishna and what is duty…?"

"You are wrong, Parth. If Dhritrashtra loved Duryodhan, Panchali loves all of you and love makes concessions. It's natural to exercise a blind spot for people you love. Panchali knows that if we have to identify a single individual, event or idea responsible for the entire episode, it's me...! She believes that I could have prevented her humiliation at any point but I didn't..." Krishna sighed deeply.

There was a long silence... a soothing quietude prevailed between the two....

Then Krishna put his hand on Arjuna's shoulder...

"Parth, women are made different from men. Their sense of righteousness, their duty... their psyche is contrasting from us. They think from the heart while men think from their head.... Women have a greater capacity to love than men.... For them love is surrender, worship, a part of their existence. For men love is more or less a physical need. For women love is exaltation, it's a sublime experience, for men it's a momentary passion.... Women are by nature monogamous while men are polygamous and capable of loving more than one. Women are ingrained to forgive heinous deeds of their men but men are revengeful and driven to fight for justice."

"Then how come Panchali is so different? Why is she not like the other women? She could have forgiven Duryodhan, why didn't she? By doing to him what he did to us, how did we become noble?"

Krishna looked at Arjuna tenderly, and then as if explaining to a young student, said, "Because Draupadi thinks like a man.... She is polyandrous. She does not have the capacity for forgiveness and empathy like other women perhaps.... Let's not forget she has emerged from the flames and it's unfair of us to expect such tenderness from her.... She was created for a specific purpose... to fulfil that revenge is her prime duty. To regard her as an ordinary woman or to associate her with such fragile feelings is a folly on our part..."

"But going by what our scriptures lay down about the rights and duties of women..."

Krishna stopped him mid-sentence, "I'm informing you that women are superior to men.... They are closer to Nature and therefore to themselves.... For women everything associated with them is extremely sensitive. Draupadi falls in between these two categories. She is as embellished as powerful and as purified as fiery she is!"

Arjuna heard out Krishna in rapt attention. Krishna was perfect in his assessment of Draupadi. Once she had soaked her hair into Dushasan's blood and sobbed bitterly, she had in true sense freed herself from her past.

"Besides, blood is not such a terrifying sight for women as they are accustomed to their menstrual cycle, Parth," continued Krishna.

It suddenly dawned on Arjuna how Draupadi had disconnected herself from Duryodhan and Dushasan after the Kurukshetra battle. It was as if she had blanked out the entire episode from her mind. She never referred to the topic again as if they didn't exist for her. It was admirable how she had liberated herself from the nightmare!

Not just that, she consoled Bhanumati and Vrushali, wives of Duryodhan and Dushasan like an empress and an elder sister. She assumed complete responsibility for their wellbeing.

Krrishna! She was deserving of her title. Like Krishna, Draupadi was committed to her duties. She had the capacity to rise above all circumstances and face up to challenges without feeling persecuted....

She was able to contain herself even at the deathbed of her children! When she watched Ashwathama carry her five robust adolescent boys and place them on the pyre for the final rites, her eyes had brimmed over with tears and her heart ached with sorrow but there was acceptance too.... At a time when every family had sacrificed a soldier to the battle of Kurukshetra, it would have been imprudent of Draupadi to openly mourn the demise of her offsprings. As the queen of Hastinapur, she wanted to set an example for the countless soldiers of the kingdom by not breaking down in public.

The same Draupadi was so anguished today... so restless to meet Krishna. Riding the chariot, one constant thought troubled Arjuna..."What if Yajnaseni's fears proved true...? Could his dear friend, his philosopher and guide of his chariot and life be in serious trouble...? Had he really called out to Yajnaseni...?"

✦

[62]

Yajnaseni stood holding on to the fast racing chariot. Time and again, her eyes filled with tears. The wind around them blew fiercely and the sun was getting ready to rise.... A big orange circle was preparing to emerge in the upper half of the sky....

"The ways of the sky are mysterious," thought Draupadi.

"It is difficult to determine if the sky belongs to the morning, to the evening... or to both? The same with human life... does it belong to the dawn or to the dusk...?" thoughts crossed Yajnaseni's mind as the chariot galloped ahead...

The gallant warrior who inspired them in the battle of Kurukshetra... who supported and protected her husbands even though not participating in the battle, where could Krishna be at this point of time...?

"...Why am I so restless, so inconsolable? There has to be some reason for this suffering.... My friend Krishna had apathy for everyone and a way of accepting all.... He had a knack of absorbing everyone's suffering and turning it into his own.... He knew all along I loved him deeply but he manipulated his friend Arjuna to marry me.... Also so that the brothers remain united, he masterminded to distribute me amongst the five of them...

"...When he came to meet me before the gambling session commenced, there was so much grief in his eyes.... He was aware of what was to unfold and hinted many warnings but I failed to read his silent signal.... It wasn't as if he wasn't aware that in the final moments, I would only rely on him.... He knew everything all along...

"...That full-moon day when he went as a *shanti doot* from Uplav to Hastinapur, Krishna was aware that the meeting would be futile.... Knowing fully well that he would be humiliated, he still went as a messenger of peace from the Pandavas all the way to Hastinapur... and carried Duryodhan's affronting message back to the Pandavas... "Forget about five villages, I will not part with a needle space plot to the Pandavas..."

"...On mother Kunti's request, he visited Karna even though aware of his response beforehand.... And it was because of that meeting perhaps that Karna was able to breathe his last moments peacefully on the battleground.... Everyone knew that Karna would be absolved of the curse of Lord Parshuram in his last moments and depart in peace....

"...Raised as a *sutputra* (charioteer's son), the eldest Pandava brother had swallowed too many humiliations... Lord Parshuram, *guru* Dronacharya... and... and me as well...! I had not spared him either... I recognised his bronzed presence, sparkling with his characteristic *kavach-kundal* (ornaments) at my *swayamvar*, but when he strode like a lion to pick up the bow, I prevented him, "I will not marry a *sutputra*." At that time I had no intention of insulting him.... Deep down I longed for all the royalties to fail so that eventually to safeguard my father Dhrupad's prestige, Krishna would be forced to participate in the competition...

"...I was aware that if Karna participated there was no way he would miss the target. He was an exemplary archer... exemplary because by then the news of Pandavas' demise including Arjuna had reached all the kingdoms including Lakshagrah.... Looking back I feel, I should not have said what I did... I don't know why I called him a *sutputra* and humiliated him publicly.... He could never get over the affront... not in his entire lifetime... the hurt lurked in some corner of his heart and nagged him forever... until his last breath.... The topic brewed up even when Krishna visited him before the battle of Kurukshetra to dissuade him from joining Duryodhan.... Even at that time, there was a reference to me in their conversation. What kind of conversation could have transpired between the two men...? One, whom I loved and cherished all my life... and the other, who yearned for me all his life...!

"...*Sakha* made no mention of it but appeared visibly distressed on his return from that meeting.... When I pestered him, all he said was...

"Karna has been the recipient of everyone's curse for so long that now it appears as if he can be happy only in unhappiness.... He conveys a message for you though...."

"Then slightly hesitantly, swallowing hard he looked at me, his eyes sparkling as he repeated what Karna had to say to me, "...Hey Vasudev... tell that extremely beautiful, desirable, large-eyed, wheat-complexioned, fragile, enchanting woman that Karna has forgiven her.... Tell her that had I shot the arrow and won her heart on the eve of her *swayamvar,* there was no way I would have shared her with my other brothers in this lifetime or in the next. Tell her that if she can, try and forget the abuses hurled at her during the Rajyasabha because I have come to value her devotion and her commitment as a spouse, I have regard for her righteousness and her divinity... but it's a little too late now...!"

Even now when Draupadi recalled that moment, her eyes filled with tears.

How poignant Krishna had appeared while recounting Karna's suffering.... It was as if he had internalised his sorrow and turned it into his own.

What level of involvement was this that he recurrently transformed everyone's suffering into his own...

✦

[63]

Eclectic thoughts crowded Draupadi's mind.

Her friend, who participated in her every sorrow and experienced her anguish to the extent that he turned them into his own....

She recalled Subhadra's welcome gathering at the palace of Indraprasth. How angry and tormented she was that day...!

"...How could *sakha*... my dear friend do this to me?" Draupadi was still not willing to accept it, "Parth was always aware of my attraction to.... He was aware of my attachment... my pride and my innumerable hurts... then why would he do this...?"

It was sunset time and Draupadi felt immensely sad. On that day nothing could make her see reason. Come twilight and she longed to fight this out with Krishna. She had been bursting to lash out at him.... What further distressed her was that all of Indraprasth was rejoicing the festivities... Draupadi had never envisioned that Krishna would manipulate Arjuna into abducting his own sister Subhadra and trespass her private territory.... To notice how besotted Arjuna was with his new bride had shaken up Draupadi's self-confidence.

Downstairs in the Rajyasabha, they were rejoicing with music and colours.... One could hear the beating drums and the shrilling *shehnais* playing the nuptial tunes but Draupadi's chamber was plunged into darkness and a deathly silence.

"*Sakhi... sakhi...* where are you?" When she heard the familiar voice calling out to her, Draupadi longed to pick up every piece of furniture and fling it.... She wanted to rave and rant and beat her brow.... What was unbearable was that somebody she regarded as her confidant had betrayed her.

"*Sakhi*, where are you? Why don't you respond...?" Krishna's voice echoed all over in the dark room.

Finally, Krishna lit up a small lamp placed near by and spread some light into the room.

"You appear to be very angry," Krishna displayed his characteristic smile.

"And you appear to be extremely happy," Draupadi could not resist the sting.

"Are you sulking?"

"Not at all, I'm rejoicing..." her long hair left loose, her body devoid of any ornaments, she was seething with rage and clearly in mourning.

"I can see that... I experience your celebration..." Krishna replied and pulled a stool to be seated.

"Why *sakha*...? What made you do this to me? Aren't you aware that he didn't belong exclusively to me in any case... by your action you have further distanced him from me. Why? What did you accomplish...? I have always regarded you, loved you, so why would you be so inconsiderate towards me and bring Subhadra in between us...?" Draupadi could barely complete her sentence. She was choking and her eyes brimmed with tears.

She swallowed hard and brushed away her tears..."Tears often balm our anxieties, *sakha*.... Why is it that it's only when I cry, tremble or grieve that you seem to take notice of me...: It's only then that you find time to be beside me.... Am I wrong?"

Krishna burst into laughter. Then very affectionately, very tenderly, he explained, "It's not necessary to make every small matter into an issue of self-respect, *sakhi*. Why do you in the first place associate the episode to your self-esteem?"

"How can I not...? Do I deserve a co-wife...? Have I been like any ordinary wife? I was distributed like an object without any consideration for my feelings. I mutely submitted to my circumstances and revered it as tradition... I put my day and night, happiness and sorrow on hold only to strive for my husbands' triumph.... It was always their justice, their joys... I'm the wife who has travelled twelve years with five husbands in the forests.... A woman who served as a maid only to uphold her husbands' prestige... and yet, uncaring of my pride and honour, these husbands brought co-wives and this time a woman who is none other than my best friend's sister.... In fact, my friend masterminds the entire plan... I fail to understand your vested interest in all this, *sakha*. Is there some greed... and if so, what is it? If it's for the benefit of someone then who can that be...? Whenever there is suspicion in mind, *sakha*, it inevitably diminishes faith... I don't want empty words anymore, I want truth," concluded Draupadi firmly.

"Truth...? The truth is that Subhadra is not your co-wife. Every brother strives to get the best groom for his sister and in this entire Universe where can I find a better candidate than Parth as her husband," stated Krishna.

"I'm not against you finding the best man for your sister but in this case, he happens to be my husband. You are well aware, *sakha*, that I've never been insecure about my other co-wives, like Ulupi, Chitrangada or other queens.... But watching Subhadra today, I'm consumed with envy... I fear that Falguni will forget me."

"*Sakhi*, whatever happened to your vast knowledge, your wisdom, your analytical mind, your extraordinary intelligence...? Subhadra is a mere child.... Are you going to compete with a child?"

"She is young... beautiful... what else do men want?"

"Men want a lot more, I'm a man and I should know.... Despite Satyabhama, Jambuvanti and the other queens, nobody can displace Rukmini in my heart.... She is an integral part of my identity... and still Radha resides within me forever... Does this imply that I betray Rukmini...? Does it imply that I'm dishonest with my memories of Radha...?"

"That's up to you, but for me if my man is attracted to another woman, even if the attraction is merely physical, I consider it my failure. If that's what men crave for in a woman... I should be able to deliver."

"Men crave for other images in a woman too... mother, beloved, friend, minister and sometimes an intelligent opponent as well, but... Subhadra is none of these.... She can only perform as a devoted wife. She is subservient, while you are dynamic...."

"I don't understand what you mean. Are you suggesting that a woman should surrender to her man and remain helpless, dependant and a doormat to obtain love from him? Are you also indicating that a woman who fights for her rights, her voice, who stands alone, who questions and dares is undeserving of her man's love.....?"

"*Sakhi*, only a woman like you who has all the qualities of a *saha-dharmachari* has the right to sit on the throne. The kind of woman you are *sakhi*, you have the capacity of coping with various conflicts.... How can any other woman match up to your magnificence and substance?"

"Sure and that's the reason all my husbands bring home Hidimba, Chitrangada, Ulupi and now Subhadra, right?"

"I'm a man and you are a woman. Nature created us to be different. There's a possibility that you may not grasp what I have to state but it's necessary for me to make an effort.... It's very easy for a man to be physically drawn to a woman but it's very difficult for him to sustain this attraction.... By temperament men are arrogant. They prefer women who idolise them and submit to them. Women like you arrive in the Universe once in ten thousand years. Multiple husbands become essential for you to sustain your aura and appeal. What you describe as your involuntary choice is in fact the only appropriate solution in your complex situation. The truth is that beyond a point, all your husbands are inadequate to contain your fire. If the sun blazes persistently there will be devastation on earth... Had the moon not emerged every night and soothed all living creatures, the planet would have been destroyed."

"Are you suggesting that the power of sunlight is not an advantage but a disadvantage?"

"If we are going to get into arguments, this will be never ending, *sakhi*. An endless argument is not a solution to a problem.... Besides to tell you the truth, I perceive no problem in this case.... You are the sunlight in Parth's life.... His journey is incomplete without you, Panchali. Why just Parth, all your husbands cannot imagine a life without you. You are their anchor, their blood vein that binds and connects the brothers and the Pandav family...."

Draupadi couldn't control her tears any longer.

"I burn in my own fire, *sakha,* where do I find my quietude...? Do I borrow it from the night or from the evening... who do I plead for peace?"

"That's your fortune."

"Call it misfortune, *sakha.* It's not a blessing to burn all the time. I was cursed to be born from the fire.... They call me Yajnaseni but everyone forgets I'm a woman too."

"We don't forget that, *sakhi*... but your femininity pales in your dynamism..."

"So what is my crime, my femininity or my dynamism?"

"To be extraordinary is a crime... to be born ahead of time is a crime... to be aware is a crime too.... To obtain something you have to submit something... that's the balance of Nature..."

"*Sakha*, don't you often feel isolated? Doesn't your magnificence burn you frequently?"

"I'm the moonlight.... My sparkle is not my own. I reflect the sparkle of all the illumination around me.... That's why my shimmer does not burn me... whereas you are self-illuminated... and to burn is your temperament..."

"Krishna, you showered me with a part of your sparkle but refrained to lend me your tranquillity.... You could have, if you desired, blessed me with your composure that could have, comforted my consistent burning... but you didn't, why?"

"Because... I need this fire... I need to extinguish injustice in your burning flame... Subhadra is for the igniting of that flame, to sustain the fire that burns in your heart..."

"Sometimes I don't understand you at all, *sakha*!"

"Sometimes where do I understand myself...?"

His eyes appeared to glisten with unshed tears because in the dim light where he was sitting, Draupadi felt his eyes shining.... That's when she concluded the argument.... Any communication that could fill Krishna's eyes with tears was unacceptable and unbearable for Draupadi. She decided to accept Subhadra, called out to her maid and ordered her to light all the lamps with scented oil...

◆

[64]

"...Why are all women so similar...?" Sitting beneath the *peepal* tree, Krishna recalled the moments spent in Draupadi's dimly lit palace...

"...What is it about them that even though hailing from different strata, era and age, women think identically? What drives them to similar situations and what triggers similar reactions? Why are they so identical even in their expression of rage...?" Questions emerged in Krishna's mind and he began to laugh at himself. The four most important women in his life were no exception. They all loved him equally.... It was too late for him to reflect on all this now... when they were not with him and he merely had their memories....

Krishna sensed all of them looking at him... with expectations and abundant love....

Three rivers before him bent into the flow of the ocean.... The sunrays fell onto the waves forming infrequent patterns on the water that seemed to resemble the facial expressions of the three women....

His beloved, wives and friend... floating on the gentle waves of the river seemed to communicate something to Krishna... "Our purpose of existence is to be engrossed in you.... Every obstacle is acceptable to us because we are the recipients of your generous benedictions.... You have enlightened us with your constant discourses.... You have absorbed our rage and soothed us.... You have revered our femininity and showered us with affection...."

His eyes still closed, Krishna felt as if their eyes intermingled and infiltrated his heart. Once again, he felt a surge of pain running though his entire body and ignited an old memory of a memorable night in Dwarika....

That night when Satyabhama arrived endowed in her Syamantak ruby carried as a part of her trousseau in the capacity of the new queen into the palace of Dwarika and also in Krishna's life.

✦

[65]

The palaces of Dwarika were decorated with lights. There was *rangoli* at every doorstep and also outside on the streets. Doors were strung with colourful festoons. Every verandah in the entire town displayed men and women adorned in gold ornaments from head to toe. Mother Devaki holding the *aarti thali* waited in the foyer of the palace to welcome the new bride. She had to be greeted with the customary rituals and Devaki was looking forward to follow the customary rites.

From a distance one could hear the rejoicing of men and women celebrating the event on the streets.... Throwing colour (*abeel gulal*) all over the place and on each other, men, women and children excitedly gathered in the palace foyer to get a glimpse of the new bride.... Large crowds spread all over the streets.

One section of the palace, however, was engulfed in darkness. A solitary dim lamp flickered apologetically.

Rukmini sat devoid of her ornaments, staring into the dim lamp, her loose hair spread out on her back. Her beautiful jewels were scattered all over the bed and her magnificent apparels studded in priceless gems were strewn on the floor rolling in dust....

Rukmini felt her life had come to a standstill.... She felt desolated as if she had nobody to call her own in the vast golden town of Dwarika.... The beloved for whom she deserted her home and her family, today belonged to someone else....

Drenched in her sorrow, the beautiful woman was also extremely angry. She was angry with herself... her destiny... for she could not alter her fate...

✦

[66]

Krishna was surprised to discover a familiar face missing amidst the assembled guests.... Then he recalled his conversation with Draupadi on the eve of Subhadra's wedding.

After the welcome proceedings, yet another ceremony in honour of the new bride was organised at a specially erected palace for the new queen, Satyabhama.

Once they were through with all the formalities, Krishna stepped out of his room for a moment.

"Where do you leave for at this hour?" Satyabhama held his arm.

"I'm off to visit Rukmini," Krishna responded and tried pulling away his arm from the clutches of Satyabhama.

She didn't let go, on the contrary, stepped closer to him and rested her head against his broad chest, encircling her other arm tightly around Krishna's back, "Is it necessary to visit today...?"

"I don't conduct according to necessities..." Krishna held her tightly to him, "...But my heart tells me I must... Rukmini was absent at the welcome proceeding and this suggests that she must be upset."

"So will you cajole her...?"

"No, she is too mature and qualified for such indulgences. She will not need any cajoling but certain things will have to be clarified and then she will definitely understand..."

"Why can't you go tomorrow instead...?"

"No.... It's imperative to erase today's wounds today. Tomorrow, they would transform into a question."

"But wasn't this expected with my arrival, weren't you prepared for it, my Lord?"

"To be honest I wasn't. I didn't imagine that a woman of Rukmini's calibre could react in this manner..."

"All women react this way... even I understand this much.... Had I been in her place, I would have reacted the same way.... You are too special and it's not easy to share you with others.... Everyone craves for your undivided love and time... your exclusive attention...and love...."

"But I have never held back my love or my time.... I have showered equal attention to all of you.... It's about perspectives.... There are no conditions in love.... It's a different matter that our heart craves for more.... Our expectations rise and like the quicksand on the seashore we are forever unquenched."

"Are you indicating that the sand must never expect rainfall? And the desert must forever remain dry and arid?" asked Satyabhama.

"To desire rainfall you have to first qualify as a fertile land.... Even clouds prefer to shower over forests crammed with trees."

"*Swami*, all I desire is to be your wife... to be the sole possessor of your love and to be forever happy with you...."

"How can the cloud that is soaked in rainwater shower in a restricted plot of land...? That would result in devastation! Excess of anything is not recommended, my love. For the crop to harvest it needs sufficient rainfall.... You will be able to digest only a sufficient amount of love.... Too much love can at times become destructive."

Having said that Krishna stepped out of her chamber....

For some time Satyabhama stood dazed. She felt mesmerised by Krishna's intelligence and philosophy. The mere thought that she was the wife of such an extraordinary man, made her feel precious... also aware.

After her profound conversation with her Lord on their premiere night, Satyabhama became all the more adamant to not share her love with anyone.

When Krishna charged out of her room, Satyabhama for a moment trailed after him. Later she bent over from the verandah banister to stare at his vanishing figure. He had crossed the main gate and his *angvastram* (apparel) was flying in the breeze. She watched his lion-like waist and marble-like torso... and was tempted to clasp him in an embrace. She trembled to get enfolded into his arms. Unsure about when he would return now, Satyabhama was filled with rage. She disagreed with her Lord that it was important for him to cajole Rukmini the same day.

It could have waited....

It was easy to determine Krishna's state of mind from his hurried strides....

Watching her husband turn so anxious for Rukmini, Satyabhama that day made a promise to herself. Rukmini may be the empress of Dwarika, but she would be recognised as Krishna's most intimate and cherished queen in the kingdom. It didn't matter that she wasn't as qualified as Rukmini to engage in knowledgeable debates with him on politics or scriptures, but she would make certain that Krishna remained spellbound in her beauty, body, heart and her palace.

Still standing in the verandah, Satyabhama felt a hand rest on her shoulder. It was her favourite maid, Manorama.

Manorama had travelled with Satyabhama as a part of her dowry. She was Satyabhama's childhood companion and familiar with her temperament. She had overheard Satyabhama's entire conversation with Krishna. She was in a habit of keeping track of news. It was her favourite activity.

"*Maharani*, there is no point in feeling sorrowful. You will have to fight for your right here."

"What do you mean fight? She too is his wife and if I were in her place I would have also felt the same way."

"That's your graciousness, otherwise nobody stands a chance before your beauty and love for Krishna..." said Manorama.

"Manu, I'm not grieved because he visits her, but because he could have waited for another time to do so... not tonight..."

"That's it... I agree with you, *maharani*... it was your premiere night.... How could he desert you tonight...?"

"But I will not fritter this night away in sulking.... In fact, I will remember this moment forever.... The empress has snatched immortal moments from my treasured time and she will have to pay a price for it..."

"*Maharani*, you are not the only one here. There are sixteen thousand queens in the king's court."

"Sixteen thousand one hundred and seven..." corrected Satyabhama, "He married me despite all of them... didn't he? He loves me and that's all that matters. I don't crave for anything more.... The rest I can handle...." Satyabhama turned to look into the mirror and lingered her eyes over her tanned body that resembled well-stirred butter mixed with a dash of kohl.... She knew she was special.

"*Maharani*, please be careful... what more can I advise?" concluded Manorama.

"You are with me to bring me all the news and the rest I know how to handle."

◆

[67]

Krishna climbed the staircase of the central palace and entered the main chamber. He wasn't surprised to find it plunged into darkness. It was Rukmini's behaviour that had disturbed him. Somehow Krishna had immense faith that irrespective of other people's interpretation, Rukmini would take his action in the right spirit. She was aware of the ensuing battle for Syamantak ruby and their negotiations with King Satyaki. She was aware of all the political strategies and it was on her advice that they had compromised with Satyaki and now....

Krishna wondered how he would begin his conversation with her tonight.... "What will I tell her... how will I convince such an intelligent woman? She will have rejoinders for every statement, what if she argues that she advised me for a compromise and marriage does not fall into a compromise. She had not been this upset when I wedded Jambuvanti or the other queens, so why today...?"

His mind crowded with thoughts, Krishna sauntered across the large room to enter Rukmini's private chamber. A solitary lamp put up a brave fight against the surrounding darkness but succeeded in spreading some light into the room.

Rukmini sat with her back to the door, resting her uncovered head on a decorative stool. Her long hair went beyond her waist and spread all over on the floor.

"My beloved queen...!" Krishna treaded carefully to not hurt or annoy her. Rukmini looked up to face him. He watched her red, tear-stained eyes and felt heartbroken! He walked closer and sat beside her, placed his hand on her back… just sensing his touch, Rukmini began to weep incessantly.

"Don't… my Dwarika will flow away in your tears…"

"Let it… I will float along and join river Purnana to return to Kundinpur…"

Krishna smiled, "But Purnana flows from Kundinpur to Dwarika and not the other way round. Once you arrive in Dwarika, there is no easy way out to Kundinpur, my beloved."

"How can you say that? I will sacrifice myself into this gushing ocean…?"

"Your life is attached to mine, so how are you at the liberty to take any decision about our life without first discussing with me?"

"Do you find humour in all this?"

"Humour…?" he asked fondly, "Do I appear like a philosopher to you just now, *patrani* (queen)? Look at my plight… a new bride is sulking with me in her palace and over here, another queen is sorrowful…. One is angry because I'm visiting the other and the other is anxious because I will soon be leaving from here…." Krishna burst out laughing.

"I'm not in the least bit angry, so you are at liberty to leave…."

"That's apparent from your face," smiled Krishna.

"As if you are affected by my anger or my sorrow…?"

"How can I not be? You are my *ardhangini*, my better half. If one half of me is angry or in despair, how can the second half experience peace…? The other second half of me residing in Satyabhama's palace also is annoyed because she too is my *ardhangini*."

"Then go… cajole her…"

"That's not possible unless I have first convinced this half…"

"Today you cannot win me with your words, my Lord."

Sitting beside her Krishna clasped Rukmini in an embrace.

"If not words, then my touch?" smiled Krishna.

"*Prabhu*, all this is futile. My heart is full of sorrow… I don't know why but I'm just not able to accept your association with Satyabhama."

"If a mother has two children and the third arrives, does she find herself divided between her children?"

"We are discussing man-woman relationship, not mother-children bonding."

"And I'm discussing the unusual relationships of this Universe. If mother Gandhari could love hundred children, then why cannot I offer equal love and respect to all my queens? My love is infinite and I can spread it to the extent you desire."

"Then stay back here tonight."

"And what would you accomplish by that? Triumph… but over whom..? Shouldn't the real victory come from within oneself…? Conquering others is a tentative victory. If I stay back with you tonight, you will feel victorious both as a woman and as an empress; you will score over the new bride… but what about you as a person? As a human being you would come across as shallow, have you ever thought about that?"

"*Prabhu…!*"

"You are the queen, the empress of the town, the leader of the Yadava bloodline, their destiny! Your generous hands stretch to offer, not to ask. Even if you think of me as an object and present me to Satyabhama, you rise in our eyes. The one who offers is the one who raises his arms. The one who accepts has to always lower his arms. Satyabhama is a mere child. She is ignorant about politics, about customs and about the power of the Syamantak ruby. She's unaware of how the king has used her as a pawn in this battle…. But you are enlightened and understand palace politics; you understand these strategies of love and war… so how can you react in this manner?"

Rukmini felt as if entire palace was illuminated. She felt ashamed of her churlish behaviour.

Krishna was right. How could she have behaved in this manner? She who had lived a lifetime with Krishna, watched him closely day and night, how could she let despair damage her heart thus? She should have had sufficient confidence in their intimacy to have erased all doubts.

Rukmini rested her head on Krishna's broad shoulder and said, "Please forgive me, my Lord."

Krishna smiled, "I should be the one to plead forgiveness for causing you suffering. If I had known that you would be so distressed, I would have visited your palace directly from the welcome gathering. It's only after you granted me permission that I would have stepped into Satyabhama's palace. For me all of you are equal. I love all of you wholeheartedly and each of you resides you in my heart as a part of me… don't you know that?"

"My Lord, I don't know why I behaved the way I did… I truly repent it and feel ashamed of myself…"

Krishna burst out laughing, "So even the scholarly empress, queen Rukmini at the end of the day is a woman. I'm glad to discover that. All this while I have relished your intellectual debates… your wholesome intense love but today, discovering you as an ordinary, possessive in love and highly emotional wife has been a revelation. I'm truly privileged."

"*Prabhu*…! Are you making fun of me or maybe I'm deserving of that…?" Rukmini covered her face with her two hands feeling embarrassed. Krishna held her hands and gently uncovered her face.

"This is the solitary lamp that illuminates the palace. If you cover your face, the whole palace will be plunged into darkness again… did you know this?"

"*Prabhu*…!" Rukmini blushed.

"I don't feel like leaving from here…" Krishna said indulgently.

"You must, Satyabhama must be waiting for you…"

"Do you say that from your heart?"

"Yes, this night belongs to Satyabhama and you must give her what is her due."

"And you, what will you do now? You will sit by this fading lamp devoid of your ornaments and mourn through the night…?"

"No…no… I'll summon the maids… get them to rub oil in my hair… I'll relish a fragrant body massage… Then early morning after shower and appropriate dressing, I'll visit Satyabhama in her palace…" then slightly shyly added… "You will be there, won't you…? I will get to see your expression early morning after spending the night with your new bride…"

Krishna stood up laughing. "It's difficult to forget the first night with a bride, right?" teased Krishna.

"Can you forget it..?" asked Rukmini shyly.

"I'm bound by duty…" replied Krishna.

"And I'm bound by righteousness," said Rukmini.

"You are extremely intelligent. It's impossible to win an argument with you."

"Then why do you play the game?"

"To lose… there is a different kind of joy in losing to you that only a beloved can understand, my love…"

Krishna clasped Rukmini in a tight embrace and departed from her palace.

As he did so, her palace and her chamber were lit up with lamps.

✦

[68]

"What does the empress say? Is she still mourning?" Satyabhama asked sitting in a room decorated with white flowers and fragrant lamps.... The silk curtains hung over the vast verandah of the chamber rustled in the cold breeze emanating from the river. It was high tide in the water and the rumbling waves could be heard all the way in Satyabhama's palace....

"She will visit your palace in the morning to welcome you... I'm hoping you will take appropriate care as a hostess..."

"I will display the right etiquette to everyone at my palace particularly the empress... she's the queen of Dwarika, the caretaker of the *Brahmins*, wife of the infinite, a great politician, adviser of Pandavas, the Almighty himself...."

"Who are you talking about, my beloved? I hail from Gokul... I'm Nand*baba*'s son... Yashoda's Kaanha... I'm a simple cowherd, that's all..."

"Sure... the simple cowherd who beckons the entire Aryan race with his cane of wit... right...?"

"As you say... I have just returned from an intellectually engaging debate and considering tonight is our wedding night, can we please reserve Bharat*varsh* politics for another night... today, right now...."

"Right now...?" There was seduction in Satyabhama's eyes and voice. She was drawn to Krishna, her lips spread into an inviting smile...

"Right now I want to transform my new bride into my wife... I have to give her, her legal right..."

"Right?" asked Satyabhama.

"Yes, right to love.... There are other ways of expressing it besides the three words – 'I love you'. I want you to experience that...."

"*Swami*...!" Satyabhama blushed but willingly raced into Krishna wide spreads arms.

That night two palaces in the same compound glittered with lights. One absorbed in intense love, seduction and erotica... the other in submission, devotion and sparkle of love...

✦

[69]

Kunti and Krishna had been sitting wordlessly for a long time.... From the window of the main palace of Indraprasth, the sky appeared brunette and intimate.... Kunti appeared pained, slightly dazed.... Krishna sat quietly staring into the sky....

"Kaanha, it's okay, let it be!" Kunti finally let out a deep sigh... "As they wish... they act according to how God guides them..."

"*Bua* (aunty)... in my opinion you must make an attempt at your end...."

"Me? Will they listen to me...?"

"You are a mother... maybe they will not avoid you...."

"Kaanha, what if they don't agree?"

"Then... he will fight through the Kauravas... and one brother will kill another." Krishna announced like a forecast.

His voice was forbidding as if coming from a deep cave. Kunti's eyes brimmed over with tears.... She had been trying to control them for a while but not any longer...

"I'm responsible for all this... It's entirely my fault... I gave him birth but rejected him. When a mother disowns, then..."

"*Bua*, I request you to make one effort.... Just try meeting up with Karna only once..."

Kunti stared at Krishna... blankly... while her eyes streamed down with tears.

For a long time, Kunti cried mutely and Krishna sat quietly looking at the skyline.

"Kaanha, how do I explain to him? How will he strengthen the Pandavas…?"

"If he joins… there will be two archers among the Pandavas and that will break Duryodhan's spinal chord…"

"But Kaanha…"

"*Bua*, I have promised you that you will always be a mother of five sons.… It's not out of fear or insecurity that I coerce you to include Karna with the Pandavas.… It's because I don't wish to watch a great man, a brave soldier get defeated.… It would pain me deeply. After all he is my brother too…"

"Kaanha, you...? Is that how you feel?"

"Why? Why cannot I feel that way? Devastation is inevitable, *bua*… but I must try and save as many as I can.… Time will testify my efforts.… That's the reason I want you to meet him…"

"Fine Kaanha, if you say so, I will definitely meet him but I know the answer right away… I know that he will never…"

"He will never accept you.… But it's important that you accept him before the battle of Kurukshetra… for him as well as for yourself.… This is a battle of consent, of acceptance, of identity, of duty.… And accepting your child is the duty of every mother.… From what I see and forecast, for Karna's peace of mind… for his salvation, it's necessary that you let him know that you accept him."

◆

[70]

Krishna appeared solemn and preoccupied sitting in the verandah of Rukmini's palace.

Rukmini offered him some boiled milk...

"My Lord, what are you thinking about?"

"You are aware, my dear, that circumstances have turned grim."

"What can you do? Besides it's not the first time that two brothers are going to battle against each other for the sake of a kingdom.... This has been an old tradition amongst emperors..."

"There is a difference, my love. This battle has all the potential of perishing the entire Aryan lineage... I can visualise the bare foreheads of so many widows... the misty future of so many orphan children..."

"It's determined on whose side you are, right? And victory is inevitable for the side you belong to..."

"Do you have any idea how many sacrifices it will entail...? How much bloodshed... I don't see any solution to prevent the mayhem..."

"The solution is with your *sakhi*..." Rukmini stated matter of fact. Krishna was startled...

"Panchali...? What can she do?"

"When the opponent fears defeat, he turns desperate. This has been proved in politics..." began Rukmini.

"Duryodhan knows that he will not emerge victorious but his arrogance will prevent him to admit that..." explained Krishna, "He will listen to no one. You are aware that I went to meet him but after his affront it's difficult for the Pandavas to remain quiet. And why should they? To endure injustice is also injustice."

"Cannot there be a way out where the Pandavas get their due and there is no bloodshed... some way to get rid of the battle...?"

"You tell me how... I have no solution. If you have some alternative, I'm impatient to hear it," Krishna asked knowing fully well that there was no solution to the problem.

"Duryodhan's biggest strength is Karna, and Karna's biggest weakness is Draupadi..." Rukmini smiled knowingly.

"You are not suggesting that..."

"Yes, my Lord, but you will have to take the initiative. Your *sakhi* will not refuse you.... Granted that mother Kunti and you have failed in your attempts but if Draupadi makes the effort there is a possibility that Karna will consider fighting through the Pandavas. "

"It will not happen... Karna will never join the Pandavas."

"Do you remember what he had told you...? He had said that you cannot promise on behalf of Draupadi...."

"Yes, but..."

"He does not want to join the Pandavas, so be it, but like you, if he takes a stand to not fight through either of the parties, he breaks Duryodhan's army by half."

"One can make an attempt on your valuable suggestion, but as far as I know Panchali, she will never agree to anything her conscience does not permit and particularly in regard with Karna whose sole dream is to perish Arjuna with his arrow."

"There is no harm in attempting. One never knows Panchali may just agree and then Duryodhan will feel demoralised to wage a war against the Pandavas..."

"I have the highest regards for your wisdom and in the circumstances will try every possibility..." concluded Krishna.

"History will testify your efforts, *Aryaputra*. If the battle is inevitable we cannot do anything to prevent it.... But we have made sincere efforts and time has made note of that..."

✦

[71]

Draupadi was seething with rage, her eyes flashing... she was not sure how to react to her friend's indecent proposal. Karna was her husband's strongest opponent... he had called her a courtesan in public and condemned her.... She should go and pacify him, for what?

Why should she swallow her pride and request him to join the Pandavas...? Just for victory...?

"We have you on our side and we have justice and righteousness. Our victory is definite then why should I plead with Duryodhan's friend, *sakha*?"

"Don't forget he is also the eldest Pandava."

"For me he is the friend of an opponent and a friend of an enemy is an enemy! That's politics. How can you forget that he abused me in front of so many people?"

"So did you, *sakhi,* you insulted him by calling him a *sutputra*..."

"At that time he was a *sutputra*... besides, you know my real reason for..."

"*Sakhi*, we are on the footsteps of *dharamyudh* (battle for duty) and it's important that you relieve him of his accumulated anguish... it's important that you balm him... accept him... that would be justice."

Draupadi's eyes were fuming, "What you imply by justice is your politics, right *sakha*...?"

"If that's how you interpret it, so be it... but for the safety of your five husbands you must meet him once."

"How can you even suggest that to me?" Draupadi looked accusingly at Krishna.

"Yes, describe it as you want – as a battle of rights or a battle of duty – but it's my suggestion that you make this one final attempt..."

"Your wish is our command... we have no option but to accept your suggestion, *sakha*."

"Don't do it if you don't want to. I suggested it for the sake of everyone's welfare..."

"Everyone's welfare...? What welfare can come to anyone through this battle, *Prabhu*...? What can be positive about the anguish of young widows and heartbreaks of helpless children...? Or maybe there is something about it that I don't comprehend... like self-centredness... like politics... like power games... am I right?"

"Your words cause me immense pain, *sakhi*... I don't oppose you; all of us are right in our own perspectives.The ultimate truth can be fathomed only when we exchange places. It's only when we view it from the other perspective that we shed light and dissolve darkness..."

"Truth is like the scorching sun... we cannot escape it even with our eyes closed.... Can we escape your halo...? Your commitment to duty has an aura too but does that illuminate our lives or does it scathe us...? I question this out of curiosity, *sakha* ..."

"You have an extremely sharp and an analytical mind but are unable to grip feelings.... Everything cannot be equated with facts.... Why does a flower bloom, why does a cloud shower and why does it dry up when the sun emerges in the sky...? These are laws of Nature and they cannot be protested."

"Protested?" There was a hint of sarcasm on Draupadi's face.

"Had I protested I would not have lived as the wife of five husbands.... My father held my *swayamvar* and without my consent laid the condition of shooting the moving fish. The Pandavas attended the *swayamvar* in the disguise of *Brahmins*. You knew everything and still made certain that Arjuna shot the arrow... that's not all... mother Kunti said, 'Share what you have brought amongst five brothers' and they did. I could have protested for being treated like an object and divided amongst five... I didn't. Don't talk about protests to me, *sakha*. Where was the justice in dragging a menstruating woman into the court…? Where was the justice in defeated players losing a wife in gambling…? Not only was all this validated but the scholarly seniors of the family, present in the Rajyasabha mutely endorsed my public humiliation…. What justice are we discussing, my friend? Even you waited till the last minute to come to my aid…. If you desired, you could have perished Dushasan's arms before he could touch me…. What justice entailed in so extending my suffering…?" Draupadi was cracking with emotion. She stopped to swallow, trembling like a leaf but not shedding a single tear.

Krishna got up and filled a silver tumbler with water from a pot beside him. He held Draupadi's hand into his and handed her the vessel. Then very gently, full of affection, he held her face in both his hands. "Tell me, in this entire Universe, was there a woman, is there a woman, who could have cursed the children of queen Gandhari and the curse to have come true…? Unless you are challenged, *sakhi*… unless you burn in fury… how would you be able to ignite flames…?"

"What are you suggesting?" Draupadi felt composed after a few sips of water. She wiped her mouth with the edge of her saree.

"There is a purpose in everything I do. You may not sometimes see the purpose or it's possible that I may not want you to see it but my purpose is the reason of my existence… and my goal…"

"In other words we are routes to accomplish your goal?" There was hurt in Draupadi's voice.

"No… you are my co-traveller… my partner… somebody who takes me to my destination… my well-wisher."

"Why did you do all this, *sakha*…? For years to come, history will remember my humiliation…. The coming generation will envision me as a weak, helpless woman…."

"Helpless?" There was a smirk on Krishna's face, "How can you who aided her five husbands be interpreted helpless…?"

It was almost as if Krishna was devouring Draupadi with words, "Centuries to come will remember you as a courageous, intelligent, independent individual who fought against all odds to preserve her self-respect. There is no explaining the bonds of the heart because words fail to paint a complete picture. A person who can assist me in my goal has to be diametrically different from me... do you understand what I mean? It's no mean task to curse the sons of mother Gandhari, revered as a faithful wife and worshipped as a deity. It was imperative that the woman, who cursed her sons when the moment came, was bedazzling...! She had to exude a fire that could not be doused even by the sunlight. *Agniputri*, please don't get me wrong, revenge is not the purpose of your life. Your purpose is to dispel darkness of this era and illuminate the Universe..."

"Regardless of it, I will not visit Karna. I'm not a part of your politics and don't desire to be," Draupadi concluded and briskly walked out of the chamber door. She stopped for a moment and looked back at Krishna with a strange, pleading expression. She folded her hands and looking directly into Krishna's eyes said...

Twadiyam Vastu Govind Tubhyamev Samarpyate ।

Weeping silently... holding the edge of her saree *pallu* in her mouth, Draupadi marched out of the room...

✦

[72]

A private meeting was to be held at Duryodhan's palace today. Balram had come all the way from Dwarika just to attend this meeting.

"*Mama* (uncle), do you feel Balram will agree?" Duryodhan was in conflict.

"Why do you worry, my dear? Balram in any case is anti-Krishna. He has never been able to get over the fact that being the elder of the two, he was deprived of the throne and Krishna crowned as the king."

"How can you be so sure?" Duryodhan asked disbelievingly.

"My dear nephew, I'm your Shakuni *mama*. I know how to gauge what's going on in another person's mind. We will work on Balram's Achilles' heel. We will promise him the throne of Dwarika."

"It's very difficult, *mama*. He is not that easy to be won over.... He has been my *guru*.... I know him. He may nurse grievances against Krishna but once that cowherd stands before him and calls out '*Dau*' (brother), Balram will melt like wax..."

"If you manage Balram on your side, your party gets strong. You have *Pitamah* Bhishma, the greatest strategist, *guru* Drona, the greatest archer who produced Arjuna, your *guru* Ashwathama, your uncle, your father-in-law and so many brave soldiers and royalties..."

"All of them will be perished by Arjuna's arrow, *mama*."

"You forget Karna...? He's the only one who can match up to Arjuna's archery."

"But *mama*... Krishna will definitely visit him once and promise to include him among the Pandavas.... And if that happens, Karna will not remain mine. He hasn't been able to recover the abuse of *sutputra* hurled at him and it's not beyond Krishna's politics to include him as the eldest Pandava and promise him the throne."

"Throne...? By just thinking that he will be included as a Pandava and seated on the throne you have volunteered your defeat! If... he is recognised as the eldest Pandava, he will join the Pandavas and if... he will fight through them, they will win.... Are these your speculations or your fears?"

"*Mama*, it's difficult to arrive at any conclusion about Karna. He still feels attracted to Draupadi and that can steal him away to the Pandavas."

"You are foolish, why would Karna long to become the sixth husband of Panchali? Why would a man who was condemned as *sutputra* all his life be satisfied with a woman already distributed amongst five men...? Besides what throne are you talking about? Karna is fully aware that his demise at the battle is inevitable. He is cursed by Parshuram.... Even Lord Indra had asked him to return his *kavach-kundal*... eldest Pandava!"

"*Mama*... whether you agree with me or not, I'm convinced that Krishna will visit Karna once..."

"Let him visit.... That will not change anything. Karna is buried under your obligations. You coroneted him as the king of Angdesh and restored his self-respect at a vulnerable point in his life. He is not ungrateful to forget that. He will not let go off an opportunity to torment Kunti... or to reject the Pandavas who have isolated him all his life.... This will be his first and final opportunity and he will not miss it. He will not miss it at the risk of his death. He will condemn them... fill them with fear... fear about Arjuna's demise for if the Pandavas fear any one person, it's Karna."

✦

[73]

"I had warned you that he will disagree," Kunti was sobbing uncontrollably. Every moment spent with Karna was piercing her heart.

"And the fault is entirely mine. If a mother rejects her son, the son has every right to reject the mother. He rejected me outright. I pleaded with him several times to address me as 'mother' but he didn't.... Nobody has ever condemned me as much as him by addressing me as '*raajmata*' again and again."

"It doesn't matter; at least you accepted him. Now he will calm down. He will be able to die in peace. He will be able to forget all his anguish and all his betrayal."

"So it's definite that he will die?" Kunti felt a lump in her throat.

"Everyone who is born has to depart some day. Karna is no different."

"He's my son. If he sides injustice, he will not find salvation."

"*Bua*, don't take this to heart but Karna has never been granted justice all his life. Can you imagine a child born out of an exercise of sheer curiosity...? A charioteer finds him and rears him.... He gains knowledge in deception and is cursed for it.... Through injustice he is denied competition in archery with the Pandavas.... Through injustice he is exempted as a candidate in Draupadi's *swayamvar*.... He has been deceived and unfairly discriminated every time.... Even destiny has not spared him, so how can he escape injustice now?"

"It's entirely my fault...I wasn't able to protect my son as a mother and I have been penalised for it..."

"Penalised...? This is only the beginning, *bua*. You have to still witness the horrifying visions of bloodshed.... In the coming days you have to listen to innumerable wails... watch countless young Aryans dissolve in the dust of Kurukshetra battle. You have no option but to shed tears..."

"Kaanha... is my crime so heinous?"

Krishna continued to stare into space quietly. Kunti found her answer in his mourning, she sobbed silently. Krishna made no efforts to console her.... He continued to stare into space quietly.

The harsh reality of time to follow clouded over them like a piercing sword that splattered bloodshed all around and spelt devastation...

✦

[74]

At the private meeting organised at Duryodhan's chamber to discuss Kurukshetra battle, the deliberations were on.

Duryodhan declared that he would not part with even an inch of a plot to the Pandavas. While Shakuni and Duryodhan were wrong in over-estimating their victory, Shakuni was on the mark in his assessment of Karna and Duryodhan in his perception of Krishna.

Krishna had decided to meet up with Karna once before the Kurukshetra battle. It wasn't as if he wasn't aware of the outcome of the meeting. But to ignore efforts in fear of the outcome was not a part of Krishna's personality.

It was well established that Karna could not refuse anybody for anything after his obeisance to Lord Surya at dawn. Even Lord Indra had chosen the opportune hour to retrieve his *kavach-kundal* from him.

And Krishna also chose the same time to meet him...

✦

[75]

River Saraswati flew gently joined by the gushing waters of rivers Hiranya and Kapila.... In the transparent water of Saraswati, Krishna visualised the time gone by. It was as if the gushing Saraswati had transformed into river Ashva, and Karna standing at the shore, hands outstretched to the rising sun... was offering his prayers.

Krishna recreated the visual before his eyes...

Copper complexioned, torso as erect as a stone and hands outstretched to offer water to Lord Surya at daybreak on the river bank...

Suddenly the visual dissolved before his eyes...

Krishna failed to recall exactly how many years ago it was but even today he sensed Karna's anguished eyes staring at him, as if asking, "Why Madhusudan? Why did you reveal the truth to me...? I didn't want to hear it.... This truth has destroyed my identity.... I could neither become a Pandava nor remain a *sutputra*.... You dropped me midway, like the unfortunate Trishanku.... You only thought about the Pandavas... was it fair?"

Seated below the *peepal* tree with his eyes closed, Krishna responded to Karna's query in his heart, "Yes, I only thought about the Pandavas and I counted you as one amongst them, which means I favoured you as well."

Karna's laughter resounded all over river Trivenisangam. He roared exactly the same way he did when he kneeled down and sobbed bitterly before Krishna.

Resting beneath the *peepal* tree with his eyes closed, once again an unguarded tear trickled down Krishna's cheeks...

✦

[76]

Standing waist-high inside the water of river Ashva and offering prayers to the rising sun, Karna looked arresting. Devoid of his characteristic *kavach-kundal*, but still as alluring with shoulders well rounded like a bow and stray drops of water shining like pearls on his bronze body…

A little distance away stood his horses and his chariot…

What Krishna had to reveal to Karna today was going to cause him his biggest heartbreak but Karna didn't hesitate to face the truth. Today, Krishna had to address the *sutputra* as a Pandava.

It was a difficult task for Krishna. He had to inform the best friend of their opponent (Duryodhan) that he hailed from the Pandava family…. He was the eldest Pandava!

Krishna walked towards the river bank and waited patiently for Karna to complete his offerings.

Prayers over, Karna walked back to the shore. His divinity was dazzling as if he was an extension of Lord Surya himself.

On noticing Kriṣhna, his expression altered slightly but he recovered immediately.

He could well imagine what would have brought Krishna two days prior to the Kurukshetra battle to his doorstep.

Krishna moved ahead. Karna folded his hands to greet Krishna.

"*Namaskar* Vasudev."

"Long live and may you emerge triumphant," Krishna stated.

Karna burst out laughing, "*Prabhu* if your blessings don't come true, how will you feel?"

"These are not my blessings but my good wishes... and I have a solution for them to come true, provided you agree..."

Karna was still laughing, "You want me to join the Pandavas, right? You are aware that this isn't possible.... Arjuna and I have been competing with each other for years... it started as children in the school of Hastinapur and went on till the *swayamvar* of Draupadi..." Karna let out a deep sigh.

"That's okay; such feelings are not unusual between two brothers."

"Brothers...?" Karna looked surprised and heartbroken.

"See Karna, I'm not here to cloak my words and trap you in a puzzle.... What I have to tell you is the truth and it's very apparent.... On the side of the Kauravas there is injustice, deception and..."

"And on the side of Pandavas there is righteousness, truth, justice and you..." Karna broke into laughter, "Are you bribing me, *Prabhu*? What is this bribe for – for life or for victory?"

"You are self-sufficient. Nobody can trap or tempt you. Your entire life has been devoted to sacrifices.... You didn't hesitate to remove and donate your *kavach-kundal* too... what can I offer you...?"

There was a chilling void in Krishna's voice, "I have not come here to bribe you but to reveal you a fact.... After hearing it whether you ask for life or for death... whether you side injustice and join hands with an opponent or a brother, the decision is entirely yours, eldest Pandava..."

"Eldest Pandava... Madhusudan!" There was surprise and distrust in Karna's voice, "Do you believe that as well...?" he whispered.

"I know it's true," Krishna looked into Karna's eyes.

They appeared slightly red and for a moment the brown eyes turned moist but Karna controlled himself and said, "Maybe... but what has all this got to do with it now?"

There was a rhythm in the flow of river Ashva.... Every time it splashed against the rocks, the waves spread all over the place. There was a different kind of music in the atmosphere. The chirping birds on the eclectic trees surrounding the river bank had deserted the branches...

the sunrays had turned brighter, sharper and the brown sand was slowly turning warmer. Karna's eyes turned damp.

"What about all this now?" Karna repeated his question. Krishna moved closer, placed his hand on Karna's shoulder.

"Yes, you are Kunti's son… her eldest son. It's my desire that you acquire your rightful position. When justice conquers injustice and the victorious return to Indraprasth, it's my wish that they return home as six… not five Pandavas…."

It was time for Karna to start laughing so loudly that it resounded all over. Not able to control his mirth any longer, Karna went and sat on the river bank… still laughing!

Tears rolled down his eyes but Karna could not stop laughing. Krishna didn't say a word; he merely stared at Karna fixedly.

A little while later, he joined him, placed his hand over his shoulder sympathetically and stroked his back, "You understand the meaning of being the eldest Pandava, don't you…? You will also get Draupadi…"

"Draupadi…? I don't want Draupadi in alms. I'm worshipped as the *daanveer… Daaneshvar* Karna will not accept alms for one Draupadi…."

"I'm aware that you love her even today…"

"Don't you love her…? There is a difference between loving and possessing; and who knows this better than you, *Sri* Krishna...? Wasn't it you who got this Dhrupad's daughter Krrishna married to Arjuna…? To distribute her among the five brothers was your plan as well…? Draupadi has never indicated to me that while returning to Indraprasth, she would accompany me on my chariot. You tell me, has she ever intimated you…?"

Karna stopped to gain his breath…

"…First rejection and then acceptance without choice…" Karna's sparkling eyes turned pale, "Kunti or Draupadi… what difference do they make to Karna's destiny? All that matters is that Arjuna be secured and the Pandavas remain five…. That's the only reason I'm being accepted now, am I not? I'm not so innocent to not understand this. I'm Duryodhan's friend, after all, and I don't have to be tutored in politics, Dwarika*naresh*!"

There was a long silence between the two and the only sound that could be heard was the crashing of waves in river Ashva and the singing birds in the trees. The sun was in full bloom and even Karna's eyes appeared red.

Karna's life was a mound of too many many festering wounds.... But now that he had unloaded himself and rested his head on Krishna's shoulder, Karna sobbed bitterly... uncontrollably...

Krishna continued to stroke Karna's head...

Karna continued to sob...

"Krishna, it's too late now..." he finally said.

"I know... life hasn't been fair to you and that's why I hope that no more injustice is done to you..."

"What more injustice can occur to me? I was condemned as a *sutputra* in Hastinapur's Rajyasabha and rejected from the competition.... Panchali abused me in Dhrupad's *swayamvar*.... For years, every morning and every night my ears echoed with that one word... *sutputra... sutputra... sutputra*.... Now that word has become a part of my personality, my existence. I no longer desire to be a Pandava anymore, Vasudev.... I was born a *sutputra* and will die as a *sutputra...*"

"I understand your feelings and your arguments, Karna..." sympathised Krishna.

"You don't, you are the king, the Supreme Entity and the manifestation of God.... How can you understand the anguish of a *sutputra*...? Imagine my plight to be informed at the dusk of my life that I'm a Kshatriya... a Rajput... and a Prince! Krishna, I bow my head to you and plead you that let's bury this topic right here on the banks of river Ashva."

"Karna..."

"That's it... don't say another word to me. I don't think I have the capacity to cope with any more truths in my life. Please sanction leave to this slave of yours who is now accustomed to unfairness and injustice...." Folding his hands into a *namaskar*, Karna took quick strides to walk towards his waiting horses and chariot.

It was evident that he wanted to get out of Krishna's sight as quickly as possible…. Or was it an effort to escape his closely guarded secret…? Krishna was quiet and continued to stare after him. He wondered…

How could two exemplary archers be born in the same family…? Karna was powerful, passionate and poignant… was his identity a part of his destiny…? A whirlpool of thoughts invaded Krishna but he put a break on them by turning his back and slowly walking towards shade where he had parked his chariot.

✦

[77]

Tomorrow was the second of *Magshavar vad* (name of a month). There was no going back on the battle of Kurukshetra and in the ensuing bloodshed were to be sacrificed the lives of heroic soldiers of the entire Bharat*varsh*. Depending on their perspective of right and wrong, everyone had sought their direction and joined their camps.

The battle was to commence the following morning and the opponents had put up tents on either side.

Considering the magnitude of equipped armies and so many wild animals prowling in the dark and dense forest, there was an unnatural silence in the atmosphere. A silence where one could hear the rustling of the leaves.... Far away, the sun was setting and the skyline had turned red. In the morning perhaps the earth was to display the same colour.

Everyone knew that the morning was to bring news of death... death of dear ones.... Nobody knew who amongst them were to be sacrificed in the name of duty. Nobody, except Krishna....

Krishna had promised Kunti that, "Your five sons will remain immortal..." and to fulfil this promise, every soldier in the Pandava tent knew that Krishna would leave no stone unturned...

He had summoned a collective meeting with all the soldiers in the Pandava tent on the eve of the battle. This was the eve of the first of *Magshavar vad*.

A dazed Arjuna sat quietly in one corner on the floor. Eldest brother Yudhishthir lost in his thoughts was pacing the floor... his face reflected his mind frame.... Bheem holding on to his *gada* seemed all prepared for the war....

While Yajnaseni quietly looked at Krishna… a thought crossed her mind.

"Why had Krishna summoned a collective meeting on the eve of the battle? What could he have on his mind…?" She had some inclination that perhaps Krishna would make them traverse a trial by fire during those moments…. Perhaps he wanted to test their weapons on the eve of the battle, not the usual weapons comprising wood and iron… or bones and knowledge… but weapons of heart!

For in the real sense, the battle had to be fought from the heart…

…Krishna's arrow-sharp voice resounded in the atmosphere.

"We embark on the battle of justice tomorrow…. As the soldiers of this battle, it's imperative that we don't carry any baggage to the battlefield. It's important that everyone sheds their worries and travels light…. Only those who pursue this battle in complete acceptance will achieve success…"

Draupadi darted a piercing glance at Krishna…

"What are you saying, my Lord…? I don't understand it completely," Arjuna managed to speak a few words after a long silence.

"Everyone will have to drop their inhibitions and admit to their weaknesses, here, in this tent… now…!"

"What does that mean?" Yudhishthir suddenly got up from his position and fixed his gaze on Krishna.

"We are accustomed to storing too much in our hearts. Our hearts are full of love, condemnation, lust and other yearning; and all this gets frequently entangled and therefore we live in denial. This battle for justice seeks purification, sacrifice, optimism. There is a difference between admission and ego. Ego is destructive, while admission is another expression of acceptance. It's my request to all of you that you shed all your worries, your entangled feelings and drop them right here…"

Then after a brief while added…

"Everyone will make a gallant effort to admit and accept others and themselves…. Those unable to face up to themselves will be unable to face the challenge of war. That is why it's vital that all of us face up to ourselves…. Yudhishthir, shall we begin with you…?"

Everyone was silent as if assembled in a graveyard. Yudhishthir took a long time to begin. He looked at everyone present in the room...

All the faces staring at him appeared sorrowful. There was a pall of gloom in the atmosphere...

He locked his eyes with Yajnaseni seated at a distance.... There was rage, repressed pain and questions in them....

Yudhishthir swallowed, lowered his eyes and began in a soft voice...

"I'm Yudhishthir, eldest of the Pandava sons... and perhaps the reason behind all of us gathered in this room today. It's my weakness for gambling that has driven us to this summit today. I attached more importance to the game of cards than I did to my own brothers, my wife, mother or my people... and I have paid the price for it! Today, assembled in this room on the eve of the battle, I comprehend that I have accepted injustice in my silence. I prided myself for never speaking a lie but by not protesting against deception, I have inadvertently supported it. Now my only goal is justice..." Yudhishthir felt choked. It was difficult for him to continue talking.... His eyes brimmed over with tears....

And along with him eyes of several others.... He cleared his throat and began afresh...

"...The bitter truth being that we have embarked on this battle for the sake of Draupadi. The Pandava sons have made a woman the reason of their battle... I'm shocked and also pained by this realisation.... The five men recognised as the most gallant warriors in the entire Bharat*varsh* have made a woman an excuse to wage a war.... Shouldn't we at this point pause and forgive Duryodhan? How can he be held responsible for me gambling at the Rajyasabha or for my pawning Yajnaseni...?"

He stopped to gather his breath...

"...It was all the result of my wrongdoings, so how can we punish Duryodhan for the injustice? Explain to me Krishna, why this deception...? This way history will remember Draupadi as the wife of husbands who treated her as an object and staked her in a gambling session... as men who could not preserve her honour and prestige.... Krishna it's my belief that even if we win this battle, history is not going to blow our trumpets!" Yudhishthir took a pause and one could hear him breathing for a while....

...Once again there was a long silence and everyone waited with bated breath. Bheem sat with his eyes down cast all the time twirling his *gada.*

Krishna walked up to Bheem and seated beside him. He placed his hand on Bheem's shoulder.

Bheem looked at Krishna with pleading eyes but there was determination in Krishna's eyes and Bheem had no choice but to follow orders.

"Bheem, what do you wish to say…?" Krishna's voice was melting as butter.

"Nothing… I wish to say nothing… I will definitely perish twenty to fifty tomorrow and my victim toll will increase every day..." Bheem responded without looking at Krishna, his eyes fixed on his swirling *gada.*

"This is not admission… it's arrogance," Krishna began to gently pat Bheem's back, "Bheemsen, son of air… what is weighing you down? The ease with which you inhale fresh air into your lungs and later exhale impure air out of them, you need to exercise the same ease in cleansing your soul, Bheemsen!"

Bheem looked up. There was an unusual consolation in Krishna's voice. He felt reassured in a manner a small child feels on reunion with his separated mother.

"Speak up, Bheemsen. Open the windows of your heart. We have to submit ourselves before we enter the battlefield…" Krishna indulged Bheemsen like an infant.

Bheem continued to swirl the *gada* creating a deep impression on the flooring of the tent.

"Yajnaseni… Panchali… Draupadi is my only weakness." Bheem's voice suddenly raised and cracked…

Draupadi looked at Bheem… and everyone was shell shocked!

"Good… this is admission…" Krishna was encouraging of Bheem.

"The first time I set my eyes on Yajnaseni, I regretted not being an archer… Arjuna is foolish…" everyone was stunned.

Bheem's outburst had turned everyone uncomfortable… except Draupadi who looked at Bheem full of tenderness….

"If I were in place of Arjuna, I would have never agreed to share her with others…. Yajnaseni is my strength and also my weakness… my blood boils at the memory of her humiliation… I swear to ruin the Kauravas… to grab Duryodhan and to rupture his thigh and fulfil our revenge of her humiliation…." Bheem's face was red with anger and he was breathing heavily. His chest expanded and contracted like an airbag. He picked up his *gada* in fury as if leaving for the war right away.

"…Had *bade bhaiyya* (elder brother) not prevented me at that time, I would have hacked Dushasan's arms in the Hastinapur Rajyasabha itself… I would have slit Duryodhan's chest… what is the purpose of keeping quiet then and waging a war now…? Let bygones be bygones. We will definitely seek revenge for Draupadi's humiliation but that certainly cannot erase the painful memory…."

Bheem was quiet for a while…

"…A helpless Yajnaseni imploring with folded hands to everyone in the Rajyasabha is an image that does not leave my heart and mind. Injustice has occurred and by challenging it now, we cannot alter the marking on the wall. I love Yajnaseni and to safeguard her respect, I'm willing to stake my life…."

His voice was loud and booming both inside and outside the tent.

Krishna began to stroke Bheem's back again and gradually Bheem calmed down…. So did everyone around him.

A while later, in a barely audible voice Bheem continued…

"Hidimba or other women would never have come into my life had Yajnaseni been married exclusively to me. To get to spend one year with her after a separation of four years was never acceptable to me. I wanted Yajnaseni entirely to me as my wife…" Bheem stopped to look at Draupadi.

There was an unusual connection, a bond of immense faith and undying affection between them.

Another long pause and Krishna decided it was time to intervene.

"Parth…!"

Arjuna looked up startled. Seated on one folded knee, his elbow resting on the other leg stretched out, his *angvastram* was flying in the breeze. There was a strange restlessness about him.

Hearing out his elder brothers, Arjuna was unsure of what he ought to say. For some time, he continued to look at the flooring and then very slowly, he lifted his eyes and looked at Krishna.... Then quietly, almost like a whisper Arjuna began...

"As I begin to speak, innumerable images conjure before my eyes...

"...my father Pandu's demise... our palace in Hastinapur... *Guru* Drona, his blessings that I become a supreme archer... Draupadi's *swayamvar*... and the Rajyasabha at Hastinapur.... The gambling session, our exile.... Hadn't we all suffered enough the first time for us to give in to *bade bhaiyya's* blunder and participate in it the second time? The outcome is that Yajnaseni paid the price while we watched on mutely...."

He stopped to take a deep breath... "Despite all that happened, Yajnaseni continued to be on our side.... The princess of King Dhrupad travelled forests, dressed in leaves but fulfilled her duty as a wife. And what did we give her in return? She was disrobed publicly in our presence but we did nothing to help her.... And today, we pat ourselves that this great battle is to restore her honour..."

He took a small pause, looked around and continued...

"...Let's face it... don't we yearn for the kingdom...? Don't we want Hastinapur back...? If not, why the gambling session, why the exile and why Lakshagrah...? Why perform the *ashvamedh yajna* (offering to fire) for Indraprasth...? This is politics... by describing it as a battle for justice, what are we trying to prove ourselves...?"

Another long pause...

"...How can we be ready for a battle even if it's a battle for justice that is won over the bloodshed of our own brothers, friends, *Pitamah*, uncles and innumerable relatives...? I'm utterly confused. I fail to understand what I can attain by killing my own people on the battle front tomorrow? What are we trying to prove? What justice are we going to pursue and what injustice are we going to vanquish...?"

Arjuna appeared pale. Tears streamed down his face and he felt choked. It was difficult to believe that that the most valiant archer recognised as *Gandivdhari* was sobbing like a child today, questioning the right from the wrong.

"Is this justice, Madhusudan? Haven't we erred as well...? Despite a wife like Yajnaseni, all of us brought home Ulupi, Subhadra and other co-wives.... I have done grave injustice, Madhusudan... to everyone... I have no right to fight this battle of justice...!! If you ask me I'm willing to offer you my head but liberate me from the trial of Kurukshetra."

Arjuna appeared frozen but his voice was cracking from time to time...!

"...I want to express many things and at the same time I don't want to say anything. I'm completely taken aback, too many thoughts cross my mind and suddenly I feel blank... I'm in acute dilemma and it is distressing." He paused, swallowed hard. He lowered his eyes yet again and continued...

"...I had never imagined that the blessing to become an exemplary archer will thus transform into a curse.... It feels as if the entire battle rests on my shoulders. Everyone expects that... I will fight injustice... but those oppressors... opponents... however you want to describe them are my own people... my brothers who I have grown up with.... How can you forget that? *Pitamah* Bhishma who has reared us... my various uncles... grandfather... friends... all of them are my own people..."

There was an awkward silence...

"...Is it fair to destroy all of them to grant justice to just one Yajnaseni? You tell me, Madhusudan, why cannot Yajnaseni forgive all of them? Is it all only Duryodhan's fault? Has my eldest brother Yudhishthir followed the path of justice? If not, how can Duryodhan become an opponent? Why should we embark on this battle...? The bitter truth is that we are as much to be blamed.... The truth is that we have no right to punish Duryodhan or Dushasan for the humiliation of Yajnaseni.... The truth also is that I'm not qualified to fight this battle...."

Arjuna wiped his wet eyes with his apparel and looked at Draupadi. Her eyes were fuming; she could not believe what she had just heard. She looked at Arjuna startled. What was her dear husband saying and why? Why was he nursing second thoughts on the eve of the battle...?

Arjuna completely dry-eyed but voice still cracking continued, "Madhusudan, this isn't fair.... So many lives trampled upon for what purpose...? You tell me, my Lord, is it fair to take revenge of a private humiliation through a battle?"

Draupadi attempted to rise from her seat but Krishna caught her eye and forbade her.

She was seething with rage...

She longed to walk out of the tent and get some fresh air...

But it was Krishna's order that nobody would leave the tent until the meeting was over.

Heavy-hearted and a mind completely blank, Draupadi wondered what new strategy Krishna had up his sleeve...

Now Krishna turned to Nakul... cheerful, sharp featured and everyone's pet Nakul was perhaps still ignorant of the horrific moments to come in their life. Devoid of any anxiety, he perceived the forthcoming battle as a natural event and eagerly awaited the next morning. As a Kshatriya, there was no fear in his eyes and the fact that Krishna was with them reassured him completely.

He said without the slightest hesitation, "I have nothing to say.... The ideal situation would have been that there was no battle.... But now that there is no option, so be it. I love my wife Draupadi and I will fight for her happiness, her honour... I will fight for the right of my brothers... I will fight to restore justice and perish injustice... That's all! What else can I say? I don't fear death. I'm aware that if you are with us, we will be victorious..."

Krishna burst into laughter.... He was touched by Nakul's simplicity and single-mindedness at a grim moment like this.... Next, Krishna looked at Sahdev...

Sahdev had been sitting patiently and reflecting for a long time. He folded his hands to Krishna.

"I will not say anything... I don't want to express anything..." Sahdev announced determinedly.

"...Because if I speak it will become a forecast... I belong to the unfortunates who can read mysteries of time..." Sahdev was trifle hesitant, then continued...

"...But even the one who predicts future cannot alter destiny. I stand before time and visualise events... whether it's the bloodshed of an individual or of injustice, the colour is red... I had hoped that all blood would be retained in our veins, not spurted all over on the floor. We look for answers in our prayers but sometimes don't find them. It's something we are not ready to accept..."

Then as an afterthought added... "To foresee what is to occur but to not be able to share it with anyone is a tragedy that burns me all the time.... Still I don't feel so weighed down that I need to unleash... *Prabhu*, please pardon me and liberate me from this cycle of birth and death. I have lived my entire life like a blank slate and that's the kind of end I would desire..."

"Blank slate," Krishna smiled briefly and looked at Sahdev... "A slate scribbled with innumerable words but all indecipherable.... But as you wish Sahdev... this is not the court of Chitragupt... I'm merely a..."

"I understand you, my Lord... I understand how you feel but I request you to try and understand my perspective. Words are often misleading, *Prabhu*, particularly my words because everyone will interpret them with their own perception. I'm aware that I will have to eventually speak my mind and if I seriously begin to express myself there will be calamity.... That is why I desired exemption..."

"Calamity has already occurred, *vatsa* (son), what more calamities can come beyond what we have endured?" said Krishna.

"My words wittingly or unwittingly transform into a forecast... I'm scared to predict any more events on the battlefront, my *Prabhu*... as the husband of Draupadi I failed to safeguard her honour in the Rajyasabha... now I will fight to restore her respect... I don't have anything more to confess..."

"Fine, as you wish..." Krishna turned to look at Draupadi.... She appeared composed but questions rotated in her eyes as if caught in a whirlpool.

Draupadi felt slightly dizzy.... She could hear her heartbeats.... She knew it was her turn now and yearned that Krishna would spare her from the interrogation....

Krishna fixed his gaze on Draupadi....

"*Sakhi!*" in these two alphabet of one word, there were many questions or maybe Draupadi heard them.

Draupadi prayed that Krishna should not ask her anything, yet deep down, her heart was restless to confess what she had never expressed all these years....

There was a feeling of déjà vu... Draupadi was conscious of a strange conflict arising within her.... The feeling was akin to what she experienced many years ago when she first set eyes on Krishna during his visit to their palace to meet her father.... Today Draupadi experienced the same feeling of conflict, part fear and part attraction gripped her mind...

"*Sakhi...!*" Krishna repeated his address and everyone waited for Draupadi's response...

This was a bigger test than her *swayamvar.*

Today's test did not involve expertise in archery but the courage to open the floodgates of an unusually beautiful, intelligent woman's heart... a woman who was to express her feelings towards her multiple husbands who perhaps loved her with the same intensity!

She was the woman who was the reason why everyone was present in the room...

She was the reason why everyone was still together...

Daughter of King Dhrupad and created from the flames, Draupadi was a dazzling persona who had innumerable princes besotted with her and which included likes of Karna and Duryodhan.

She was a woman who had incessantly fought for her self-respect...

Her five husbands were as curious to know what went on in the woman's mind who had surrendered to them in body, word and action all these years.

"Why me...? I'm not a participant in the battle, so why must I make any confessions?" Draupadi said what came to her mind spontaneously. Krishna looked at her with an expression that made her uncomfortable.

"You may not be going to the battlefield but you are the cause of the battle and the remedy as well."

"I don't understand, *sakha...*" Draupadi feigned ignorance.

Her eyes resembled the fear of a little child caught stealing sweets...

Bheem was right, Krishna thought. Draupadi was distractingly attractive.... She was an extraordinary woman!

"I didn't understand, *sakha*," Draupadi repeated herself.

Krishna tried to control but a smile spread across his face, "Somebody as intelligent as you cannot understand my question...? Will anybody believe that...?"

"*Sakha*... what can I say, my entire life has been a problem. I was created to seek revenge... emerged from the fire and have been burning ever since. I've lived my entire life like a flame. What do you expect from me?"

"Admission... acceptance..."

"Acceptance...? Would I have, survived so much without acceptance? I have accepted every moment, every situation, every injustice, shock, sorrow, pain including my horrifying humiliation..."

"I agree you have *sakhi*, but on the eve of the battle I want you to relieve yourself of all your burdens... your innumerable anxieties and yearnings... grievances and limitations that you have been festering within your heart... I urge you to unload those hurts and free yourself..."

"You ask me this, *sakha*? Is there anything about me that you are unfamiliar with...? Are there any secrets from you... what is it that you don't know...?"

"*Devi* this is not about you and me...."

The expression in Draupadi's eyes changed. It was as if she had suddenly decided to reveal her intimate secret in public today.

"Vasudev, can there be anything more intimate or private than dragging a menstruating woman amidst the Rajyasabha and getting disrobed in public view...?"

"This is not a moment for bitterness.... It's a moment for unconditional acceptance.... It's a time to acknowledge each and every incident... individual, moment and relationship encountered in our life..."

Everyone was looking at Draupadi. She was indeed very beautiful... wheat complexioned, hair as dark as the night and long enough to cover her hips, rosebud mouth, who would believe that this attractive, slender personality was a mother of one daughter Meenakshi and five robust sons…?

Draupadi appeared unusually fragile…. Unknowingly she was consumed by an engulfing sweetness. There was something spellbinding about her in exactly the same way that there is something mesmeric about a nubile sixteen-year-old.

"Vasudev…" everyone was staring at Draupadi… waiting in anticipation to know who and what Draupadi would admit to.

"When my father addressed me as 'Krrishna' I had no idea that this word would one day become a part of my life…. *Sakha,* nobody recognises and understands truth and sorrow the way you do…. If I speak the complete truth on the eve of the Kurukshetra battle… there will a battle right here inside the tent. To offer equal intensity to all five husbands is not easy, Madhusudan… and if what I have to say incurs the slightest crack then…"

"…Then it will not diminish your self-respect in our eyes, Panchali…" Arjuna immediately interrupted.

"*Priti Parthen Shashvatam*!" Krishna sought this blessing from Mayaḍanev and filled our lives with love…. "You are at liberty to express what you want, so say what you desire fearlessly, Panchali."

"You Falguni…? And you *sakha*… do I need to express myself to you? All of you are aware of what is inside my heart and in time to come so will other generations…" Draupadi got up from the meeting. She had been feeling claustrophobic for some time and was relieved to get some fresh air outside the tent…

Panchali's eyes were slightly moist but she didn't lose composure… "When my five husbands were watching me disrobed, I had raised my arms seeking your help…. Isn't that sufficient proof of our unique friendship? Our relationship of trust and distrust is as constant as our breathing…. To be alive we need to periodically inhale and exhale…. I, Krrishna, daughter of Dhrupad, today open the floodgates of my heart to my husbands and to you…! Now there is no baggage… no sorrow… no grief… no pain… what I'm about to say has been locked inside my heart and pierced some corner of it for years…. Vasudev… Madhusudan… *sakha,* every moment of my suffering has brought me closer to your heart.... Whenever I have encountered injustice I have faced it head-on. I was never worried because I have always sensed you by my side, holding my hand.... All I pray now is that I receive the same kind of love from you in every lifetime.... I want nothing more than that...." There was a long, meaningful silence while everyone was drawing their own conclusions to her oratory.

But Panchali's outburst hadn't ended, "*Sakha*... why is it that it's only in our suffering that we find you close to us...? Is it because you prefer it that way or is it necessary for us to be in the depths of despair, to feel tormented and troubled to have you beside us...? Inside this tent on the battlefield of Kurukshetra just your presence amidst us is so reassuring.... But why is it that you become our guide only during the battle, why cannot you play the·charioteer of our life and lead us in our moments of happiness as well? If I'm reborn, I would like to have you as my friend again and this is possible if you so desire."

Krishna recalled his first meeting with Krrishna....

She was sixteen, tanned and bewitching. Her shimmering black hair touched her feet and she had lost her heart to Krishna at first glance. In that era, when every princess dreamed of marrying the perfect man, Draupadi was no different.

At her *swayamvar*, when every king and heroic warrior of the entire Bharat*varsh* was assembled with the sole intention of taking her home as their queen, Lord Krishna had arrived at the venue with a different objective.

The incident of Lakshagrah was still fresh in his memory....

At the podium of competition attended by the likes of Duryodhan, Karna, Shishupal and Jarasandh, Draupadi was delighted to spot Krishna and thanked the Almighty for his arrival.

Seated with her eyes cast down, Draupadi mistook Arjuna's dark feet for Krishna's feet as they passed her and sent a silent prayer to God to take those feet to victory.

When Arjuna shot the arrow and emerged victorious before Draupadi, waiting to be garlanded, Draupadi had missed a heartbeat....

...This wasn't Krishna. Her eyes had filled with tears as she turned to look at Krishna standing beside Arjuna with sad, helpless eyes....

Draupadi felt betrayed by Krishna....

Well aware of her feelings for him, Krishna had deliberately opted out of competition to ensure Arjuna's victory and inadvertently rejected Draupadi. This non-acceptance pierced her heart like a thorn. When Draupadi looked at Krishna, there was accusation....

Krishna hadn't forgotten that expression in all these years.

That Yajnaseni, created for the sole purpose of revenge could be so vulnerable and contain so much compassion, who knew this... except Krishna?

And yet, her vulnerability, her compassion, her fragile sporadic feelings like the splash of water remained locked in her heart and drenched her....

The others merely saw the smile that surrounded Agniputri. Those close to her scathed in her beauty, her sparkle and her dignity but failed to sense her moist heart... not even her five husbands. For to experience her dew drop nature, one had to first endure the fire and nobody dared that!

There was less shame, inhibition and more of anger in Draupadi's eyes as she stood attired in solitary apparel in the Rajyasabha that fateful day. Dushasan had not disrobed her clothes that day; he had stripped her self-respect...

Even today what pained Yajnaseni was not so much that her husbands watched her being disrobed mutely but that Duryodhan affronted her self-respect and condemned her honour for which her husbands were entirely responsible.

Draupadi felt less insulted about facing the elders in the family during her menstrual cycle but more livid about being staked in a gamble, as if she were an object....

In a trembling voice that shook up the entire palace she had asked...

"Did my husbands first lose me or themselves?"

Tears streamed down her face out of humiliation, not helplessness.

Krishna had watched Draupadi's eyes turn moist on several occasions and they reflected different emotions at different phases which only he understood. Today, recalling those innumerable moments, Krishna soaked in their memories.

"Na Me Mongh Yach Bhavet..." Krishna recalled his own words that he imparted to Draupadi while filling her with extended apparel on that fateful day, "The way you cry today, so will the queens of all these wicked men in time to come... *Na Me Mongh Bhavet...* I promise you, my words will not go futile..."

Krishna could hear his five ingredient conch, a sound that had become a part of his consciousness.

Only he knew the pain of sacrificing flute and substituting it with a conch... Krishna was aware of the frightening days to follow after the Kurukshetra.... And that's why he described the battle as *Pran Udven Jatevya.* He knew that what was to follow was going to be remembered and condemned by history for many generations.

On that eve of Kurukshetra, Krishna's rich voice was chanting...

Yatodharam Stato Jay... resounded in all directions.

✦

[78]

When Arjuna's chariot made way into the gate of Dwarika, it was mid afternoon.... The horses were frothing at the mouth after running for two days without a break....

Draupadi's hair was dishevelled and face layered with dust. Finally, Arjuna loosened the reins....

When the chariot crossed the main entrance, Draupadi was surprised to discover the royal streets deserted. The roads that forever buzzed with activity were barren except for a few stray Yadava women walking past. All the gates of the golden fortresses were firmly clasped. There was something ominous in the atmosphere.... Draupadi looked at Arjuna... "What could be the matter, Parth? Why do I have this sinking feeling...?" Arjuna, wordless, placed a hand on Draupadi's shoulder and rode the chariot towards the central palace....

The central palace sparkling with various golden pots surrounding all the doors belonged to empress Rukmini.... The palace was surrounded by a cluster of eight smaller palaces belonging respectively to Satyabhama, Jambuvanti and Krishna's other queens. Despite being late afternoon, the refectory adjoining the palace was empty... almost lifeless....

The place that was always vibrant and bustling with maids and assistants running up and down was today unusually quiet and that worried Draupadi.... Her heart missed a beat and she looked at Arjuna again. There was terror in her eyes, an indication of something untoward to occur.... Arjuna found it difficult to look into her eyes....

The royal guards outside the palace appeared disenchanted and listless....

Arjuna rode the chariot inside the stable of the central palace. Except for a few very young mares and some aged horses, the stable was more or less empty.

Arjuna lent his hand to aid Draupadi alight from the chariot.... Both appeared slightly weary after the excessive travelling.... Their eardrums still hummed with the whistling breeze....

Her feet almost staggering Draupadi limply walked to the main entrance.... The saree covering her head was dragging on the floor... her eyes were dry out of longing of many lifetimes.... She was parched and yearning to quench her thirst.

The staircase to the central palace was silent. In normal circumstances, the foyer was crowded with ministers and subjects wanting to meet Krishna. Even when Krishna was not in Dwarika, this spot was crowded with his well-wishers.

As she climbed the staircase, Draupadi recalled her first visit to the palace after Krishna married Rukmini. She remembered the elaborate welcome ceremony Rukmini had organised in her honour....

She had been coming to Dwarika for years and every time she was welcomed with fanfare but they were rituals devoid of personal touch. For the first time, the same ritual became special because it involved the personal touch of the lady of the house.

Draupadi experienced a difference in fragrance to the customary ritual after she was welcomed by Rukmini in Dwarika.... She was showered with flowers and pearls before she could step inside the gate.

"She is my *Vasudevasya sakhi*..." Rukmini had said folding her hands in a *namaskar*. There was a mischievous smile on her face that day....

Rukmini was younger to Draupadi and much younger to Krishna. When she failed in her attempts to dissuade brother Rukmin from arranging her alliance with King Shishupal, she wrote a letter to Krishna carried over by a Brahmin called Suden. That letter from Rukmini entailed merely seven *shlokas*....

The *shlokas* enunciated her feelings for Krishna and a threat that if he did not prevent her impending wedding to Shishupal, she was determined to end her life....

That evening when Draupadi had returned from her routine stroll in the garden, Krishna came to her carrying Rukmini's letter in his hand.

Draupadi was able to read Rukmini's face in the letter....

Two mischievous Krishna-obsessed eyes brimmed over with abundant love on the paper.... The image was in many ways a reflection of her.... They had the same intensity, obsession and yearning to submit to him....

Draupadi had laughed and without the slightest sarcasm suggested, "Even I never invested this kind of faith in you, *sakha!*"

"Really...?" Krishna reacted playfully.

"*Sakha*, she is in every manner deserving to be your empress and it's your prime duty to abduct her from her present surroundings.... She's intelligent; even I've heard stories of her knowledge and beauty.... Only a woman like her is qualified to be the queen of Dwarika..."

Krishna had looked at Draupadi's limpid eyes and dived into them like one dives to swim across to the shore....

...Later Krishna had especially sent for Draupadi to travel to Dwarika to meet Rukmini.... She remembered their first meeting.

"*Vasudevasya sakhi...!*" Rukmini had said joining her hands in a *namaskar*, "My husband's friend, *sakhi*... we welcome you to Dwarika..."

Draupadi could sense her dancing eyes even today, her cheerful face and her affectionate hand into her own....

Arjuna held Draupadi's hand....

Draupadi appeared frightened, almost unsure of herself. Like a little child, she clasped Arjuna's hand into both her hands and began climbing the staircase to the central palace.

✦

[79]

Rukmini looked at Draupadi wide eyed...

Draupadi completely stunned, stared at Rukmini's blank expression. Rukmini had just finished recounting the story but Draupadi disbelieved every word that she uttered....

Arjuna stood motionless, then without exchanging a single word, went and stood in the verandah. Far away at the bank of the river, the sun was setting on the horizon. The orange skyline resembled a blood-splattered battlefield that Arjuna questioned with darting eyes....

A pale darkness was gradually descending on the palaces of Dwarika.... It was as if the darkness had determined to spell ominous news at every doorstep. Only this morning the Yadava men folk from all homes had set out for the grand carnival and by the evening Dwarika had turned so gloomy, desolate and restless....

It was only in the morning that all the golden chariots and the beautifully decorated horses had assembled in the foyer of the central palace and one by one departed for the splendid celebration....

It was only in the morning that all the Yadava men had embraced their wives and left for the festivities to Prabhas Kshetra. It was all just a few hours ago and yet... this evening at Dwarika without Krishna was so lonesome... so bereft and so incomplete...!

Draupadi, flabbergasted was staring at Rukmini with wide eyes. A Dwarika without *sakha* was more forbidding than a graveyard.... There was something haunting about the silence....

"So now..." Draupadi looked at Rukmini.

"Time has spread its dragnets.... The drinking session must have commenced at dusk in Prabhas Kshetra..." Rukmini's voice was as cold as death.

"But *sakha*..."

"You... you could not arrive on time *Vasudevasya sakhi*!" Rukmini surveyed Draupadi in a manner that made her uncomfortable.

"Does it mean that now *sakha*...?"

"...Will not meet you.... The Yadava carnival will seek the devastation of all the Yadavas... and that will mark the end of the golden era of Dwarika," Rukmini was sounding like making a forecast. Her eyes cold and stoned, face devoid of expression, she was composed as if waiting for time to beckon her and liberate her....

"Parth..." Draupadi could barely find her voice....

Her eyes streaming with tears, throat parched and experiencing difficulty in breathing, she screamed "Parth..." so loudly as if her voice was going to crack....

Arjuna heard Draupadi's voice calling out to him while standing in the verandah and missed a heartbeat. Rearranging his apparel, he rushed inside the room....

"Parth..." Draupadi's voice was barely audible now. Arjuna almost banged into the corridor pillar before he could rush to pick up a fainting Draupadi in to his arms... she had fallen unconscious.

Arjuna carried her to a nearby cot and laid her on it....

"*Sakha*... Parth... Prabhas... *sakha*..." Draupadi was speaking incoherently. Though unconscious, Draupadi's eyes were still streaming with tears...

A dazed Rukmini who had not shed a single tear all this while, was moved by Draupadi's helplessness. Her eyes brimming over with tears she told Arjuna...

"There's still time... try and reach Prabhas.... If you will fail to meet *Prabhu* at the last minute, then Panchali..." Rukmini could not complete her sentence.

Arjuna looked at Draupadi.... This was the woman he loved immensely.... She had spellbound her five husbands in her attraction and in her devotion to them.... She had never discriminated between them both physically or emotionally.... She was the queen of Indraprasth... whose mere glance was sufficient to put the biggest emperors into a tizzy.... She was the woman even Duryodhan and Karna had secretly desired....

And this woman... loved Krishna so passionately!

The woman who had sent off her five husbands to the warfront without a tremor and courageously applied *tilak* on them had today, on news of Krishna's final departure, broken down completely!

Is this what she had hinted at when she expressed herself on the eve of the Kurukshetra battle when she said...?

"When my father... when my father addressed me as Krrishna I had no idea that this word would one day become a part of my life... *sakha,* nobody recognises and understands truth and sorrow the way you do..."

So this was that crack!

Strange that such insight should pierce through a small crack...

The queen, who had remained steady as a rock after the demise of her five adolescent sons, was today rattled with just the speculation of a tragedy involving Krishna. Arjuna could have never imagined this.

He was gripped by vintage images involving Draupadi and Krishna.... He went into a flashback recalling various moments, expressions, interpretations... and these memories seemed to say "Hurry up, Parth... if the soul is no more, the body will perish away soon..."

Draupadi was still unconscious... still talking incoherently.

"*Sakha...* I'm on my way... I will reach you... wait for me *sakha,* Krishna..."

Arjuna picked up the unconscious, blabbering Draupadi into his arms. Her hair had ripped open and dragged on the floor... so did a part of her saree... and her arms hung lose outstretched. Her bustier strings had loosened as a result the apparel had pushed down and her cleavage was prominently evident. Her gold and pearl necklaces also had pushed behind and hung lose along with her hair and her saree.... Her legs were lifeless and coiled on the knees...

Arjuna carried her and marched towards the chariot.... For a moment Rukmini stared after him.

She had no intention of stopping him and sent a silent prayer for the two to the Almighty... "O Lord, please make sure that this woman wins the race of time.... It's for the wellbeing of everyone.... Do take care, Lord... *Shanti Shanti Shanti*...!"

✦

[80]

Resting against the tree trunk, Krishna opened his eyes slowly and looked all around him.... It was mid afternoon and the sun was blazing.... Protecting him from the scorching heat and providing him shade was the thick foliage from the *peepal* tree guarding him like Sheshnaag... Jara was still sitting beside him on his haunches...

"Can you hear the bells of the chariot?"

"No, my Lord.... There is no one in sight..."

"Illusions..." a mischievous smile played on Krishna's face, "Strange are the ways of the heart... you yearn for the one you wait... and you believe that they will be able to reach you..."

"You are waiting for Arjuna, my Lord...?"

"Yes, Arjuna too..."

"Will someone be accompanying him, *Prabhu*...?"

"That depends on the person..."

Krishna was unable to keep his eyes open, his throat was parched. With his eyes closed, he sensed all kinds of colours around him.... Peacock feathers floated around him gently stroking his face.... Bells chimed in his ears.... Was this the sound of Radha's anklets running on the streets of Vrindavan...? Or was it the chariots of Indraprasth preparing to welcome the king of Dwarika...?

...Were they the bells from Rukmini's *chandanhaar* (elaborate necklace)... or were they the delicate flowers studded on Satyabhama's bracelet creating music in his ears...?

...Was it the sound of mother Yashoda's clanging glass bangles while churning butter in Gokul or was this mother Devaki's bare hands incessantly stroking his brow while her two gold bangles on either wrist slipped down from time to time to created this unusual sound...?

It was difficult to determine from where so many different sounds originated in Krishna's ears.... He shut his eyes lightly and once again composed himself to wait for his visitor...

✦

[81]

"What do you think you are doing, *sakha*?"

"Shouldn't I be contributing something too when we are hosting such an elaborate *yajna* (prayer)...?"

"But this...?" Draupadi sounded alarmed.

"Let go off my hand, *sakhi,* everyone is watching..."

Draupadi blushed and immediately let go off Krishna's hand...

Later in the night when everyone assembled in the courtyard under the open sky comfortable in the gold seats specially put up for the occasion, suddenly Arjuna burst out laughing...

"I have never seen Yajnaseni blush like this..."

"But that shouldn't provoke such laughter..." Bheemsen was a trifle irritated.

"When I told *sakhi* that everyone is watching, she immediately let go off my hand as if it's a crime to hold another's hand..." said Krishna

Arjuna was still roaring with laughter... "Crime it is, when you are the wife of five husbands to hold hand of your friend in public view..."

"He was picking up soiled plates of the guests... how could I allow him...?" explained Draupadi shyly.

"You prevented and in the process your *henna*-painted, ornament-adorned beautiful hand held my hand in public, who can be this fortunate?" Krishna burst out laughing and once again Draupadi felt embarrassed and blushed.

Arjuna continued to rock with laughter. Yajnaseni continued to blush and all this further aggravated Bheemsen.

It was all in good humour but beneath the banter, deep down Krishna was fearful of the time to come... if only he could somehow prevent the forthcoming moment.... But he didn't know how to.

Suddenly, his eyes searched Sahdev's who was quietly sitting in a corner. As soon as Krishna caught his gaze, Sahdev lowered his eyes.... It was as if the two had communicated several secrets in silence....

"I feel like eating fruits, *sakhi*..." Krishna requested.

"I'll get them right away..." Draupadi got up at once.

"Where are your maids?" Arjuna held Draupadi's hand.

"For *sakha*, I'll bring it myself..." Draupadi relieved her hand and went inside the house....

Once again, Sahdev and Krishna exchanged a glance but this time, it was Krishna's turn to lower his eyes....

Draupadi returned with a large gold vessel filled with fruits....

As she did so, walking through the dark lobby, her earlobes sparkled with her *ratna phool* studs, but more sparkling than her diamonds were her bewitching eyes and shining raven hair at the moment slightly unkempt because the long tresses tied into a bun had loosened considerably and dangled on her nape... a few strands of hair having fallen on her face. Her long, sharp nose, two petals like lips and a small rounded cleft... her swan like neck as if carved from wax and below the neck, where you cannot resist your gaze her large, well-rounded breasts....

Her waistline was so slender that it could be held between two palms and over it hung an ornamental gem studded waistband... the sound of her anklets gradually approached closer.

"Here, *sakha*..." she placed the gold vessel before him....

Krishna picked up the knife accompanying the vessel and began to slice them.... As his eyes met Sahdev, the latter began laughing without reason.

Before Krishna could respond to Sahdev's laughter, the knife had pierced into his hand and it was bleeding profusely. Before anyone could react, Draupadi had slit her priceless silk apparel to bandage Krishna's bleeding fingers....

Arjuna, Bheemsen and Yudhishthir were stunned....

Sahdev smiled briefly and got up.... He looked at Krishna and laughed again. Nobody could understand his mysterious laughter except Krishna.

Krishna held Draupadi's hand....

"Krrishna... *sakhi*... today in the presence of everyone, I promise you that when the time comes, I will provide you as many number of apparels as in the threads of this bandage.... That's my word of honour...."

Sahdev laughed once again.

"I will never need so many apparels, Vasudev.... After living in the forest for so long, I prefer clothes made out of leaves. I'm no longer comfortable in these expensive fabrics and now I kind of feel myself attached to my leaves and ornaments made out of flowers. I don't know how many threads entail in this bandage strip but I would request you to instead bless me that the ties of our relationship remain eternal.... Promise me that no harm should ever be done to our precious bond, Govind."

Krishna held Draupadi's hand affectionately, "Do I need to make you this promise, *sakhi*?"

All eyes present in the room filled with tears. How pure and at the same time intimate was their bonding.... What possible name could be given to a relationship like this? Friendship, love or something else...

✦

[82]

"If my husbands were defeated before they lost me in the gamble, what gave them the right to stake me…? What kind of politics is this? My question is directed to you *Pitamah*… *Maharaj* Dhritrashtra, *kaka* (uncle) *shri* Vidur…. Why? Why did you accept this stipulation…? I'm the daughter-in-law of this family…. Are daughters-in-law lost and gained in gambling sessions? Is this your tradition?" Draupadi's tear-drenched scream was echoing in the Rajyasabha.

All heads were bent and none dared to look up as Draupadi raised one disturbing question after another.

"I'm asking you something, I want answers to my questions…" Draupadi's voice lashed like hot flames.

"Questions…? Slaves don't have the authority to question…they merely follow orders…. So keep quiet or I will tie a bandage over your mouth, the way mother Gandhari ties over her eyes…" Duryodhan laughed mockingly…

"You ask me to remain quiet but what about history, Duryodhan?"

"History will remember you as the queen of the Kaurava family…. Forget about these five impotent husbands who lost you in gambling as an object…"

"So how different are you from them? They lost me and you won me as an object too, didn't you?"

"Victory has its own glory; the losers have nothing, except humiliation…"

"Duryodhan, I need to pose you a question.... In fact I need to address this question to the entire men folk of the Kaurava family present in this Rajyasabha.... Did my husbands lose me first or themselves...? If they lost themselves first, do they have a right to stake me? What does justice say, what about politics, what about duty...?"

"Nobody says anything.... Everyone has submitted to Duryodhan and for generations to come everyone will remain quiet..."

"That's what you believe, you wicked soul..."

"If you speak an extra word, I will get you disrobed here in the Rajyasabha in full view of everyone."

"I wish you do that, for as of now I'm still composed.... As yet you haven't caused me sufficient suffering to be able to curse you.... Torment me more, so that I can curse the destruction of the entire Kaurava clan..."

Once again, Duryodhan burst out laughing and the sound reverberated in the domes of Rajyasabha...

"You...? You will curse?"

Karna who had been quiet for a long time could not contain himself any longer.... He decided this was the right time to join and seek revenge for his old wounds.

"Only virtuous women curse... and a woman living with five husbands cannot be virtuous. Panchali... alias wife shared by five husbands..." Karna laughed sarcastically.... He sounded as bitter as poison.... After all these years, he still felt tormented by Draupadi's insult of him at her *swayamvar*.... He had woken up many a night startled...

"Quiet... Yajnaseni is my name... I was created out of fire... fire which is as bright as pure it is... I'm Draupadi, daughter of King Dhrupad... revered and worshipped among the handful women of this era.... How can impotent men like you who couldn't remain faithful to your single wives, understand the devotion and complete surrender of a faithful wife committed to her five husbands...? You will never understand my endurance, my large-heartedness.... It's not in the capacity of an ordinary woman to sustain unity amongst her many beloveds.... It would have been the easiest thing for me to make them quarrel among themselves... but I held them together in my love, my devotion, my truth and my purity... I accepted all the conditions, all the insults, all the piercing comments and mockery hurled at me to continue my duty as a wife and never looked back..."

Tears streaming down her cheeks she continued....

"...Just imagine what could have transpired had I even for a moment faltered from my path of commitment? These five husbands, who are seated before you, would have all travelled different directions. The string that holds the pearls is often invisible but it is strong and clutches collective rows of beads together. I have performed that role... kept everyone together and united..."

Draupadi stopped to wipe her tears.

"...I have never understood how loving another can diminish my feelings for the former.... Some individuals have the extraordinary capacity, they are able to love more than one person simultaneously and offer themselves wholeheartedly.... In the process, their love flourishes... never decreases.... How come nobody questions or doubts a mother loving all her children equally...? Why does society always dart these arrows only when it comes to the subject of another husband or another man...?"

There was pin drop silence in the room...

"...I have been frequently penalised on this subject... I've had to time and again sacrifice my identity, my womanhood, my perspective.... Time and again, I've had to go through trial by fire to prove my righteousness.... Despite being completely faithful, I've had to prove my intentions recurrently.... The men present in this room will never understand how painful that can be.... The fact is they are the cause of my present condition...still that does not alter my faith or my honour.... The purpose of my existence is to seek revenge. If I desire, I can exude flames from my body and perish my husbands this very moment who dared to gamble with me like I was an object..."

She stopped to look at the seniors...

"...What happened to your *Kshatriya dharma* to drag a menstruating woman, devoid of ornaments and attired in single apparel into Rajyasabha.... I'm the daughter-in-law and my prestige is the prestige of the family. You *Pitamah*, *maharaj* Dhritrashtra, *kaka* Vidur, *gurudev* Drona and all the gallant and knowledgeable people present in this court, weren't those who gambled the children of this family as well, then how come, none of you prevented them...? Just imagine somebody who was never glanced by the wind when indoors or gazed by the sunlight when outdoors, this Yajnaseni, today stands scantily dressed in public view.... And the reason for my condition is my own husbands! They have wronged me time and again and every time, I have forgiven my five husbands... I do it once again. But I don't forgive you both, Duryodhan and Dushasan.... You will have to account for every insult hurled at me, every tear shed from my eye.... Arjuna's every arrow and Bheem's every attack will challenge your follies and injustice.... You will apologise to me for your mocking laughter today.... You will come on bended knees and plead forgiveness.... Today I, Yajnaseni, the daughter of Dhrupad and the wife of the Pandavas take the pledge in front of all the learned men of the Kaurava clan... until I dip my hair in the blood spurted out of the split chest of Dushasan... I promise, I will not tie my hair. Dushasan, you have pushed a woman to her extreme threshold... and a scorned woman is like an animal.... It's very difficult to get a woman to this stage, for a woman by nature is forgiving, compassionate, loving and fragile.... If devastation is the ugly side of civilisation, vengeance is the other side of virtuosity.... Today, I sense this burning poison in my veins.... Until I soak my scalp in your blood, I will relive this torment in my memories.... This is Draupadi's... Yajnaseni's promise to you... until then you will burn in the fire of my vengeance, and so will you Duryodhan and the entire family of Kauravas..."

Draupadi's long tears travelled all the way from her eyes to her cheek, nose, and neck right up to her chest.... She was frothing at her mouth... and trembling with rage.... She resembled a fluttering leaf on a cold, breezy day.... Her outstretched arms to announce her curse stopped midway... instead in a booming voice that echoed all over the Rajyasabha, Draupadi began to chant loudly ...

"*Hey Govind... Hey Gopal... Hey Govind... Hey Gopal...*"

Her arms were outstretched. It was as if she no longer feared being disrobed by Dushasan.

Her chanting pierced the conscience of everyone present in the room.... Her husbands sitting with their heads bowed all this while, gradually looked up.... Dushasan held one end of Draupadi's saree into his hand and looked at Duryodhan....

Duryodhan laughed wickedly indicating Dushasan to begin the process....

Dhritrashtra, Vidur and *Pitamah* Bhishma looked crestfallen as if someone had painted black all over their faces....

Draupadi's voice boding evil resounded in all four directions... "*Hey Govind... Hey Gopal... Hey Govind... Hey Gopal....*" Her hands were outstretched, her eyes closed in faith and tears trickled down her eyes. Her voice gradually turned louder....

There was something menacing about the atmosphere as if everyone assembled in the room awaited for something portentous to happen.... Dushasan was still pulling Draupadi's apparel....

Draupadi appeared disconnected with her surrounding. There was radiance on her face, a rhythm about her chanting as if melody had combined with truth and entered her body.

Dushasan was pulling... still pulling... still pulling....

"*Hey Govind... Hey Gopal...*
Hey Govind... Hey Gopal...
Hey Govind... Hey Gopal...
Hey Govind... Hey Gopal...
Hey Govind... Hey Gopal...
Hey Govind... Hey Gopal..."

An unconscious Draupadi in the arms of Arjuna was speaking incoherently.

✦

[83]

Arjuna had picked up Draupadi and was breathlessly running towards his chariot....

It was as if he had understood that his soul mate, his *guru*, his friend was breathing his last moments and there was a possibility that he would not be able to meet him.

✦

[84]

The sun had settled in the middle of the sky on the bank of river Hiranya. Jara was sitting cross-legged beneath the *peepal* tree. Krishna's eyelids were half shut. He was composed but engaged in an inner dialogue. It was as if the subconscious Krishna was talking to the conscious Krishna.

"...So who are you waiting for, Kaanha?" the subconscious asked the conscious.

"...Nobody...!"

"...Is that so...?"

"...Yes... because I know that the one I wait for will not be able to reach me..." responded the conscious.

"...So you admit that you are waiting..."

"...Hmm... waiting for undisturbed sleep... that's all.....'

"...Not someone you have left behind... and are waiting for?"

Krishna smiled with his eyes closed. "What purpose will it serve waiting for that person...? She will not be able to make it either way, besides she may not even be aware that..."

"...Of course she does, so many complaints, incomplete communications, hurts and so many questions to be resolved... surely you are aware of all that...?"

"...But she will come, won't she..?"

"...It's not necessary that she visits in person.... Can't you sense her touch, her laughter, her sulking and your cajoling her...can't you hear her anklets, smell her fragrance…? Isn't all that a proof of her presence in the ambience…"

"…All that is within me…and has always been…"

"…It's you who has been in an eternal dilemma of 'yes' and 'no'… wasn't she always beside you in all your troubles, pain and your happiness? Then why worry now…? Why wait for her so anxiously…?"

"…I don't know. The truth is that I'm waiting for no one…. All I'm attempting at the moment is to focus on my meditation. I'm preparing for my journey to be with the Almighty who is a part of me or maybe I'm a part of him…"

"…Truth…?" The subconscious asked the conscious, "So you admit that you are not waiting for anyone specific, right…? And you have always spoken the truth, so why deceive yourself at this point…?"

"…I'm not under any illusions. I understand and still, I don't know why but sometimes…"

Krishna's eyes were closed but in them floated a spunky, sharp featured, fair as the moonlight face. Her hair as black as the night and eyebrows dancing all the way, she displayed the candour of river Yamuna and with eyes as beautiful and innocent as a deer, she would look at Krishna full of trust and ask…

"What do you think of yourself…?" her tone was accusatory.

She was fully drenched, her long hair dripped down with pearl-like drops of water… her lips quivered with rage and her wet saree clung to her chest, also her twenty-yard *ghaghra* (skirt) soaked to her body accentuated her every curve. She stretched her hand holding a broken earthen pot still carrying some water and in exasperation emptied it all over Krishna…

"I want to know exactly what you think of yourself…. Let me inform you that pots don't come for free at my home. So what kind of a game is this to break pots of milkmaids passing by…?" Every time she exploded, Krishna would roar with laughter…. He knew that she would not be able to sustain her wrath for too long…. This was a routine affair… Krishna, Balram and their other cowherd friends would climb on to a flourishing tree and hide amidst the branches to target the passing milkmaids with their *gullel* (catapult).

The milkmaids got furious. They knew that nobody would dare such prank, except Kaanha. Yet every time he flashed his mesmeric smile and indulged in baseless arguments, every time he cajoled them and played his flute for them, they were spellbound...! Not Radha, she was different. She was not swayed by his charm....

And today the cowherds had broken Radha's pot. Balram and his other friends out of fear were not willing to descend from the tree. They knew that when Radha got angry, she spared nobody....

"Will you please tell me what you think of yourself?" Radha repeated her question for the third time.

Kaanha was still laughing. Radha came closer. The cowherd boys were aware of what was to transpire. A major war of words was to follow between the mischievous Kaanha and the volatile Radha. The boys quietly stayed on top of the tree with elder brother Balram. But Kaanha was not afraid. He stood where he was, undaunted. Radha stepped closer, looked into Krishna's eyes. Kaanha was still laughing. Radha assembled the scattered pieces of the pot and broke it on Krishna's head... some of the water poured down his face, on his mouth of which Krishna swallowed a few drops.

"*Waah*... Radhike, water at your hands tastes like sugarcane..."

"Quiet... does all this suit you?"

"You tell me, do I suit you?" Krishna mocked. The more he smiled, the angrier she got.... The cowherd boys were still on the tree trembling in fear.

Radha stepped closer, "Wait and watch till I complain about you to your mother..."

"Come, let me accompany you. Where will you come looking out for me again?" said Kaanha.

"Aren't you even slightly ashamed of yourself, Kaanha?"

"Why should I...? Only women feel shy, don't they...? And I'm not a woman..."

Radha decided that there was no point arguing with him further and changed the topic with... "Now you have to buy me a new earthen pot?"

"Sure… let's go right away," Kaanha agreed.

Radha stopped to stare at him for a while. His broad smile, mesmeric eyes, dark skin, curly hair and on it attached a peacock feather…. "What was so special about him that her anger evaporated every time…?" Radha thought to herself.

Kaanha was still waiting… "Come… come… I'll buy you a new pot painted with a peacock and a parrot…"

"I don't need the painted ones; I will sketch them myself…."

"You know how to sketch a peacock and a parrot…" there was awe in Krishna's eyes.

"Yes and that too very well. This pot that you have just broken look at it carefully…. Look how hard I have worked on the drawings."

Kaanha bent to pick up the first piece, then the next and the next…. Then slowly he walked beside Radha and offered her his flute.

"Here… decorate it with your drawing for me…"

"On this?" there was surprise in Radha's deer like eyes, "This piece of wood…?"

"Silly girl, this is not a piece of wood…"

"Then, what is it?" Radha shrugged her shoulders and turned it over to survey it.

"This is a flute…"

"A flute, what's that?"

"It's a musical instrument… when I blow into it, it creates life…"

"I don't believe it, how can that happen…?"

"You don't believe it?"

"Not at all…. You are an accomplished liar and everyone in the village endorses that…"

"But I will not lie to you."

"Why…?"

"I don't know but I don't like lying to you. When I look into your eyes, I speak the truth unknowingly…"

"I don't believe you…. Go away… I don't wish to speak to you…"

"Don't speak to me but listen to me playing the flute, won't you?"

There was approval in Radha's eyes… an approval filled with curiosity.

"Go away… I have no time to spare for your piece of wood to create music… you play it and enjoy yourself…." She hiked up her flared skirt a bit to be able to walk more freely…. Next she patted her wet hair and re-arranged her saree.

Then fully aware of the effect of her beauty, she sauntered with a gait. She must have barely sauntered ten steps, when out of the blue she was swept away by the most mesmerising sound…. It was as if the sound was pulling her to it… like a magnet… full of desire and magic…. It was a sound difficult to resist!

Radha did not turn back but it was difficult for her to proceed as well…

She could feel the sound drawing closer to her. Involuntarily Radha closed her eyes, drawn to the enticing sound, feeling like a snake enveloped in the spell of the snake charmer's *been*…

"Radha…" The voice calling out her name and emerging from the same direction sounded as musical…. She stretched her hand to hold the voice and felt she had caught on to a branch clustered with flowers. Radha was not sure if this was a dream or reality and she didn't wish to know…. What mattered was that she continued to float in the rhythm of that music… the fragrance of the flowers… the magic of these moments…! Sometimes tossing her, sometimes crashing, swinging and spreading frothy waves all around like the gushing river, she was willing to be swept away in the tide…. The music was piercing into her heart… and she was enveloped in the magic like a serpent dancing to the rhythm of the *been*…

This was an unforgettable experience…. Like the life-giving plant *Sanjeevani*, the music had given her a new lease… transformed her into a new Radha.

◆

[85]

"*Ma... ma...*" a young woman emerged from the kitchen into the corridor and Radha turned to look at the woman who had addressed her as 'mother'.

Though middle-aged, Radha was only slightly grey on the temples and depicted stray lines on her forehead.... Her skin still sparkling and body still agile, her curves were evident from the tightly pushed bustier over which was draped a red, transparent fabric. Her hair still black and attractive was tied up in a large bun that could be held in two open palms.

A few strands hung over her forehead and drooped all the way to her cheek.... She was seated before the churning pot; and her large deer-like eyes were moist today. They were looking far away, as if searching for something. She had stopped churning the pot and the tattoos on her idle arms guarded by her two red armlets were in sync with her silent red lips...

"*Ma... ma...*" an attractive, young woman was shaking her up.

"Radha *ma*... O Radha *ma*..." Radha looked startled, stared at the young woman before her.

"Where are you lost...?" the young woman asked her.

Radha moved her eyes without turning her face to look at the younger woman. She stroked the young one's face with her slightly knotted but slender hands.

"Nowhere... I was merely..."

"I notice every day that you are lost in your own thoughts. Your eyes fill up without reason. What is it *ma*, has someone hurt you...?" The young woman took Radha's hands off her face and held them in her own to sit cross-legged beside her.

"No... no... nothing unusual..." Radha responded, her eyes still moist.

"*Ma*, is there something that you are not telling us...? Is there something that's troubling you?"

Radha stared at her unblinkingly.

"How are you able to read what's inside my heart...? I sometimes feel that God sent you to me because he forgot to bless me with a daughter," Radha responded.

"You are changing the topic," interrupted the younger woman.

"I don't know why *beta* but I have a sinking feeling.... It feels as if something untoward, ominous is occurring somewhere..." Radha relented sensing no escape from her investigation.

"Of what kind, *ma*...?" the woman appeared startled. She looked deep into Radha's passion-filled eyes, "Have I done something wrong...? Are you upset because of me...?"

"Of course not, silly girl... In fact I live to see your face every morning... You are my joy... so full of affection..."

The young woman stared at Radha, "Then did *bapu* say something to you...?"

"No... no...." Radha interrupted.

"Then what...?" the woman asked.

Radha kept quiet for a while.... She looked into space... into the faraway white clouds and whispered, "It feels as if the cycle of debts has completed..."

"*Ma*..." the girl sounded confused.

Radha was still staring into space. It was as if she was talking to somebody standing there... "I knew it all along... all you needed was an excuse.... But remember one thing, just as you couldn't leave Gokul without my permission, you will not be able to..."

"Who are you talking to, *ma..?*" the woman followed Radha's gaze in the direction of the sky. White clouds spread out on a brown sky resembled large cotton balls forming different shapes and patterns.... Radha's eyes seemed to be searching for someone specific in these clouds...

"*Ma*... O Radha *ma*..." the woman broke Radha's spell once again.

"Hmm...?" Radha looked startled.... Then as if pierced by a thorn, she got up abruptly and without offering any answer, moved in the direction of the kitchen.

The younger woman, Shubhra, continued to stare after Radha and thought that even at this age Radha's swagger could put any young girl to shame.

"Shyama..." Radha called out from within. The young woman for quite some time was addressed by her mother-in-law as Shyama.

The two women shared a unique bond not easily understood by others. Shubhra alias Shyama doted on her mother-in-law and Radha lived her youth through Shyama...

Radha even today vividly remembered the turning point in their relationship. It was soon after Shubhra's marriage. One day, Shubhra had a massive quarrel with her husband Aryak. Radha was unsure of what transpired between the two but Shubhra wept all night and refused to eat dinner. Radha tried consoling her, so did her husband Ayan. The father-in-law dropped all inhibitions to sit face-to-face with his daughter-in-law, but Shubhra was beyond reason.

Radha couldn't sleep a wink that night. Next early morning when she woke up, she was surprised to discover Shubhra still seated against the pillar in the corridor. Shubhra stared out in to the sky blankly.... Her eyes reflected the plight of the previous night.... Radha came and sat beside her. Shubhra sensed her but didn't acknowledge her. Radha also didn't deem it fit to disturb her. She gently stroked Shubhra's head and Shubhra snuggled into her arms, and rested her head inside Radha's lap... and gradually Radha's lap soaked in Shubhra's tears.

They continued to sit in the same position for a long time... Radha didn't ask a single question and Shubhra offered no explanations but finally it was time for confessions.

The skyline had changed colour. Shubhra rose from Radha's lap.... She looked at Radha's questioning eyes and pleaded, "Tell me *ma*, is it a crime to love...?"

"No my dear, love can never be a crime." For a while both were quiet.

Then Radha's eyes filled with tears, she stroked the younger woman's face, "The tragedy with us women is that our love has to translate into surrender... we have to continuously give without expecting anything in return... and even then, we are not spared of interrogation! In our society, it's not significant that the beloved is the husband but what's further distressing is that the husband also is not a beloved...."

Shubhra held on to Radha's hand stroking her face, "*Ma*, have I ever failed in my intentions? Have I faltered in my duties? Have I caused you or Aryak any hurt? Haven't I served and fulfilled my duties with body and mind towards Aryak... but what can I do about my heart...?"

"It's not in your control.... Nobody's heart ever is in their control..." completed Radha.

"*Ma*, what can I do if a corner of my heart still soaks in the first shower of the rain...? What can I do if that corner remains damp...? What can I do if no sunlight or summer can dry up that corner...?

Radha stared at her daughter-in-law wordlessly.... Then pulling her closer, she rested her head on her chest and stroked her gently saying, "Shyama..."

Shubhra looked at Radha.... Looking distantly into the red sky; it was as if Radha was reading the time gone by. Hadn't she heard this story many times before? Radha sighed deeply then continued...

"For a woman, her beloved is her entire life.... He is the reason of her blossoming and the reason of her wilting away. Men and women have different interpretations of love.... For men it is receiving all the time, whereas for women it is flowing like a river.... Just as a river pours her sweet water into the ocean, the woman submits her love.... It's the nature of love and fragrance to always offer. Love that flows like the river in a single direction nurtures every drop while within the boundary but once it crosses boundary, there is a disaster! It leaves behind a trail of muck and mourning.... That's why we say love is like air held in a fist....

The fist is empty and yet not really.... Our lines of destiny are entwined with marriage and though after a while the colour of *henna* fades away, the lines of fate refuse to disappear. They come firmly clasped with us at birth and we have no choice but to tread the rest of our life dictated by them...."

That day, till daybreak, the two women shared their lives in silence.... And ever since Shubhra transformed into Shyama for Radha!

"Shyama..." Radha called out from inside.

"*Ji ma,*" responded Shubhra and went inside the room...

Radha was still contemplating on Shubhra's earlier comment on her. Shubhra wasn't wrong. For the past many days, Radha had been feeling unusually restless. The sound of the flute hounded her everywhere she went whether she was eating, drinking, sleeping... churning butter... feeding the cows or milking them....

For a long period of time, the flute had stopped following her; or rather she had prevented the sound from chasing her.

It was for this very reason that she had stopped visiting river Yamuna. She had even steered away from the river bank to fetch water ever since Kaanha left Gokul for Mathura.

"How many years ago was that?" Radha tried to recall as her eyes burnt before the wooden fire. She was kneading the flour for *roti*, while her heart pounded with innumerable memories.

Shubhra sat before her, clearing the stones from the rice but her eyes were fixed on Radha. She had never seen her mother-in-law so preoccupied, so vulnerable. In the many years of knowing her, Radha had always come across strong; yet today, her eyes filled up recurrently.

Shubhra wondered what could be hurting her mother-in-law so much. She deliberately dropped her plate to test if Radha got distracted but Radha's mind was elsewhere.... She had unthinkingly touched upon the plate over the fire without first putting on the *roti* and burnt her fingers. Shubhra dropped her rice plate and charged towards a large vessel filled with butter, scooped out a generous mound and rubbed it over her hand. Within moments, the burn got transformed into a big round blister.... Shubhra looked at Radha. Radha lowered her eyes, her expression one of being caught while stealing.

"*Ma*, are you missing somebody?" Shubhra asked gently.

Though it was many years ago, Gokul was still rife with stories of their romance. The cowherd boys and the milkmaids often mentioned a certain married woman in the village even today.... These stories had reached Shubhra's ears as well. Radha preferred not to respond to Shubhra's query and disappeared inside her room. She shut her door and flopped on her bed. Facing the bed on the wall was an ornate mirror carved in wood. Radha happened to glance into the mirror.... She stared at her reflection for a while, and then burst into tears.... Her wailing could be heard outside in the corridor and also in the kitchen.... Shubhra was conscious of her heartache but thought it appropriate not to agitate her. She continued with her chores and didn't disturb Radha by knocking on her door.

With time, Radha's sobs became louder and the heart-wrenching cries filled Shubhra's eyes with tears but she engrossed herself in with her domestic chores.

Late evening when Ayan and Aryak returned home with their daily grains, they sensed the atmosphere grim. Shubhra appeared dragging her feet. The men assumed that the two women, who never had any differences, today got into a tussle and decided to stay out of it....

After dinner, Radha was sitting in the corridor all by herself.... Aryak and Ayan had retired to their respective rooms.... Shubhra came quietly and seated beside her. She took Radha's hand into her own... and stroked it for a while. Then without looking at Radha asked, "How far is Dwarika from here, *ma*..?"

Without responding Radha withdrew her hand in exactly the same way she had withdrawn her fingers from the firewood earlier in the day.

"*Ma*... I'm asking you..." Shubhra asked Radha again in a soft voice.

Shubhra's determined voice pierced into Radha's heart. There was a nip in the air and Radha shivered in the breeze.

"I don't wish to go to Dwarika..." Radha said softly.

"Who is talking about visiting...? I was merely investigating how far it is located from here."

"How would I know?" Radha responded.

"Haven't you always stated *ma* that rivers and women flow in one direction and when they change course or leave the shore there is chaos...?"

"I did, my dear, but when the heavens open up and there are heavy showers even the rivers cannot control themselves.... Not wanting to, they break away from their shores at times..." Radha was staring blankly into the sky, "Even if the entire Dwarika comes to me now, it serves no purpose because it's like sand held in my fist that will soon slip out..."

"Is something distressing you, mother? Are you frightened about something?"

Radha turned to gently look at Shubhra, "Everything has always transpired according to his desires.... And that's how it will continue.... If he was really concerned about our fears and anxieties, if he really cared for our feelings and attachments it would have never come this far..." Radha responded and went back to staring into space, "Also how many people can he feel concerned about...? He has his duties... his goals... his deadlines..."

"Who are you referring to, *ma*?" Shubhra questioned.

"My child... let it be..." Radha whispered.

"Don't ask me his name if I take his name, the *kadamb* tree will wither away all its leaves. The water in river Yamuna will break the shores and rush to merge the paths between Gokul and Mathura.... Even the Govardhan Mountain will shake up and this entire game will be destroyed in a moment..." Radha covered both her ears with her hands, "I cannot bear this sound any longer... who is playing the flute so loudly...? Stop it... please stop this sound of the flute.... If the melody doesn't stop, my veins will burst... I can feel my head pounding.... Please, please stop the sound of this flute..."

She sensed the flute sound drawing closer and closer and unknowingly shut her eyes.... Wrapped in the melody of the flute like a snake mesmerised in the melody of *been*... Radha fell into a trance....

"Radha..." the voice calling out to her was emanating from the same melody... she sensed a hand stretching out to her and it felt as if she had caught on to a branch filled with flowers. Radha wasn't sure if this was a dream or reality and she didn't wish to either... she wanted to savour this music… savour the fragrance of these flowers… and relish the magic of these moments, that's all… she wanted to surrender to the jumping, splashing, crashing waves and remain there….

The music pierced through her heart making her restless…. It followed her and wrapped her in the melody spreading its magic like a snakebite spreading its poison all over her body….

For a moment, Shubhra considered asking her mother where the sound of music originated from, but then didn't need to, because slowly, she began hearing the notes as well. It was as if the flute had invaded her body and filled it up with music. She could sense her adrenaline rushing. She felt as if the entire Gokul was flowing in the rhythm of this extraordinary music….

She placed Radha's head into her lap. She opened her tresses and gently began running her fingers into them… while the two anguished women were mourning a damp corner of their hearts… consoling each other's sepia memories with tears and sighs… the two men of the household, unaware of the Yamuna floods that had broken the dam and burst into their home were sleeping soundly….

…The sound of the flute had crept through the cracks of the walls and invaded into the veins of the two women… throbbing and turning them restless!

✦

[86]

Resting beneath the tree with his eyes closed it was as if Krishna was travelling the streets of Gokul... visiting the palace of Indraprasth.

Draupadi's sparkling and questioning eyes stared at him from the sunlight in the sky... and asked, "Who are you thinking about at this moment, *sakha*?"

A little later, Rukmini's faithful eyes, full of love but drenched in sorrow floated on the waves and trickled beneath Krishna's feet as if stroking him to gently ask, "Are you too much in pain, my Lord?"

A while later Satyabhama's dark, seductive eyes full of desire as if caressing every fibre of his body but full of pain and complain seemed to ask, "Why did you betray me, *Prabhu*?"

Radha's limpid eyes as deep as the water in river Yamuna and as restless as a fish were covered with dark clouds of anxiety, anger and fear.... They bent over Krishna's face like a *peepal* branch swaying in the breeze and asked, "Kaanha, you lied to me, didn't you? You deceived me and didn't come back after all...?"

The four images seemed to intermingle before Krishna's eyes.... He tried hard to separate them but it was like separating the rivers entwined into Trivenisangam.... He tried, but like rivers Hiranya, Kapila and Saraswati, the images of Radha, Rukmini, Satyabhama and Draupadi blended and floated before Krishna's eyes turning them moist from time to time.... Krishna made one more effort but it was futile.... He opened his eyes.

It was mid afternoon. The changing tides in the river and the scorching sunlight fluctuated like a flickering flame.... The *peepal* leaves fluttered in the cold breeze of the sea.... Krishna closed his eyes and waited in anticipation for that one voice...

A voice that would wake him up from this trance.... He was reminded of his own words again...

Sarganmandir Tashva Madhya Chaiyahmarjunah ।
Adhyatmavidha Vidhana Vaadah Pravadtamahamah ॥
Akshranmakarodism Dwandvasamaskiya Cha ।
Ahmevakshyah Kalo Dhataha Vishwatomukhah ॥
Dandah Damyatamasmi Nitirasim Jigishatomah ।
Maunanchaivasmi Grihanagyanan Gyanavtamahomah ॥

"Hey Arjuna, I'm the middle as well as the end of the sky and other parts of Nature; in short, every creation, sustenance or destruction is a part of my magnificence. I'm the knowledge... I'm the awareness... I'm the conflict in time of despair...

"...I'm the shape in the alphabet spread out in all the scriptures. In grammar, I'm the adjective, the preposition, the noun and the adverb. In tense, I'm the past, the present as well as the future. In the cycle of *karma*, I'm the provider and also the receiver...

"...In times of injustice, I'm the oppressor so that those without values learn righteousness. I'm greed, ambition and also success. I'm the silence that preserves secrets and also knowledge that spreads awareness...."

Daruk had gone to fetch Arjuna but had still not returned because it was only on reaching Hastinapur he learnt that Arjuna and Draupadi had left long ago to visit Krishna in Dwarika.

He wasn't in Dwarika... not in Gokul... neither in Hastinapur... nor in Indraprasth... so where was Krishna?

For the first time it occurred to Krishna that even he wasn't aware where he was.... In a fervent desire to be everywhere all the time, he was not able to reach anywhere...!

◆

[87]

The full moon night was dancing on the waves of river Yamuna.... At times the water gently flowed and sparkled and at other times, it gushed along with muddy water.

The moonlight filtered through the *kadamb* leaves and Radha's face shone like silver. Her eyes were shut and head resting against Krishna's chest.... He ripped apart her long hair gathering dust on the floor and roved his slender fingers into them. His other hand was entwined into Radha's arm and rested on her chest; Radha was playing with Krishna's fingers with her free hand...

"Can I leave now, Kaanha...?" Radha asked with her eyes closed, tears streaming down all the way to her cheeks and behind her ears. Krishna caressed her, "How long can I hold you here...? It's my misfortune that I will never greet the morning sunlight looking into your eyes."

"Kaanha... my mornings are destined for someone else.... Call it my fortune or misfortune but it's my nature to keep a commitment... and it's your temperament to not steal me away... I'm bound by promises... I'm helpless..."

"And I'm bound by time... my time is running out."

"Today it's your time to leave... someday when it would be my time, I will depart too," stated Radha.

"Won't you stop me?" asked Krishna.

"If you were going to stop by my preventing, would you have gone away in the first place...?" asked Radha, "All of us have to reach our determined destinations. Me to my home and you to yours..."

"Let me look at you in the direction of the light..."

"Why?"

"Your eyes are damp," observed Krishna.

"That's what you feel... because you look at me with moist eyes..." explained Radha.

"Will you cry when I depart?" asked Krishna indulgently.

"Why, would you feel pleased if I say yes...?"

"Is it possible that I would rejoice when you are in tears?"

"Well, that's how it has been all these years, Kaanha.... You harass me, make me cry, break my earthen pot and hound me with your timely, untimely rendition of the flute... and when I drop everything and come searching for you, you go and hide somewhere deliberately.... Isn't this harassment?"

"That was just a... just... just a game, Radha."

"And this...? What is this?"

"This is reality," declared Krishna.

"Sometimes it's a game for you and sometimes it's reality, so what happens to me Kaanha, where do I fit into all this...?"

"You are a part of me, therefore a part of my game as well as my reality. What I cannot experience directly, I experience it through you..."

"Kaanha..." Radha responded in a sharp tone that pierced into Krishna's heart, "So you will determine everything, right...? Our love for each other is your decision.... Your love for others also is your decision...? My long exile... my tears and anguish is your decision as well... also the fact that I'll never be able to forget you and yearn for you all my life...?"

Krishna came closer to Radha, held her hand and placed it on his lips.... Radha began to hear the flute out of the blue...

For a long time, the two were lost into each other's spell... oblivious of their surroundings...

Then suddenly, Radha withdrew her hand from him and said, "I wish to tell you one thing Kaanha..." and without waiting for his response continued, "When you travel on a long journey with someone, you unwittingly transform into the path.... The traveller often forgets if he's on a journey or if he is the destination.... You've determined to depart, and depart you will Kaanha, but just remember to trade the path as a voyager.... In your long journey, take care not to transform into a never-ending destination..."

"Radha, I'm going to fly away into the sky... all my ties on earth will soon end. The lines on my palms will be layered in dust and it will not be possible to view my reflection even in a faded mirror.... In fact the more I will try to wipe that dust, the more the image will dissolve..." Krishna's voice was drenched in tears but his eyes were dry staring far away into the sky.

"Why do you have to leave Gokul... what are you being deprived of here...? You have the cows, your mother..." then slightly hesitantly, "And me... I'm here too... what else do you want...?"

"Me... when did I want anything? I'm going to distribute everything I had brought with me before I leave..."

"Before you leave, what does that mean? Are you going somewhere?" Radha sat upright.

"Yes, I have to move ahead and I have no right to turn back. I'm time and I cannot look back Radhike, even if I want to.... Even if you want to..."

"I don't follow all your complicated conversations. In any case you have always done what you wish. Tell me honestly, have you ever lived your life thinking about others...? Whatever you believe in becomes the truth and whatever you follow, becomes duty.... Congratulations Kaanha..." Radha's voice was sinister and salty like the water of Yamuna.

"I accept I'm independent and only an independent individual has the freedom of choice. I depart because I wish to and I arrived here because I had no other option. Radha, the one who is independent is also responsible. He has the responsibility of liberating others because only a free soul can grant freedom to others. If I get bound what will happen to the freedom of so many who are suffering...? Have you ever thought about them? I know you are not self-centred and I cannot be because I'm detached from self, so how do I elaborate this further?"

"Without you, everything will be lonely and desolate here."

"I will always be here and eternally beside you…. Our journeys are a process of our minds my beloved…. In reality, there are no such exercises. What exists is a time span of our journey from one point to another and it's this journey perhaps what we term as our identity…"

Radha stared at Krishna perplexed while he continued…

"…At this moment, we are lost into each other but the moment before and after are moments consumed in travelling. Every moment of our existence is gradually leading us to our departure. End is inevitable; the only thing we don't know is when…. That's the only question we don't have an answer for. If we did, our journey would never be as interesting nor as challenging, do you get that, my love?"

"Kaanha… I understand just one thing that I cannot live without you…" confessed Radha.

"Life is consistent, my beloved, it continues to flow like river Yamuna, sometimes with pristine, sparkling water… and sometimes with mucky and muddy water, but the flow does not stop, whether I'm there today or not there tomorrow…"

Radha snuggled closer to him. Disturbed by his revelation she was crying bitterly on his broad chest…. Krishna was drenched in her tears and uncontrollable sobbing. He stroked her back affectionately and stared far away into the space….

He was well aware of his departure from Gokul… and in a way was getting prepared for it. Krishna had to reach his final destination and that too in the decided timeframe…

[88]

On reaching Dwarika when Draupadi learnt about Krishna's journey to Prabhas Kshetra she let out a scream…

"Parth…" Arjuna who was standing in the verandah heard her scream and missed a heartbeat. He charged inside the room, rearranging his apparel…

"Parth…" Draupadi's voice had turned into a whisper. Arjuna stumbled into the corridor banging into a pillar and made it just in time to pick up a collapsing Draupadi… Draupadi closed her eyes.

Arjuna lifted her and put her on a cot near by… "*Sakha*… Parth… Prabhas… *sakha*" Draupadi was speaking incoherently.

She was unconscious but her eyes were still streaming down with tears…

"*Hey Govind… Hey Gopal… Hey Govind… Hey Gopal…*" Draupadi was blabbering in a semi-conscious state, her eyes still closed.

Arjuna picked her up and charged breathlessly towards the chariot…

By now even he had assessed that there was wide chasm between his soul mate, *guru*, friend and them!

Arjuna laid Draupadi inside the chariot, held the reins in his hand and whipped the cane….

The horses neighed as if understanding that today was a day to fly faster than the wind and take their master to his destination…. The chariot was flying in the direction of Prabhas Kshetra…. After a while Arjuna seemed to have second thoughts and turned the horses to the river bank.

A solitary boat was rocking at the shore. There was a possibility that the Yadavas, who had travelled by the golden boats the previous night, didn't consider the wooden boat appropriate for their carnival.

Or maybe Krishna had deliberately left the boat behind as an indicator to reach him via this route.

Arjuna lifted the unconscious Draupadi in both his arms.

The wet sand on the shore was still afresh with many foot imprints... many were swept away in the high tide of the previous night.... On spotting two beautiful, flower-like footprints there was no doubt in Arjuna's mind that they belonged to his dear friend and Lord *Sri* Krishna.

Arjuna tried waking up Draupadi and shook her up vigorously, "Yajnaseni, wake up, Yajnaseni... see, here are the footprints of Lord Krishna. He has not gone too far... can even the high tide dare to wash away his footprints...? He's the destiny... he's the time and nothing can happen to him... so wake up, Yajnaseni... and look...!"

Her voice barely a whisper and still blabbering... "*Govind... Gopal... Govind... Gopal...*" Draupadi opened her eyes....

She stood before the footprints and her moist eyes streamed down filling up Krishna's foot impression in the sand with tears.... Firmly ingrained in the wet sand, the footprints were now filled to the brim with Draupadi's tears and suddenly Parth remembered what Krishna had told him. "Tears are our feelings overflowing from our eyes.... When words fail and we are at loss of expression, tears complete communication...."

Kneeling beside the lotus footprints, Draupadi's saree and her strands of hair mingled in the wet sand. Her eyes full of worship for *Sri* Krishna's footprints, the words inadvertently slipped out of her mouth...

Twadiyam Vastu Govind Tubhyamev Samarpyate ।

✦

[89]

After the departure of Arjuna and Draupadi, the palace appeared desolate. Rukmini felt crushed by Draupadi's obsession for Krishna. Feeling diminished, she asked herself why she allowed Krishna to go... Why did she not travel with him... why did she succumb to his argument...? Rukmini was filled with self-doubts.

It pained her that she didn't value Draupadi sufficiently. For a woman living with five husbands to contain so much love for her husband was quite extraordinary. Unlike other wives, Rukmini did not feel envious of Draupadi, on the contrary she felt overwhelmed by her bonding with Krishna.

Krishna would often say, "If we look for specific identities in men and women, men thrive on ego and women on envy. In reality, envy is a passive emotion of ego and ego is an active emotion of envy."

Rukmini comprehended why Draupadi was able to survive in love without envy and was therefore in many ways superior to her five husbands. The brothers had been through troubled waters and all of them deep down nursed internal conflicts with regards to her. But rather than aggravate or provoke them, Draupadi retained a rare balance with her wisdom and composure. And it was because she was so committed that they were able to survive so many crises. Interestingly, the one she desired, worshipped and loved the most also remained the only unblemished, unquestioned relationship of her life.

It was the other way round for Rukmini. Whenever Rukmini turned competitive vis-à-vis Satyabhama or any of Krishna's other queens and expressed outrage, he would pacify her and say, "Most of what troubles us is self-created. We perceive love as one-on-one relationship but love is more intriguing than that and subsequently we create further problems for ourselves. Love is a flower that can blossom for anyone at any time unannounced. It has no trappings and it comes without pressures. The more the trappings and the pressures, the brighter is the possibility of our preventing the blooming of the flower.... We are so cautious about it that we refrain from the experience and in time to come get accustomed to a life without love. Ironically, we are willing to accept a life without love but unwilling to accept that someone we love can also love someone else..."

...Today, Rukmini for the first time understood the enormity of the message.... Draupadi's love for her husband was full of surrender, eternal and non-controversial! That's why their love remained unbroken forever.... Years ago, when Rukmini had addressed Draupadi as '*Vasudevasya sakhi*' and welcomed her into the palace, she hadn't in her wildest imagination dreamt that this friend could be so close to her husband's heart....

...So many years later as she watched Draupadi depart from the palace with Arjuna today, Rukmini felt she had erred in not escorting Krishna to his final journey. She began preparations to leave for Prabhas Kshetra instantly.

"I couldn't leave with him but I can certainly follow him," she thought to herself, "In any case, isn't it the duty of a wife to follow into her husband's footsteps? And today, when everyone is trailing to his destination, why must not his queen and his better half do the same?"

Without thinking any further, Rukmini stormed out of the palace and landed on to the staircase. As she walked down the steps, she turned back to look at the palace for one last time. This was the staircase she had once climbed, step by step, holding on to Krishna's hand. She had walked on the carpet of flower petals all the way upstairs. Then, she had Krishna's hand in her own.... Today, she walked all alone on a bare flooring... the flower petals beneath her feet was Krishna's magnificence and in his absence the fragrance had disappeared from her life...

"Will I find Krishna?" a thought crossed Rukmini's mind... "Am I running out of time...?"

On the staircase Rukmini said a silent prayer in her heart, "Oh Lord... please look after my husband wherever he is... provide him happiness and peace... please spare him from pain and sorrow.... Pass on his sorrows and pain to me instead..."

Rukmini took quick strides and walked out of the central palace to proceed towards the passage leading to the quadrangle outside. Created out of white marble, the quadrangle was surrounded by *ashoka, gulmohar, garmado* and *kesuda* trees but they never looked as wilted as they appeared now. At the centre of the quadrangle was a colourful fountain, surrounded by a small pond inside which floated beautiful lotuses.... Whenever Krishna was in Dwarika and the Rajyasabha was in progress, this area was crowded with audience and forever buzzed with royal guards, ministers and subjects.

This was the quadrangle where Krishna had greeted Sudama.... He had come running barefoot all the way from his palace to this quadrangle to welcome his dear friend. For a moment, Rukmini relived that entire moment. The quadrangle had witnessed so many carnivals in Dwarika. It was here that the subjects always celebrated all their festivals. They sprinkled the entire surrounding with colour and decorated it with different plants (*aasopalav*) and flowers, Krishna participated in these festivities with a lot of exuberance. It was as if his entire existence was one big carnival. He had lived every moment of his life as a celebration and now he was all set to celebrate his end!

On many full moon nights, Rukmini had spent long quiet hours beside him in this quadrangle.... Words were not necessary during those intimate moments as both didn't feel the necessity to express. *Sri* Krishna had an ability to transform every moment spent with her into something special and unforgettable.

This was also the same place Krishna spent many late nights talking to Draupadi as well. Rukmini had often watched them from her verandah and wondered what the two could be talking about. There were times she even felt trifle envious. That her husband so easily shared his thoughts with another woman diminished Rukmini. She resented not sharing the same level of intimacy with him and felt inadequate about Krishna not sharing his innermost thoughts with her....

But she made sure never to reveal these anxieties to Krishna.

Only once when Draupadi and the Pandavas were visiting Dwarika and Krishna returned late night to Rukmini's chamber, he was surprised to discover her awake.

"Not asleep as yet, *Devi*?" he had asked.

"I was waiting for you… you spent a long time with your friend…. I thought you would now return only in the morning…" Rukmini responded.

Krishna laughed, "Whatever time I spend with *sakhi* is insufficient…"

"That's true and we have to be content with the remaining time for us after that, right *Prabhu*?"

Krishna came closer to Rukmini. "My beloved, I detect slight bitterness in your tone. Are you jealous of *sakhi*?"

Rukmini's eyes filled with tears, "I'm not envious of anyone but yes, I'm affronted by your action."

"Beloved, I'm often affronted by my own actions… and that is why I have determined to gradually loosen my bonds and liberate myself…."

Rukmini continued to look at him.

"Liberate?" she finally asked.

"Yes beloved, I'm trying to detach myself from the various worldly relationships and making an attempt to bond with God…"

"But haven't you always lived your life thus…? Like the lotus flower in a pond… surrounded by water but always untouched!"

"You understand everything… are aware of everything and yet complain of feeling affronted… you have complete right over me, my beloved, but so have other people…. I belong as much to you as I belong to the several people…. I have never held back in my showering to you… but the doubt arises when your expectations rise above my affection…. That's when you feel hurt…. I have no right over my birth, my life or even my death. I was created for the wellbeing of mankind. That's my duty and also my identity…

"…It's not only Yajnaseni but everybody has turned anxious post Kurukshetra battle…. Life will take a while to settle down after the mayhem. As a woman, she is more vexed and also articulate about it. She has lost her six children…. The triumph is nothing but a revenge fulfilled for her and yet we cannot overlook that she is the queen – Bharat*varshni* – as a mother, don't you empathise with her pain? Don't you worry about the future of this vast kingdom…? So isn't Draupadi justified in her sorrow? Try and understand this, my beloved, despite being the wife of five husbands, Draupadi is extremely lonely and distressed…. I'm the only one she can share her pain, her anguish and dilemma with…. It's because she trusts me implicitly and you as my wife doubt your own husband and complain of him hurting you…?"

Rukmini was speechless. She clung to him tightly as if wanting to immerse herself inside him. She suddenly felt extremely contented that she was the wife of her Lord!

She felt flattered that the queen of Bharat*varsh* was so devoted and so full of reverence towards her husband. Doubts subsided within Rukmini. She felt overwhelmed by her husband's extraordinary presence.

That entire night she lay awake engulfed in Krishna's embrace. She felt euphoric about being the wife of such a magnificent man. The man born for the welfare of this Cosmos… the man who had submitted his entire life and now his death to a purpose… just the thought of how special he was endeared him all the more to Rukmini who basked in the intimacy.

Rukmini broke from her reverie. She crossed the quadrangle and moved ahead. On the right side was Satyabhama's palace…. Large verandahs layered with creepers… beautiful golden cages housing parrots… and magpies hung from the ceiling…. The pillars in the verandah were made in gold in and studded with priceless colourful gems. Satyabhama's exotic palace was reflective of her aesthetics and erotic personality.

Without doubt, her palace was the most beautiful in the entire kingdom and Satyabhama also had the maximum number of maids to attend to her.

She ordered new ornaments every day and boasted of the largest and choicest collection of apparels and perfumes….

She believed that the only way to keep Krishna tied to her was to keep him under her beauteous spell.

She was the youngest of all the queens and therefore everyone including Krishna pampered her and overlooked her various shortcomings.

Krishna was drawn to Rukmini's wisdom and patience. He had great respect for her magnanimity.

And Satyabhama, though never expressing it, resented this; she felt envious of Rukmini.

She resented Krishna's deep and silent bonding with her, their constant, telepathic connection. It filled her heart with immense pain as if she was less loved and less intimate with Krishna even though this wasn't true. Nevertheless, Satyabhama continued to feel envious....

As Rukmini stormed out, she happened to glance at Satyabhama's palace. Satyabhama was standing in the verandah. Her eyes lifeless and body devoid of ornaments.... Attired in white apparel but without her characteristic *karnaphool* necklace or the beautifully braided large bun... her dark, long, shining hair was loose, spread out on her back. The eternal mischievous smile had vanished from her face and she looked dazed. The once immensely beautiful and vibrant Satyabhama today resembled a stone statue erected in the verandah of her palace.

Rukmini looked at Satyabhama; she felt something piercing in her heart. She was seized by an urge to run and embrace her... mollycoddle her... she was tempted to console her....

Satyabhama was staring into the space but suddenly noticed Rukmini. Her eyes reflected no recognition... she appeared static.

Rukmini didn't think it appropriate to disturb her privacy and moved ahead. She had to reach her husband soon.

She must have walked barely twenty steps when she heard a voice call out to her... "*Didi* (elder sister)... *didi*..."

Rukmini stopped. It was Satyabhama. She came charging towards her. She held Rukmini by her shoulders and turned her to face her. Then looking directly into her eyes, she asked point blank... "Our Lord is not returning, is he?"

Rukmini stared at Satyabhama... how blank and hollow were her eyes... as if they had enveloped the entire desert within them... desolate and filled with betrayal...

Rukmini lowered her eyes, unsure of how to respond to her questions.

"*Prabhu* isn't coming back... please tell me, *didi*...?" Satyabhama repeated.

Now Rukmini had no choice but to tell her the truth. She gently lifted Satyabhama's hands and pulled her closer. Rukmini clasped her in an embrace all the while stroking her back.

"You are right, *Prabhu* has left for Prabhas Kshetra and from there he leaves for his heavenly abode..."

"How can he... how can he do this...?" Satyabhama asked distressed. Her eyes flashing with self-pity and overwhelming love for her Lord. She wasn't willing to accept that Krishna could actually depart without informing her....

"*Didi*... is it possible that you have misunderstood... that there's some mistake...? I don't think *Prabhu* would go away just like that... without intimating me... without taking me along... I don't believe it's possible..."

"It is the final journey where everyone travels alone..."

"But I'm his dearest... his most intimate... I am... am I not?" Satyabhama raised the topic in expectation that Rukmini would confirm her query and clear all her suspicions. She needed the reassurance to subside all her anger and despair forever.

"But of course you are..." Rukmini echoed her feelings; Satyabhama was clinging to her like a child.

Rukmini gently stroked her hair, "There was no one dearer or closer to *Prabhu* than you.... You are his life... his better half... his beloved..." Rukmini indulged her as one would indulge a small child.

That was enough to break down Satyabhama....

"Please forgive me, *didi*... I've always been jealous of you... have resented your bonding... your intimacy with Lord... your position of an empress bothered me and my resentments prevented me from becoming his cherished queen. On his final journey, he confided in you... sought your leave... not mine..." she could not stop sobbing....

Satyabhama was cleansing her accumulated hurts through her tears. It was as if truth had emerged like sunlight in her heart and cleared all the clouds. This was the first time she understood Rukmini's significance in her Lord's life.... For the first time she was able to strike a realistic assessment of her relevance in his life.

Rukmini deemed it a fitting moment to enlighten Satyabhama with what Krishna had enlightened her at a significant point in her life. She said…

"He belongs as much to you as he belongs to the several people…. He has never held back in his showering to you…. The doubts arise when your expectations rise above his affection…. That's when you feel hurt…. He has no right over his birth, his life or even his death…. He was created for the welfare of mankind. That's his duty and also his identity…."

Satyabhama felt consoled…. The Krishna she had lived her entire life with was in the true sense understood by her only today. The Krishna she was forever in search of was discovered now… in his absence.

Perhaps this is the true sign of divinity… as long as you search God, yearn for him, you don't find him. Then he emerges on his own, like truth, straight from your heart… soul… mind and every fibre of your existence…

Today, *Sri* Krishna's Satya had encountered truth.

Today, Satyabhama in true sense had become Krishna's *ardhangini*.

Rukmini consoled Satyabhama till she was sufficiently composed, then intimated her about her trip to Prabhas Kshetra…

"Would you like to join me?" Rukmini asked her.

"No *didi*, I will stay here… in Dwarika… it is so full of his memories… his fragrance…. All the moments he spent with me here are still afresh… I will live in those memories…. The Krishna I lived with day and night but could never make my own… I will do so now…. This palace is still rife with the dust found below Krishna's footsteps…. The domes here still echo with his voice…. I can still visualise him sitting in the verandahs of all the palaces… I can see him before my eyes celebrating the festival of *Janmashtami* in this very quadrangle… throwing colours and enjoying himself thoroughly…. I will celebrate all those moments again with a new perspective… I will recreate and relive all my moments spent with him… I will never leave Dwarika now till my last breath… because my Lord, my life, my God resided here… resides here and will reside here for ever and ever…"

Satyabhama was talking without any pauses… delirious and disconnected…..

Rukmini decided to let her be and proceeded ahead. She ran down the steps and walked to the road leading to the main street of Dwarika.

Rukmini was on the solitary, deserted road of Dwarika all alone; when she heard the bells of Krishna's chariot.... She was familiar with the sound of these silver bells. She had waited many late nights in the verandah of her palace only to hear its music.

Every evening when she heard the approaching bells in the foyer of her palace, it was a moment of celebration.

"*Maharani...maharani...*" She heard Daruk calling out to her.

The voice of Krishna's charioteer was not a stranger to her. She stopped, turned back to notice that Daruk was racing towards her on the chariot.

Maybe Krishna has returned... Rukmini fooled herself and searched the chariot with false hope... it was empty.

"Where is *Prabhu*?" Rukmini asked Daruk.

"Where are Parth and mother Draupadi?" Daruk asked her.

"Why?" Rukmini's heart missed a beat... was it out of fear or...

"I have come to fetch them..."

"Not me..." the answer was on Rukmini's lips but she bit her tongue.

"Come soon, mother, or else..." Daruk could not complete his sentence.

Rukmini also had sensed the ominous and without asking any further questions seated inside the chariot as they raced towards Dwarika's river bank....

"Why are we taking this path?" Rukmini asked him.

"Mother, we will reach faster via the river.... There's a possibility that we may still be able to meet him..." Daruk replied hesitantly and full of concern.

"Does it mean...?" Rukmini felt a lump in her throat. The coming event had cast its shadow and Daruk's chariot, her increasing heartbeats and hallucinations turned Rukmini increasingly edgy and restless.... When they reached the river bank, there was no ferry on the shore....

"I will soon organise a boat..." Daruk informed and disappeared.

The river was in high tide and the footprints of the Yadavas were more or less washed away. Big waves came rushing to the shore and wiped away some more footprints...

Suddenly Rukmini discovered a familiar footprint and sat beside it.... Her eyes brimmed over with tears.... These were the footprints her hair locks drooped over when she knelt at her Lord's feet every morning.... These were the footprints she worshipped with *chandan*.... The footprints of her Lord... of *Sri* Krishna...! They were deeply immersed in the sand. The impression engraved in the sand was filled with water.

Rukmini's streaming tears were making an offering in the water filled footprints.

Daruk arrived and stood beside her....

He looked startled. He could not believe how the footprints filled to the brim with water could contain Rukmini's tears without spilling over. What was further surprising was that not a single tear had dropped out of the carved footprint....

It was not just Krishna... even his footprints were accepting of everyone. The Lord had equal compassion and affection for everyone. The purpose of Krishna's life was wholehearted acceptance.

"*Ma*, the boat has been organised, let's go..."

Rukmini got up. She touched the footprint to her head and covered her head with her saree to escape the scorching sun. She seated beside Daruk inside the boat and slowly they proceeded towards Somnath.

✦

[90]

When Arjuna and Draupadi anchored the boat at Somnath shore, the sun had come down.... The yellow rays spread across the water in the river adding sparkle to the waves....

It was high tide, so it was difficult to sail the boat close to the shore and the two had to get off amidst the gushing water. Draupadi stepped down and began walking briskly... as she did so, she splashed water all around her. It wasn't easy to walk that path and she did so holding Arjuna's hand. Together they walked towards the Somnath shore...

They stopped before the glorious Somnath Temple comprising silver pillars. The enormous domes were studded with rubies and gems. This magnificent temple was built by Krishna....

Draupadi had often visited Somnath Temple with the Pandavas. She had immense faith in this shrine and the miraculously emerged *shivling* within.... There is an old belief that Lord Somnath blesses you with your choice of partner....

There was no time to visit the temple so Draupadi stood out, closed her eyes and bowed her head to pray to the *shivling.* "He, who has always accepted everyone, please accept him with the same affection and honour, O Lord Shiva, O Shambhu.... Please grant him a peaceful and painless demise.... That's all I ask for, my Lord...."

Then as if conducting a simultaneous conversation with Krishna, she whispered incoherently... "O Govind... you have given so much to all of us... peace, affection, honour and joy... I submit all that to you today.... *Prabhu,* I'm not sure if you will be there to accept me when I reach you. I accept you wholeheartedly at this moment and return to you all that you've showered me with.... I pray for your salvation... pray that you are able to traverse this Cosmos to the heavenly abode without obstacles. That's my only sincere prayer to God... I'm aware that I may need the same prayer for myself soon for everything submitted to you is reciprocated and we are duty bound to accept whatever you shower on us.... That's the truth... the beginning... the end... and the enlightenment..."

Twadiyam Vastu Govind Tubhyamev Samarpyate ।

Her eyes were closed and engrossed in a prayer. Draupadi felt Arjuna's hand rest on her shoulder... she opened her eyes.

Suddenly everything had calmed down.

It was as if a divine flame had been ignited within her and dispelled all her anxieties. She felt composed and accepting of reality. Eventually, everyone has to connect with the Almighty. It's a new beginning when the soul discards its old clothes to adorn new ones.... This was the cycle moving into the second phase....

When Arjuna placed his hand on Draupadi's shoulder and looked into her eyes, there was a reflection of *Sri* Krishna in them.... He recalled the time his chariot was parked in the middle of the Kurukshetra battlefield. He was feeling demoralised even before the battle could begin.... On the opposite side were his brothers and other relatives. On his side were his own people fighting for justice. Suddenly Arjuna recalled Krishna's oratory to him at that moment...

Vasansi Jirnani Yatha Vihaya Navani Grahanati Naroparani ।
Tatha Sharirani Vihaya Jirnanyanyani Sanyati Navani Dehi ॥

Just in the way a human being discards his old clothes to adorn new ones, similarly the soul, which is the owner of our body, discards its old body to reside into a new one.

Prabhas Kshetra was not very far away but because there were no chariots around, Draupadi and Arjuna had to walk to the destination.

The two must have barely walked a few furlongs away from the Somnath Temple when they began to notice corpses of Yadavas scattered all around. Those who had managed to escape the violence and reach this far had collapsed on their way, some of them had bled profusely before breathing their last....

A shiver ran down Arjuna's spine to see so many valiant soldiers vanquished.... He collected the corpses and in an attempt to bid them a dignified farewell began to cover them with their apparels. Those who were grievously injured and hacked, Arjuna extended to attach the broken limbs to their anatomy.... In doing so, he completed their last rites. Arjuna bid adieu to all those who failed to get a deserving farewell from Krishna.

Slowly Arjuna understood the significance of his journey. The Lord wanted him to accomplish his incomplete task and that's why perhaps summoned for him.

When they reached Prabhas Kshetra, they saw rows and rows of extinguished pyres.

So many handsome, robust bodies mingled with different components and reduced to flickering flames.... It was poignant to watch the innumerable smoke rings create various patterns in the skyline....

Arjuna began assimilating ashes from respective pyres.... He looked around him for a suitable vessel to collect the ashes.... There were many drinking glasses and bottles scattered around but none deserving to hold the precious powder and therefore Arjuna poured it in his apparel.

"What are you doing, Parth?" Draupadi asked him.

"The final rites of all of them have been performed by *Sri* Krishna. But he has left the ritual of immersing the ashes into water for me. At a little distance from here is Trivenisangam, I will immerse these ashes into the river and pray that their souls rest in peace..." Arjuna replied.

"But where is *sakha*?" Draupadi could not hide her impatience any longer. Arjuna had exhausted a lot of time in performing the final rites of the Yadavas and then in accumulating the ashes. Initially Draupadi didn't think it appropriate to hurry him up but watching Arjuna consume more time in pursuing the exercise, Draupadi could control herself no longer.

"I thought we have come all the way to meet *sakha*..."

"We haven't come, we have been summoned by him... *Sakha* has called us here to complete his incomplete tasks," Arjuna replied as if suddenly understanding the bigger message of *Karamyogi*....

"…We will find him soon. By beckoning us on this path, he has indicated us to complete his unfinished tasks… I'm confident that *sakha* is not in this premises of Prabhas Kshetra… He wouldn't be able to survive amidst so much violence and devastation… I have a feeling he's taken shelter in a quiet place… a temple or perhaps beneath a tree to calm himself down…. We will find him soon…"

"But when…?" Draupadi was getting restless.

"When he desires…" Arjuna responded with utmost faith and submission, "When he desires, he will emerge from nowhere…. Until then, it's our duty to accomplish his goal. He knows his duty and will emerge at the right time…. We always get the results when we do what has to be done with faith, focus and submission…."

"Parth, I don't know why, but I feel as if he is waiting for us…. We must first go to him and adhere to the rest later."

"He never waits for anyone. But till we are able to reach him, we describe our journey as waiting…. We are waiting for that summon. Till he grants us permission to be in his presence, we have to wait for that moment…."

Finally, all the ashes were collected in Arjuna's apparel and tied into a knot.

"Let's go, *Devi*…" Arjuna invited.

"But *sakha*…?" Draupadi was upset. She was not willing to spend any further time on travelling to Trivenisangam to immerse the ashes and further delay their meeting with *sakha*. She was unusually restless and her head was spinning. She tried her best not to flare up but it was beyond her control. She was seething with anger towards Arjuna's untimely philosophy.

"Please let us find *sakha*, Parth. I'm not going to return from here without meeting him."

"Nor will he depart anywhere without meeting you," Arjuna replied with a smile… "Why would he call you all this way otherwise…? Calm down, my beloved. We will meet *sakha* very soon…!" He flung the apparel knotted with ashes over his shoulder and began walking.

Draupadi dragged her feet….

The two walked towards Trivenisangam…

✦

[91]

Far away in the horizon, Krishna's eyes seemed to be searching something. His last breaths were stalled in anticipation. Who was he waiting for? Draupadi, Arjuna, Rukmini, Satyabhama, Radha or was it the Almighty himself who had been hovering around him for quite a while to take him along with him. Peacock feathers dropped all over him and mingled him into their colours. The sound of the flute continued to play inside his heart and mind as if singing a farewell tune. He was all set to depart and yet held on to his last breaths tightly clutched in his fist.... Why?

Maybe Krishna didn't know himself what was obstructing him. What can prevent a person who lived his entire life for the wellbeing of others...? What can possibly torment a soul like him in his last moments except for some yearning... some unfulfilled desire...?

The land of Trivenisangam was burning in the scorching heat of the afternoon sun but the river bank was pleasant due to the cold breeze coming from the water. There was a nip in the air and the *peepal* tree beneath which Krishna sat trembled from time to time. Krishna sitting with his eyes closed would ask Jara, "Look around, my brother, can you spot someone...?"

Then going by Jara's silence, he would understand that the person... the people... he had been waiting for had not yet arrived....

"...Will I have to leave without bidding goodbye to my dear ones..." a thought crossed Krishna's mind and he immediately sought answer for it.

"Everyone who matters in my life has bidden me farewell long ago. Had they not, I wouldn't have come this far. It's because they liberated me wholeheartedly that I've been able to reach this far without worries or baggage. The time to meet my loved ones, to linger over goodbyes is over.... Now without waiting any further, it's time to separate the heart from the mind and spread my wings in the direction of salvation...'

It was as if Krishna was having an inner dialogue... "Waiting is futile.... To wait every day, every moment for something is not living but yearning.... Instead of forever waiting to receive something, it's better to accept one's every breath as an extension of life.... That would be meaningful and truthful... and who can understand this better than me? Those who live today, in the hope that something may transpire tomorrow, will live tomorrow in the hope that something may transpire the day after. They fail to live life abundantly because they are rooted in future, ignorant that tomorrow and day after will be an identical exercise.... Whatever has to be will be and it will be in the present. Those living in the future are like birds trapped in a cage forever dreaming about freedom! When they die, their tragedy will be that they didn't live their lives to their heart's content.... It's one without hope who doesn't mind ending his life today. It's always a dying man who asks if there is rebirth.... It's because he wants to be reborn!"

Once again Krishna was reminded of his own words...

Na Hi Prapashyami Mamanupadyat
Yacchokamucchoshanamindriyanam |
Avapya Bhumavasapatnamriddham
Rajyam Suramapi Chadhipatyam ||

"If I'm granted all the powers of the Cosmos or even half the powers of the heaven, there is no guarantee that I can wipe away the worries of all the angels."

"Is freedom from life freedom from yearning?" wondered Krishna. He was breathing his last moments but something deep and intense was bleeding his heart, not allowing him to spread his wings and fly away. Something was holding him back.

◆

[92]

They could see Trivenisangam from far.

Rivers Hiranya, Kapila and Saraswati emerging from three different directions entwined in a collective rhythm and submitted into the ocean. Its pristine, sweet water without the slightest resistance, submitted into the bigger flow. Draupadi wondered what was so compelling about the ocean that the rivers yearned to be swept away by the larger waves.... The waves reminded her of a woman's journey restricted within two shores....

"Didn't all women submit their desires, dreams, ambitions, attachments to their partner and become an extension of his identity? Why cannot women have their own identity and on those few instances when they did, why did they have to answer so many questions...? Why must a woman always feel so stifled and inadequate to express herself...?" Draupadi's eyes turned moist. Walking barefoot on their way to Trivenisangam, she searched for a familiar figure beneath a shady tree. Her heart yearned to spot the face that was the purpose of her existence....

"...Why do I have a sinking feeling despite being so closely connected to *sakha*... why am I so anguished, so insecure...? What is it that prevents my mind to accept that if he has called me this far, he will definitely wait for me...? There's no reason for me to feel as edgy and restless when I'm nearing my destination..." Draupadi reflected staring at the vast expanse of sand spread all around the shore. The sun was setting on the scorching water of the three rivers. Warm, golden, singing water of Hiranya... pristine water of Saraswati, so transparent that you could decipher the smallest black and white pebble settled deep beneath... and the gushing, loud waves of Kapila almost in competition with the pounding heart of Draupadi.

Suddenly Arjuna's eyes fell on Jara at a distance. He was seated with his back to them, hands folded. Beside him was evident a yellow silk fabric. Arjuna clutched Draupadi's hand and wordlessly dragged her towards the spot.... Now Draupadi also was able to spot the yellow fabric....

Draupadi's feet burnt running barefoot on the hot sand. She was unaware when her saree had blown away during this arduous journey. Her hair was ripped and wind blown. With great difficulty and with heavy breathing, Draupadi strived and struggled to somehow accomplish the last stretch. Completely exhausted, she could no longer wait to get near Krishna's yellow apparel.

As she dragged her feet, Draupadi stumbled upon a large rock. Her apparel had got tangled into her toe and Draupadi had missed a step falling on her forehead. Blood streamed down her face all the way down to her neck and below.... As she staggered ahead, the sweat on her face mixed with blood... Draupadi tried to wipe away the mess with the edge of her saree realising only then that the saree had flown away in the breeze...!

Every step was getting difficult for her but she trudged along, her eyes fixed on the yellow apparel beneath the *peepal* tree. She had not stopped chanting "*Hey Govind... Hey Gopal... Hey Govind... Hey Gopal...*" since she began the journey...

Arjuna walking behind Draupadi for a moment considered to run back and fetch Draupadi's saree. But watching it roll over in dust, he saw no purpose. There was no point stopping Draupadi even for a moment now.... He let her go ahead.... It's only when she stumbled upon the rock and fell on her forehead that Arjuna let out a scream... "Panchali..."

Sitting beneath the *peepal* tree, his eyes shut, Krishna could not help laughing, "The heart has no reasons.... You hear echoes of those you wait for all around you.... It's hallucination, what else...?" Krishna thought to himself.

That exact moment, a slightly breathless Jara announced, "*Prabhu*...! They have arrived..."

Krishna opened his eyes. He seemed confused, "They...?"

Krishna wondered who Jara was referring to. He had summoned so many of them. Then in his mind, he said, "Let me check who had heard his voice first. Who out of the many people he had called out to had arrived at his doorstep first...?" He attempted to get up and look around.

A stumbling, staggering Draupadi with her hair dishevelled and body drenched in blood and sweat and uncovered by a saree was now just a few steps away from him...

"*Sakha*..." she let out a scream that could quicken anyone's heartbeat.

"I had faith that you would come. I had faith that my friend would not let me depart without giving the final rites to my body...."

"And me, haven't you called me as well...?" asked Draupadi.

"Falguni and you have never been separate for me. I've always perceived the two of you as one image. To be honest, I don't know myself, if I love you more because of Falguni or I love Falguni more because of you, Panchali..."

Draupadi seated at Krishna's feet. She was weeping as blood trickled down her face, neck, chest, drenching her entire body. She was drained and parched. She was so pained at the moment that she longed to cry to her heart's content. One look at Krishna's bleeding foot and she grasped what had transpired. She understood there was very little time left now. She wanted time to stop ticking and hoped against hope for a miracle.... But she knew it was not to be....

"I will not let you go, *sakha*... you will not be able to leave..." Draupadi said and held Krishna's hand into her own.

"Everyone has to leave someday.... Also where am I going, just on another journey...? When time calls you, you too will have to leave.... You know this very well *sakhi* and still argue with me...?"

"Why hasn't time come for me as yet...? If you desire you can alter my time span..."

"That's not in my hands, *sakhi*. Everyone has to wait for their time. I did..."

By now Arjuna had arrived at the spot too. He kneeled at Krishna's feet, bowed his head and began weeping, "We will be forlorn and incomplete without you.... There's no meaning to our life without you, Madhusudan." His voice was choking; tears flew incessantly, wiping the blood stains incurred from Krishna's wound on the floor.

One hand holding on to Draupadi, he stretched his other hand to stroke Arjuna's hair. He laughed slightly and then shut his eyes. Then very softly as if in immense pain, he said, "I don't have the energy to orate the entire *Gita* to you once again…. There's no time for it either, Parth… so rise and move towards the path of enlightenment… achieve your goal."

"What goal is left to be achieved now, *Prabhu*?"

"Liberation…! Your own and of others… the goals you have accomplished so far were transitory and futile… your real goal awaits you now… it's before your eyes… so go and find them and seek salvation…."

Then folding his hands in a *namaskar* to both, he said, "It's time to liberate me too. As long as both of you remain attached to me, it's not possible for my heart to seek freedom."

Arjuna looked up, "*Prabhu*, you were always liberated, always infallible, detached, disconnected…."

"But in the end, a living mortal…" Krishna completed his thought, "And all human beings need to be liberated, Parth…"

"You too…?" Draupadi asked. There was yearning in her eyes. She longed to ask him a question she had resisted for many years… ever since she was sixteen and when she first set her eyes on Krishna at her maiden home in Panchal Kingdom… the question that had haunted her but she had never found courage to ask….

She was still in a dilemma whether to do so when she heard the Lord call out to her…"Krrishna…!" Hearing him address her by this name rattled Draupadi's body and mind…. She felt so overwhelmed that she longed for the earth to open up and envelop her. Beyond this one word, Draupadi had no desire or expectations out of life. It was her most cherished moment.

Arjuna looked at Draupadi.

Her eyes were filled with pathos for a friend. He placed a hand on her shoulder. He empathised with her feelings and in a strange way, identified with her vulnerable condition. Slowly, he got up and deciding to leave the two of them alone for a while, began strolling towards river Kapila.

[93]

"Parth..." Draupadi tried to prevent him from leaving.

But Arjuna proceeded towards the river Hiranya as if he had not heard her.

"Krrishna..." Krishna addressed his namesake again, "To love is not to possess.... To desire their happiness and to endeavour for the same is also love..."

"It isn't... not for a woman."

"And I'm not a woman..." Krishna teased Draupadi, smiling mischievously.

"But I am a complete woman... desired by many but submitted only to my husbands.... Still something pierces deep inside my heart.... You tell me *sakha* what is it that has remained incomplete and causes pain after all these years...?"

"Desire... there is no controlling over desire, right? I must not desire you because you have always been beside me and reside in my heart... I have never revered your femininity as a gender, for me it was always your strength, your righteousness, your identity. Our relationship is an interaction of two individuals and consequently cannot translate into the conventional man-woman emotions..." declared Krishna.

"I suggest you talk for yourself and don't include me in your assessments..." retorted Draupadi, "I very clearly wanted love from you since the first time I set eyes on you in Panchal. My heart has ever since only craved for you.... During my *swayamvar* too I hoped that you would shoot the arrow and emerge victorious but you… you led me to suffer a life of incompleteness… all alone!"

"Didn't you say *Twadiyainasti* Govind…? There is a possibility that I'm responsible for the void in your life but you have accepted this void as part of your destiny…. And when you submitted yourself in totality to me, you submitted the void as well, thereby returning to me what was given to you by me…" explained Krishna.

"You are revered as the complete man and cited as a beacon of perfection, so how can somebody like you talk about incompletion? Think of what can happen to the Universe if they discover that the image they worship as a God is in his final moments admitting to imperfection…" Draupadi's tone was sarcastic. She tried to regain composure and looked at Krishna.

"Acceptance is my duty *sakhi* and I will do so under all circumstances. Whether we discuss completion or incompletion, they are different sides of the coin… one ends where the other begins and vice-versa. They are opposites in their meaning but when you encounter them, you discover that they are interrelated. It's because life itself is full of contradictions. There are multiple images of a specific moment but we interpret them according to our changing perspectives."

"Words… once again words… can't you for once drop the baggage of words and reach out to me in purity of feelings…? Can't you for once tell me the truth…? Please *sakha* that will be my freedom…. The only way I can absolve all my anxieties, my sufferings, my various insults and my eternal quest for truth is if you accept me in totality…. Only then can I find peace… tranquillity *sakha*…" implored Draupadi.

"But when have I not accepted you, *sakhi*…? Don't you know that acceptance is my prime duty…? That I accept everyone… everything."

"No, you haven't accepted me, *sakha*."

Krishna began laughing, "*Sakhi*, you tell me, how does one accept oneself? You are a part of me. In fact there is a possibility that it's your incompletion that has made me complete. It's these minor inadequacies in each other that assimilate as competence…"

"Have you ever loved me… this is one question that has forever tormented my femininity, my identity. Whenever I have thought about it, the question has pierced my heart, causing me immense pain and suffering. I want to know the truth *sakha,* so tell me the truth today without fear or inhibition.... Forget about morality, forget that I'm your friend's wife... forget about societal pressures and confess to me, *sakha*.... Tell me please if you have ever loved me...."

"I have... I have loved you immensely; but for me love is not what comprises between spouses. Marriage is not the outcome of love for me. Love for me has never been restricted to a river flowing from one shore to another. It is the air spread out in the entire Universe. Just in the way we need to inhale fresh air and breathe freely to live, we need love to enter our lives and enrich us... The air exits in our closed fists, behind locked doors.... It's impossible to survive even a moment without it. Yet, we are never conscious of it... my love for you *sakhi* is like that invisible air in the surrounding... my love for you is my eternal appeal for your welfare, your honour, your happiness.... It's been my endeavour to fulfil your every wish, *sakhi*....

"Love for me is not to be able to touch you or to live with you... I disagree that love is only about living together.... For me love is breathing under the same sky... to be able to look up and visualise your beautiful smile. I have consistently and intensely loved you *sakhi* and do so even now.... It's possible that because I had never communicated this incomplete expression to you was preventing me to depart... I say this to you that I will love you even when I'm no more... I don't know why people disconnect love with death....

"Love is eternal and there is no reason why we cannot remain connected even after death.... The truth is that the Krishna you love, the Krishna you lament your incompletion to, is in fact the Krishna of your imagination, that's the Krishna you desire...! He is not the husband of Rukmini, not the son of Devaki, not the friend of Arjuna, but just your own Krishna. He is exclusively for you, *sakhi.* You belong to him wholeheartedly and he to you.... The Krishna you love, loves you immensely as well. Have faith in me, whatever you have asked, belongs to you and will remain with you.... Nobody can ever take it away from you."

"*Sakha*...!" Draupadi was beleaguered, "This is the most enriching moment of my life and after what you have just said, I don't desire anything more..."

"Then do I have your leave now?"

"So you are determined to go?"

"Where have I come from that I need to depart? I have always been here and will continue to remain so. Before leaving the body, this soul is compelled to fulfil its duties.... This is one of them, *sakhi*.... If your heart remains connected to mine, how my heart can be free... and until my heart is free, my soul cannot find salvation. It's my responsibility towards you, towards your affection..."

"My affection will draw you back to this earth, *sakha*... I will meet you once again in person..."

"This is attachment, *sakhi*...."

"So be it... I feel attached to you because I'm a human being..."

"So where am I the Almighty? You are the only one who has never treated me like a deity..."

"*Sakha*, why do you confuse me...? All I want to know before you leave my hand is where does my destiny take me from here...?"

"Your destiny inscribes five names of your husbands, *sakhi*. There are four directions but you are spread out in more.... And what makes you ask me this question now, at this point and put me in conflict? Calm down... outside the cycle of questions and answers is an infallible, disconnected, detached life... a life of complete tranquillity. Today this tranquillity has beckoned me, tomorrow it may beckon you."

"When... when will it beckon me, *sakha*...? This body seems a burden now... I'm tired of dragging it... I yearn to get rid of this cycle of relationships... I yearn to break free of these transitory emotions... I yearn to cross over and look at the world from the other side.... It has to happen to all of us... everyone..."

"*Sakhi*... still so many yearnings... so many desires...? How will you be able to cross over with so many yearnings and scrutinise from the other end? To be able to do so, you have to become lighter than air.... You will have to abandon all your baggage and wipe away the lines of fortune. You will have to erase all memories and get back to the blank slate where you started. Then, time will spread its arms and beckon you, hold your little finger and personally escort you to the other side.... As of now, only I can travel. Piercing through innumerable moments, I break free walking towards an infinite halo that's a part of me or maybe I'm a part of it. When the time comes, the halo envelopes us into it... it has to..."

"*Sakha*...! I, Panchali, Draupadi, daughter of Dhrupad, Pandav wife, daughter-in-law of Kuru family, release you from my several attachments and affection; I relieve you from all my responsibilities and in the process relieve myself from the bondages...."

Her voice choking, she repeated, "*Twadiyam Vastu Govind Tubhyamev Samarpyate*." This time there was a ring of truth in the words. One could hear her voice resounding in all ten directions of Hiranya, Kapila and Trivenisangam. The echoes hounded again and again. And Krishna closed his eyes peacefully. So did Draupadi, breathing slowly, chanting prayers to God.

Aum Purnamadah Purnamidam Purnatapurna Mudachyate ।
Purnasya Purnamadaya Purnamevavashishyate ॥

✦

[94]

Watching river Kapila entwine into the gushing flow of the ocean, a thought crossed Arjuna's mind. A river that travels such a long journey has many doubts. Her journey entails so many tides and bends but she calms down as soon as she nears the ocean. It's as if joining him, she finds answers to all her questions, solutions to all her uncertainty and becomes free.

Arjuna felt Draupadi was in a similar condition. Seated at the feet of Krishna, she had resolved all her conflicts and calmed down.

"The way *sakha* had resolved all my queries on the battlefield of Kurukshetra, he has cleansed Draupadi's soul today. She looks so serene. To clear misgivings and bring peace to all is Krishna's prime goal and to think that this exquisite, knowledgeable soul responsible for enlightening our lives will no longer be with us makes me feel dejected.... Who will now resolve my conflicts, who will calm me when I'm anguished, who will console me when I'm sorrowful and reassure me of his guidance...?"

Then Arjuna recalled what Krishna told him long ago and repeated it to himself...

Udvederedatmanatman Natmanamvasdyetya ।
Atmaiv Yatmano Bandhuratmev Ripuratman ॥

All of us have to safeguard ourselves. We have to take care to protect our souls, for in the end we are the caretakers and also the oppressors.

Arjuna began walking in Krishna's direction.

Draupadi and Krishna were seated with their eyes closed.

They appeared unusually tranquil as if safeguarded from a threatening storm. Arjuna joined them and felt composed as well. He closed his eyes and began stroking Krishna's feet.

The longer he stroked him, the better Krishna felt. His pain decreased gradually and Krishna felt at peace with himself.

And yet, something deep down was still churning within him.

Who else was still binding him? Whose attachment was hindering his journey? Who was he waiting for? Whose questions still remained to be answered?

✦

[95]

When Rukmini landed at the Somnath shore, she noticed Arjuna's boat and understood that they were driven in the direction of Krishna.

Only she didn't know which that direction was…

Krishna had confided into her about Yadavas exodus to Prabhas Kshetra but how devastating the journey would prove, she had not the slightest idea.

Walking briskly from the Somnath Temple in the direction of Prabhas Kshetra, she didn't spot any corpses. But at regular intervals, she encountered extinguished pyres strewn with ornaments, garments, soiled utensils, chariots, weapons and could imagine the tragedy…

Her heart fluttered with fear. The thought that her sensitive husband had to endure so much filled Rukmini's eyes with tears.

He had a way of absorbing everyone's suffering and in the bargain had to witness the end of his own brothers, friends, children, grandchildren, and subjects. All his well-wishers had to perish before his eyes and turn into flames.

"How did he undergo so much suffering, how did he contain this suffering…?" thoughts disturbed Rukmini.

"This is the *Satyika* necklace… I recognise it," said Daruk….Then he lifted the blood-stained apparel and said, "This is *Krutvarma…*" then "*Charudesham*, this *Pradhyumananuj Gad…*"

Daruk picked up the apparel and the ornaments and identified them. He recognised each and every crown, necklace, armlet and many blood-stained garments scattered all over the place. Daruk gathered all these, one by one and mourned their loss.

Rukmini felt deeply grieved. Standing amidst the dismantled ornaments and dispersed apparels, her terrified eyes hunted for Krishna's Vyjayanthi necklace and *pitamber* (apparel) secretly hoping to not find them....

It was a painful exercise.

Like a man possessed, Daruk ran helter-skelter picking broken pieces of belongings. When he couldn't take it any longer, he just dropped them on the ground and cried. He spotted a sandal with intricate carving. Rukmini's eyes fell over it too. She screamed "*Naath*..." and ran to pick up the silver sandal. She held it close to her chest... then touched it to her eyes and head....

She curiously looked around the place for the missing sandal... far away till their eyes could see there was no sight of it....

Innumerable thoughts flashed Rukmini's mind. Horrific images began conjuring in her mind. She reflected how deeply her Lord must have suffered to have gone through this ordeal. Temporarily relieved to not find the missing sandal, she prayed to never discover it in the same condition as the Yadavas.

Rukmini wondered what could have occurred. The speculation of it sent shivers down her spine. Her streaming eyes, dropped over the blood-stained sandal.... Rukmini's tears were an offering gradually washing away the blood stains....

She pondered where he could have gone... in which direction? Rukmini turned restless. Daruk came beside her and helped her to rise. Rukmini clung on to the sandal as if she was holding an idol. Wide eyed and heartbroken, she blankly followed Daruk, holding his hand. Daruk had determined his destination from the trail of blood stains on the ground. All he did was to follow the blood stains.

A little away, the two discovered the second silver sandal immersed in a pool of blood. It was evident to Daruk that his Lord was seriously injured.... The blood drops were an indication that Krishna had limped his way to be able to reach where he was.

Daruk knew that his Lord couldn't injure himself until he willed it. He was a witness to his divinity on the Kurukshetra battlefield where despite being in the midst of violence, no harm could come to this miracle worker.

So who was this who had dared to cause such agony to his Lord? If he set his eyes on him, he would kill him instantaneously. Daruk was consumed in his deliberations; holding Rukmini's hand, he followed the blood trail on the ground.

"Don't worry mother, Lord will be safe wherever he is...."

Choking over her words Rukmini responded, "That's evident from his blood-stained sandals... so why do you offer me false condolences, Daruk...? *Prabhu* had warned me before leaving Dwarika that the time for his bonding with his body had ended.... If that's true my guess is that he would have gone into *samadhi* long ago and attained salvation. He has detached himself and it's unlikely that he would wait so long for anyone. It's unlikely that he would be yearning in any desire, so to hope that he would still be clinging on to life... holding his every breath would be our foolishness, Daruk..."

"Mother, but it's also not possible that *swami* can go away just like that."

"He had sought permission when he left from Dwarika. All he has to now do is to sit in meditation and transport his life into *Brahm*. It's that simple for him. What makes you think Daruk that he would prolong his suffering only to wait for us? He must be impatient to join the Almighty...."

Then after a moment, slightly dejected, she added, "That's why he deserted me and came away.... When taking the nuptials, holding my hand he had said... '*Naati Charami*'... until death do us apart, so what happened to that promise? He walked all alone towards salvation, leaving me here to miss him and mourn for him. Why did he do this, Daruk...? Wouldn't I have walked the path of salvation with him?"

"Mother, why do you agonise so much...? Don't we know that he will not go anywhere unless he fulfils all his responsibilities? The rising doubts in your heart are an indication that you are destined to meet him. He's not so selfish that he would go away without clearing your cobwebs. He will resolve all your conflicts... then liberate himself... trust me mother and let's speed up our steps. This blood trail is going to lead us to our destination."

"That's true, Daruk. You have assessed him even better than me. You are right. My outrage is a proof that he is perhaps waiting for my queries. If he had gone into meditation by now, he would have cleared my every doubt and suspicion. The fact that these doubts reoccur is a proof that he has to go through the exercise of calming me. Maybe at this moment he is anxious to meet me as well.... Let's rush Daruk... I can't wait to bridge the distance between my *swami* and me...."

There was a spring in Rukmini's feet. It was as if she had inhaled Krishna's fragrance in her surrounding and now didn't need to follow the blood drops to reach her goal. She moved instinctively in the direction of Trivenisangam.

She could hear her Lord calling out to her and she sent a message to him through the passing breeze, "Wait for me, my Lord... I'm not too far away... just a few moments more.... Please don't be in a hurry, my Lord."

A little distance away, on the high tide of river Kapila, Krishna was haunted by a tear-filled image telling him, "There's so much still to ask you, my Lord... so much to express.... It feels as if we have hardly communicated with each other in our long association.... Now when time beckons and you depart for your journey, it makes me realise that I have so much to discover... so much to experience... and share.... There is so much to complete in our communication.... Please wait for me, my Lord...."

Krishna opened his eyes. Draupadi watched his intriguing expression and asked, "Who else is to come, *sakha*? Are you still expecting someone?"

"*Sakhi*, this isn't waiting, it is suffering. Somebody in agony is bleeding my heart and it's so intense that I cannot be free unless I relieve this person of her anguish."

"Who is it, *sakha*...? Let's face it, all of us are equally anguished about your departure. We are so dependent on you that it's impossible to visualise our life without you.... You've been a part of our happiness and sorrow and we will be tormented without you.... But someone is deeply causing you pain at this moment.... So who is this who chains your soul and obstructs your flight...?"

"Who can it be *sakhi* besides my *ardhangini*? She is restless to meet me. When I left Dwarika and she bade me farewell, it wasn't a wholehearted goodbye. Her eyes pleaded me not to go and she chains me even now. Her image comes to my mind again and again. Her imploring eyes… her outstretched arms… her glittering lips and her furrowed, trembling eyebrows…. The image that comes to my mind isn't at peace too…"

"When we visited Dwarika…" Draupadi said softly.

"You visited Dwarika…? Then why didn't Rukmini come along with the two of you? Didn't Satyabhama insist on accompanying you as well…?"

"There was no time for all that, *sakha*. Only I know how I have held on to my breath to reach here."

"She will come, Draupadi… Rukmini is a very intelligent woman. She understands that if she isn't able to relieve me off her bondages, I cannot depart peacefully and will therefore certainly visit me. It's important that she liberates herself… and liberates me… she will come…"

◆

[96]

Rukmini was very close to Trivenisangam. She could spot Draupadi seated at Krishna's feet and beside her Jara, hands folded, dumbstruck. He couldn't get over the magnificence of Krishna who knew everything but went through the motions like he didn't.... Jara felt blessed to have witnessed the Lord in his four-armed transcendental *avatar* and speculated if the people assembled here were aware that they were amidst a divine soul....

Jara was still in the process of comprehending the outpouring of Draupadi and Arjuna, when Rukmini arrived breathless. She threw herself at Krishna's feet, her face soaked in perspiration and tormented, exactly the way Krishna had described her. Her eyes were imploring as if determined to prevent Krishna from going anywhere.... It was evident that she wasn't ready to break her chains binding him as yet.... Her expression looked as if she was going to burst into tears any minute.... Her face full of sorrow and arms outstretched... her lips quivered... and eyebrows trembled, she was unable to contain herself....

She kneeled and bowed her head before Krishna. Soaked in sweat her *sindoor* (vermillion powder) on the head had smeared all over... so had her powder *bindi* on the forehead. As she bent her head over Krishna's feet, the red powder mingled with the blood oozing out of Krishna's foot colouring her forehead into a flaming red.

"What's all this... my Lord... why must it happen? Is this exercise necessary...?"

"My beloved, I told you when I left Dwarika that our time to be together has ended. You bade me farewell but not wholeheartedly.

Something… somewhere prevented you from letting me go and that's why I've had to wait for you here today…. You had to travel this long journey to meet me. Now grant me your leave." Krishna smiled at her indulgently; he signalled her to come close. Rukmini drew closer. Then very affectionately Krishna placed his hand on her cheek.

"Wipe away your tears, beloved… you are a *Kshatriya* woman…. If you weep while bidding farewell to your consort, you shame the royalties. To be courageous is part of your *Kshatriya dharma*."

"That's when the husband leaves for war and this is no war," stated Rukmini.

"This is a war too, my dear… a war between life and death…. This body is making excuses to not depart while the heaven pulls me to bliss, it beckons to my soul…. Unless you are willing to grant me leave, how will I be able to embark on this journey?"

"*Prabhu*, when the husband leaves for war, there is hope that he will return soon and the wife would have the opportunity of welcoming her victorious hero, but in this case…" Rukmini felt a lump in her throat and she could not complete her sentence.

✦

[97]

The sun was gradually proceeding towards the west. As it did so, the bright rays turned subdued and the sun got ready to set. The shadows of everyone seated beneath the tree had extended considerably and imbued with a sense of doom.

It seemed as if history had decided to imprint them in the sands of time. And the orange sun, as if aware, quietly travelled its path casting a cursory glance....

The water in the rivers appeared to be turning pale yellow.

The sun was slowly creeping into the *peepal* branches... its rays less scathing and the golden light more enjoyable now....

Krishna cast a fleeting glance on the setting sun. It was time for his life to set as well.... He let out a deep sigh and then continued his conversation with Rukmini.

✦

[98]

"You are so scholarly, you understand *shastras*, you are knowledgeable about the cycle of life and death… you are aware that the body has to perish… besides our bonding was of two souls."

"Was…? What do you mean by 'was' *Prabhu*? Has our relationship ended?"

"At some point, you have to let go off all relationships with the body…. It's time to complete all the rites…. That's why we practise *pitrutarpan*…. our offerings for our dead parents. These are exercises to free the souls from their bodies…. The Krishna all of you know is just a body…. When my soul travels out of my body, I will transform into a piece of wood and a pile of ash…. The image you love today is attractive only as long as it breathes. When the body decomposes, this beautiful face will become grim and then all of you, who love me so dearly, will not love me any longer. That's why, my beloved, religion emphasises on the importance of *agnisanskar* (burial) in human life. Everything grim and impure is destroyed in fire…. The flames absorb all debris, all negative vibrations and purify them with the chanting of '*swaha*'…. After the offering, everything is purified, be it gold or human conscience."

✦

[99]

Looking into Rukmini's eyes, Krishna was reminded of the many beautiful evenings they spent together.

On that day too, Rukmini was staring at him unblinkingly, her eyes full of trust and affection...

Krishna was reminiscent of many passionate times spent with her. He recalled the times she had pampered and spoiled him with love.... He valued her compassion and had the highest regard for her wisdom and maturity....

He had lived his marital life with her to the fullest. He recreated those joyous moments before his eyes again.... Eyes closed, he visualised her gloriously illuminated palace that basked in the sparkling lights....

The sunrays bounced on the fluctuating waves of the three rivers.... In a strange way, the golden lights on the water were similar to the twinkling lights inside Rukmini's palace.

◆

[100]

"But my Lord, why is it that in all these years, I failed to understand you completely? Despite so much time spent together and so many intellectual discussions, why was I never able to reach out to your soul...? Could it be that during all our meetings, you remained divided in compartments...? Every time I held you in my arms, I sensed your mind elsewhere.... You were always clouded in problems and sufferings of people.... In all the time we spent together in so many years, we were never alone, my Lord. There was someone amidst us, even in our most intimate moments...Some invisible force that I could not see, didn't know, never touched but sensed all the time. The truth is that you could never be entirely mine and always visited me accompanied by someone. I'm not certain if it was the same person every time or perhaps different, but there was always someone for sure. You knew this all along and so did I..."

Krishna began laughing, "Women are so intuitive. Men can never be as perceptive even if they want to. They say it's difficult to read a woman's mind because she fiercely guards her secrets.... Today I discover that her heart is more transparent than water and one can spot the tiniest pebble settled beneath. My beloved, you don't need to ever express your pain or rage to me in words, for I can always read it in your eyes, your touch... I always have..."

"So why didn't you do anything about it...? Why didn't you ever give me the time I craved from you? In all earnestness, what did I desire out of you? Did I desire this title of the empress, this throne, these beautiful apparels, ornaments or a glorious palace...? Wouldn't I have possessed all this had I married *raja* Shishupal as well...? I had not penned you a love letter for all this…! If I dared to drop inhibitions and hold a torch to the most magnificent man of the Aryan race, it's because I desired to live my life with you…" explained Rukmini.

"Then why this regret, this repentance now…? You have lived your life with me, have become a part of me, and becoming a part of me is submitting yourself. I regret not spending sufficient time with all my loved ones. But then my time has never belonged to me. I'm duty bound to anyone who needs me at any time. That's the purpose of my existence and you surely know that, don't you? My beloved, the truth is that you don't love me for this or that reason. You just love me and transmit your infinite love to me eternally. When love is focused on one individual, it becomes restricted like the water surrounded by a dam. A love like this turns suffocating and draining. It's arrogant to think that someone can only belong to you and you to him, and arrogance you know has nothing to do with love," elaborated Krishna.

"But my Lord, is it not natural for a married woman to desire to spend time with her husband alone, is that asking for too much? I didn't expect you to spend every night at my palace; I didn't expect you to bring me flowers, new garments or gifts every day… but to expect that whenever you visit me, you leave aside all your worries, responsibilities and questions outside my doorstep, the way you drop your crown before entering my chamber is not expecting too much, my Lord…!" pleaded Rukmini.

Krishna felt heart wrenched looking at Rukmini's tear-filled eyes. He thought to himself all women asked for so little…. All they wanted was love. Boundless, undivided, eternal, infinite love…

The truth is, it's very simple to make women happy. They have very little expectations and very few demands. Still, men fail to comprehend their feelings because of which women constantly feel inadequate and incomplete. Somehow, they fail to be at peace even after finding their life partner. It's because the husbands never completely submit themselves to their wives….

Then looking at Rukmini, Krishna stated, "You talk about bonding, my beloved, but marriage is more than a bonding, it's a union. My anxieties, my responsibilities, my preoccupations and my concerns are all a part of me, so how can you expect me to leave them outside your doorstep every time I visit you…? The truth is I'm wholesome because

I contain the anguish and the anxieties of so many around me. If I discard all these, I would not be myself, I would be inadequate, won't I be, *Devi*...? When two individuals are drawn by an invisible force to something precious, they describe it as love. They fulfil their commitments to each other and express themselves freely. It's because they are independent and devoid of fear. That's why we say that two seeds can never be united because they are closed, while flowers can, because they bloom and are inclined to attachment..."

✦

[101]

While Rukmini and Krishna were engrossed in this intimate conversation, Daruk after running helter-skelter managed to obtain *ghabajaryu* (medicine plant). He crushed the leaves on a rock and made a paste out of it. He was about to pull out the arrow out of Krishna's foot and apply the ointment when Krishna stopped him, "Let it be, my friend, all this is futile now.... Let the arrow remain where it is.... It's only as long as the arrow pierces my foot that I'm able to prolong my breath.... Freedom from pain will be freedom from this life.... No ointment can cure my wounds any more, my dear..."

"But, my Lord..." Daruk tried to say something.

"I'm grateful to you for bringing *maharani* Rukmini to me. Had you not escorted her all the way, there's a possibility that I wouldn't be able to breathe my last peacefully.... Now, I will able to leave freely and it's because you have aided her journey.... You have all your life driven my chariot and I'm grateful to you for that..." Krishna folded his hands.

"I'm grateful to you, my Lord, for giving me the opportunity of serving you. It has been my privilege."

"You are a clean-hearted, pure person. You have been by my side till my last moment, served me faithfully; you have given me everything I expected from you.... You are at liberty now Daruk to find your own path..."

"My path is with you, my Lord... where do I go without you?" Daruk was weeping uncontrollably.

Krishna got up with great difficulty, placed his hand on Daruk's head and said, "*Sarve Janah Sukhina Bhavantu Sarve Santu Niramayah*.... That all of you remain happy and in good health.... May you live long, Daruk, may all your wishes come true and may God be with you... *Tathastu*..."

✦

[102]

Rukmini silently participated in the conversation between her husband and Daruk. Arjuna and Draupadi sat frozen like statues. Everyone was deep down praying for Krishna's relief. Then suddenly, Rukmini revived her dialogue, "*Prabhu*, is it possible that salvation is self-centred…? I may not be able to prevent your freedom, but have you thought over it that in your quest of liberation, when you let go off my hand, you do me injustice…?"

"Beloved, one has to travel alone on the path of salvation. We have been entwined ever since the *hastmedap* (marriage), so where does the question of letting go off your hand arise…?"

"These are all intellectual arguments, *Prabhu*, and love has nothing to do with knowledge. Love isn't so simple that it can be expressed in words. It's an intimate experience and you cannot take away my experience from me. My quest, my loneliness, my yearnings were my own and you were never a part of that, were you?"

It was as if the sun was eavesdropping their conversation and deliberately moved at a snail pace…. The sun knew that when it was time for the Lord to exit, the earth would plunge into an eternal darkness. It would be the most poignant exit from the Universe. The sun was aware that it would be the most ominous moment to follow and deliberately delayed its departure.

Krishna sighed, "That's true, all of us are eventually alone and we have to carry our baggage by ourselves. But, my beloved, there's a vast difference between being alone and being lonely. We often mistake one for the other and this influences our interpretations as well. Being alone is being introspective and productive and it has positive outcome. Being lonely, on the other hand, results in one feeling dejected, distressed and demoralised...! It has negative, pessimistic interpretation.... My dear, loneliness is a part of nature and nobody is free from it. Everyone comes to this world and has to leave alone..." Krishna was speaking in a trance.

"Then why does everyone get married?" asked Rukmini, "Why do we raise a family, why do we build relationships with siblings, relatives and friends...?"

"Actually, loneliness is a part of human life; only we don't accept this or rather don't want to accept. We like remaining strangers to ourselves. Those who come to terms with it, slowly begin to enjoy it. They relish these moments and are at peace with themselves. It's possible to be within yourself and remain in a crowd.... It's only when you come to terms with being alone, that you emerge complete and it is irrelevant that you are divided amongst many...."

"What about love...? It's not possible for women to seek love from various sources. Happiness for women usually comes from just once source, her man."

Then looking at Draupadi seated beside her, she added, "Everyone is not as special as Draupadi... I'm an ordinary woman...! I love just one man and expect him to fulfil all my desires. All I wanted was a regular life of happiness like an ordinary woman, that's all.."

✦

[103]

Krishna took a whiff of the air and recalled his fragrant moments with Rukmini.... Those innumerable moments when Rukmini got upset and sulked with him.... He recalled how he would pamper and indulge her until she was pacified. Today, Rukmini had actually behaved like an ordinary woman. It's strange that somebody as brilliant, as scholarly and knowledgeable as Rukmini could react in this manner.... Probably all women were identical when it came to matters of heart, irrespective of how intelligent or superior they might be.... Krishna seemed to agree with the theory at this moment...

✦

[104]

Krishna consoled Rukmini and said, "Beloved, you know very well that you are not ordinary and can never be. How can Krishna's better half be ordinary? I don't say this out of pride. When I narrated the *Gita* to Parth and said, 'Among the elephants I'm Airavat, among trees I'm *peepal*, among the cows I'm Kamdhenu, among the rivers I'm Ganga… and among the women I'm Rukmini', I meant it…. My beloved, you are supreme and therefore play a vital role in my intimate life. Love is not at the mercy of reasons. It survives on a spiritual halo. The more enlightened you are, the more your love expands. The more you spread your wings, the more you blossom and enrich as an individual…"

Krishna spoke with great difficulty now. He wiped his eyes and concentrated on his breathing which had slowed down considerably. His injured foot and loss of blood had turned him weak but that did not deter him from expressing himself, "Those in love and later in marriage always have high expectations of their attachments. Somehow they always feel love diminishing out of their marriage…. They feel love is not what it used to be. The fact is that love should bring awareness…. Different people have the capacity to make you feel complete in different ways. It's their presence that adds sparkle to your life. Love grants you the freedom to be yourself in happiness and sorrow. If you will depend for everything on that one person, how can you, my beloved, ever find freedom and happiness in your life…?"

He stopped to take a breath. "The time we got to spend with each other was the best time of our life. Our happiness was correlated and we relished many joyous moments. We have given a lot of sustenance and contentment to each other…. There's a possibility that you have submitted more to me than I have to you, but it has been a qualitative, a fruitful marital life.... It's better that you look at the positive side rather than repent and regret of all that you could have got from me or expected out of me..."

Rukmini wasn't the only one absorbing Krishna's words of wisdom. His sermon had cleared many doubts in Draupadi's heart as well. Watching Rukmini so serene and soulfully connected to her Lord, something resolved inside Draupadi. Suddenly all her anxieties abated. It was as if all her anguish had been cleansed in a watershed.

Rukmini was in a trance. Her Lord, her *swami* loved, respected, regarded her and felt concerned for her, what more could she want? He was right. Their moments spent together were extraordinary and eternal. For the first time, Rukmini viewed them in a different perspective. What she had so far regarded as futile moments now appeared full of mirth and melody. For the first time, there was a different glow on her face. It was the glow of a woman who had lived her marital life to the optimum. Unable to contain herself, she said...

"It would have been a big loss, my Lord, had I been deprived of this conversation with you today. I have in all earnestness tried to be an ideal wife. Yet somewhere deep down, something always ached.... Today, you have relieved me of that pain.... You have, with your gentle hands, cleared the clouds and filtered light. When I look back today, I realise that what I perceived as your rejection was in fact your effort to provide me space.... What I envisioned as your intrigue and mourned the recurring reserve, was your caution to safeguard me from hurt.... What I considered deprivation of time was your commitment to the wellbeing of others.... Every time I turned reflective, it was your way of bringing me closer to myself. How superior and special you are from the rest of the men who treat women as objects of desire.... You stand apart from the rest of them because only you seem to endorse what our *Vedas* profess in the seventh step of *saptapadi* (marriage vows) where a husband undertakes his wife as a friend. Please forgive me, my Lord, for misjudging your magnanimity and suffering unnecessarily...."

Krishna heard her out uninterruptedly. When she completed, he said, "The question is always the same but we need to view it from a different perspective. We get embroiled in expressions and lose intentions. In doing so we belittle our relationships.... The mind is the male side of a human being while the heart is the female side... and every time there is conflict, the mind reigns over the heart. It's only when heart rules the mind, we take compassionate decisions. Men are different from women in the way they think and act. They are meant to be different. It's in the interest of women that rather than compete with their counterparts, they concentrate on their virtues and blossom. The best way to resolve conflicts between mind and heart is to remain alert. If we can just experience emotions and only when need arises, carry them over to our mind, there's a possibility that we can reduce conflicts in marital life…

"…My beloved, I have loved you intensely… and have valued your submission…. It's my ardent wish that if I'm reborn, I would desire you as my life partner and will pray for that to happen…."

Rukmini sobbed bitterly and broke down. She was filled with remorse that after living with Krishna for so many years, she had failed to fully comprehend him. She regretted misreading him. A thoroughly remorseful Rukmini fell at Krishna's feet and sobbed uncontrollably.

Krishna's affectionate hand was caressing Rukmini's back, as if saying… "Get rid of all your anxieties and liberate me now…. Unless and until your heart sets me free from your attachments and your responsibilities, I cannot depart for my final journey…."

"My Lord, at this very moment, I return to you all that you have showered on me…"

Twadiyam Vastu Govind Tubhyamev Samarpyate ।

Rukmini declared while brushing away her tears. She raised her head to look at Krishna. His eyes were closed as if in a trance. Rukmini's heart missed a beat. She stretched her arm to touch his heart. His eyes still closed, Krishna pressed her hand against him with both his hands….

"There's still time, beloved…. It seems I will have to linger over this body for some more while… I will have to adhere to somebody still remembering me…. Even now I pierce someone's heart…. There are still some questions to be answered somewhere…. Those beautiful eyes who seem to look at me and say, 'Kaanha… will you really go…? Will you not think of me even today…?'"

"Radha…" Rukmini's heart missed a beat.

"Will she come…?" Draupadi seemed to ask herself.

✦

[105]

"*Ma*... why do you cry so much so much...?"

"I'm not crying..." Radha wiped her tears.

"Are you going to pretend with me as well...?" Shubhra held Radha by her face and looked into her eyes, "Don't I know you sufficiently... besides, is there anything about you I'm not familiar with...? I can see that you are hurting deeply.... Tell me *ma,* who is it that you remember so much...?"

"One remembers those one forgets and I haven't forgotten him. He is within me and has been around me all the time, all these years... I have sensed his presence eternally and if he hasn't left my side why must I remember him...."

"Where do you think he would be at this point of time?"

"How am I supposed to know? After he left from here he has never inquired after me...."

Then deciding not to discuss the topic, she attempted to rise from her seat but Shubhra caught her hand and prevented her.

"Just because somebody forgets us... is it possible for us to forget them as well?"

"Look Shyama, I don't wish to discuss this any further," Radha got up adding, "I have many household chores to complete."

"*Ma*, be careful that your soul does not forever wander in yearning... that will be tragic..."

Radha felt choked and could barely find her voice but attempted to answer Shubhra, "I don't understand why you advocate his case so strongly, you don't even know him…"

Shubhra's eyes resembled a fish floating in river Yamuna, mischievous and brimming with water, "Who said I don't know him…? I see him every day in your eyes. He is my namesake… well almost… whenever you call me Shyama instead of Shubhra, I feel like responding to you from Dwarika."

"What has all this got to do with Dwarika?" Radha avoided meeting Shubhra's gaze.

"Because he resides in Dwarika and everything associated with him moves in and around Dwarika."

Shubhra was determined to not let go off the topic today and Radha was determined to not engage in any further discussions, "I don't know all that… I've heard he is a King now, the Emperor of golden town Dwarika. I've heard he is very knowledgeable, ascetic and talks about righteousness and spirituality. But the one I loved resided here in Gokul… on the narrow streets… on the bank of river Yamuna… amidst the *kadamb* trees… in the milk pots of the milkmaids and in the eyes of mother Yashoda…"

"Mother… what if he just drops by… to meet you?"

"Crazy girl, those who go away, don't come back. If he wanted to return why would he go away in the first place? He is my time… he does not have a name or a shape."

Shubhra stared unblinkingly at Radha. Here was a woman who had lived her entire life by her principles. She was an ideal wife, ideal mother and had put in a lot of efforts to sustain all her roles. At every crossing of her life, she had faced challenges without compromises. She was a woman who had never looked back… only forward.

So what was it today that prevented this mature woman from progressing? She had kind of frozen at a turning point. Not just that, she recurrently looked back as if someone was calling out to her. Today, her eyes had the sparkle of a sixteen-year-old blossoming with all the seven colours of the rainbow.

"*Ma*… I'm asking you, what if he comes here to meet you."

"Then what... even I don't know how I would react... but one thing is certain, the gates of Gokul are so firmly clasped from all four sides that nobody can leave the place and once somebody goes out, he cannot return."

"But why should it be so? I've sensed your anxiety for him, witnessed the aching void without his presence in your life... I've watched how you have spent every moment of your life waiting for him."

"It's not necessary that those we wait for must visit us.... It's not necessary that we wait either.... We wait because he is not amidst us."

Radha's eyes had a remote look as if travelling far away... "You ask too many questions, my girl.... When relationships end, we complete our debts. It means it's time to free ourselves from attachments, from the give-and-take; it's time to unite with one's soul. I'm not sure if all my debts have been cleared, but I'm ready to return whatever is necessary to initiate the process. Unless I return all that he has showered on me, how do I relieve him? He has the right to demand and has done so for many lifetimes. I've never been able to refuse anything to him so far, and will not do so in future as well.... Besides whatever he asks for, in any case, belongs to him..."

"*Ma*, I want to ask something more," Shubhra was ready to trespass Radha's darkest secrets today.... She had decided to absorb all of Radha's anguish, sorrow and turn into her own.

Radha lost in her thoughts and engaged in an inner dialogue, was well acquainted with Shubhra's stubborn nature. Unknowingly Radha sought relief in Shubhra's excessive interrogation because in a strange way it offered her insights into her consuming relationship with her Lord.

There were so many fragile memories Radha feared to confront, but Shubhra had the knack to draw those awkward moments out of her. His name and memories involving him were locked in a corner of Radha's heart but Shubhra dared to open the floodgates, spread light as if gently coercing Radha to release the repressed moments...

Radha secretly relished the process of cross-examination because in responding to Shubhra's curiosity, she was somewhere articulating her own feelings to herself. The exercise was so pure, honest and so special....

It was almost as if Shubhra transformed into an extension of herself.

Time had over the years compartmentalised Radha's heart into two specific roles. The first, where she was Ayan's wife, Aryak's mother, Gokul's milkmaid Radha… the second, a woman mesmerised and obsessed with Krishna and living her life devoted and submitted to her beloved…. The purpose of her existence was Krishna… he ran in her veins… resided in her eyes, heart and mind… and yet Ayan's wife had never failed in her moral or societal duties.

She had served the husband she was wedded to with her body, soul and mind. She had never let him down as a consort… but at the same time, her passion for her beloved had never wavered in all these years.

"*Ma*, how were you able to lead this dual life in one lifetime…?"

"This body turned lifeless when he left Gokul…. Since that moment, I have merely existed… I'm merely bidding my time… waiting… waiting for that moment when I will be liberated."

Shubhra took Radha's hand into her own and full of compassion asked, "*Ma*… have you never desired to visit Dwarika, don't you want to go and see what he does…? How can you not be curious to know how he lives and with whom? Who are the people he is intimate with, who resides closest to his heart…? Who empathises with him? Who is by his side in his moment of sorrow?"

"No…" Radha replied sternly.

"Why?" Shubhra probed.

"Because I know that once I find an answer to these, I will not be able to return from Dwarika. It's not my temperament to leave my position and settle elsewhere. And it's not his nature to accept me anywhere, except in my rightful position…"

"But mother… what about this yearning… this vacuum… this torment… these anguished moments of waiting… what do you accomplish from all this?"

"Happiness… one has to seek happiness in whatever destiny has in store for you. It's our illusion that we can transpire situations according to our desire…. That's far from truth…. We were destined to meet… our parting was pre-determined too. Every moment is created because it's destined to pass… in trying to cling on to these moments we cause ourselves needless anguish. It wasn't in my capacity to prevent him when he left.... This heartache or what you describe as loneliness is for my own wellbeing.... It's an indicator of his unbroken bonding with me. The reason I linger in his memories is because he hasn't erased me from his heart.... Feelings are like fire, if you don't ignite the flames, they extinguish gradually.... I could feel it in my heart that he has been igniting the flames every moment and that's why the fire burns within me constantly...."

"And didn't father ever question you about all this?"

"He is aware that his wife belongs solely to him. He acknowledges that I've been faithful and served him wholeheartedly. He accepts that I've lived my entire life confined within the four walls of my home. He has little curiosity for the 'other woman' residing in the body of his wife. The 'other woman' lives on her own terms without any bindings and loves somebody else..."

"Surely it's not that simple for a man to accept that..."

"Why just one man, it's equally tough on both these men to accept reality. It's not easy to love 'another man's wife' so intensely, or for that matter, 'another man' to love your wife so passionately.... But then love has never been simplistic. It comes with layers of pain, anguish, craving and many other familiar emotions.

"Yes, but love is also the root cause of all happiness..."

Radha was unable to answer Shubhra, for her entire body was captured in a melody. She felt as if the sound of the flute was emanating from every fibre of her being. She could sense Kaanha's lips smothering her and her body floating in the melody....

Suddenly all the mirthful moments spent with Kaanha clustered in her mind and danced around her.... Who better than her to comprehend that love was the root cause of all happiness... in fact she still was!

"Yes, it's true and I can say out of experience that I'm happy because I'm in love... I know that wherever he is, he remembers me and loves me. This thought is more blissful, more romantic than me having to live with him..." whispered Radha.

"If you are that blissful then what have I been observing these past few days...? Clearly some worries have been clouding you... some sorrow has been bleeding your heart because of which you have been so preoccupied and so withdrawn."

"It's because I have to liberate someone and I will not be able to do so unless I liberate myself. How can I become the cause of his suffering when I know I'm the joy of his life, his desire, his music and his melody…? Before embarking on this journey, he seeks my leave and I grant him that…. My duty now is to reassure him and grant him all that he expects from me today…"

✦

[106]

Draupadi glanced at Krishna resting with his eyes closed. His face depicted fleeting emotions as if engaged in an arresting conversation with someone. One moment smiling, another moment intense, there were myriad expressions on his face....

Rukmini, Daruk, Arjuna, Draupadi and Jara sat surrounding Krishna.

Despite so many people around him, Krishna was all alone and engrossed in an inner dialogue.

His eyes closed, Krishna saw before him a cheerful girl, sharp featured, fair as moonlight with raven black hair and dancing eyebrows. She had the bounce of river Yamuna and eyes as innocent as a deer. Looking at Krishna innocently, she seemed to ask...

"So what binds you now...? Why don't you go wherever you have to...?"

"It's only you that my soul yearns to meet now.... Unless you visit me, my soul will remain trapped in my body and long for you."

"This waiting is futile, for I will not come..."

"That's what you always said but when I played the flute you were always drawn by the rendition and came running to me, you remember that, don't you?"

"No, I don't remember anything..." she responded partly angry and partly embarrassed.

"Please come.... How will I leave without your consent?" Krishna was internally pleading to Radhike.

✦

[107]

The setting sun had turned flaming orange. Far away where the three rivers entwined into the ocean, the sun was ready to set. The river had turned saffron as if sprinkled with *kesuda* flowers. The sky was draped in an orange stole, resembling a saint, as if bidding goodbye to its ascetic ways and also to Lord Surya.

The orange rays falling on Krishna's face lent an aura.

Myriad colours of the evening had spread in all the four directions.

Even the *peepal* leaves in the fading sunlight appeared orange.

And Krishna with his eyes closed, was in a trance. In the horizon of his heart, he was lost in a heart-to-heart conversation with Radha…

✦

[108]

"How can I come to visit you, Kaanha? We have travelled different paths... from the day you left Gokul we have travelled in opposite directions. Now even if I desire to meet you, I would have to first traverse my mileage and then your mileage of the journey. The distance has become too long, Kaanha."

"It's long distance for those who are disconnected. We always remained connected holding hands, no matter how far we travelled from each other. We have never let go off our hands. Our directions may have been different but our conditions remained identical."

"Kaanha... you've always been very clever. You've always trapped me in your words and fooled me. You did so when you departed and now when you beckon me it's your word play again. But just remember, I'm not that little girl any longer to come into your smooth talk."

"For me you will always be that, Radha. When I departed from Gokul, it was with an image in my eyes. That image hasn't altered in all these years. I still think of you as the fighting, sulking, forever crazy about me Radha..."

"Why not... because you always had your way and made me dance to your tunes..."

"Alright, then you make me dance to your tune now..." Krishna had a mischievous smile on his face. He seemed to enjoy teasing her as much now as he did years ago.

"There is magic in your fingers Kaanha. The entire Aryan race dances to your tune..." Radha shrugged her shoulders like old times.

Krishna burst out laughing with his eyes closed...

"After all these years my fingers are fragrant with memories of your touch, Radhike.... Sometimes when the tip of my finger touches my nose I get a whiff of your body...."

"What about your innumerable queens...? Sixteen thousand one hundred and eight..."

"They are my wives, my *ardhangini* but you are my soul, my truth, my identity, my desire and my purpose of existence. Out of the sixteen thousand one hundred and eight queens, none is attached to my name, Radhike, except you. The Universe remembers us as 'Radha Krishna'. Your name is taken before mine..."

"Go away... these are empty talks.... Have you in all these years ever thought of me... remembered me... beckoned me...?"

"How could I call you, Radha, when you were always beside me every moment? Had I passed a single moment without you, I would have certainly called out... for I'm incomplete without you...."

"That's why you left me and went away?" suddenly Radha's eyes filled with tears.

Unknowingly Krishna stretched his hand to wipe away Radha's tears and then withdrew his hand remembering that Radha was not physically present with him.

In his memories, however, she was so vivid that he sensed her in everything around him.

"Yes.... Precisely for that reason...! Had I stayed with you, I would have been absorbed in your affection... I would have made no efforts to seek or accomplish anything outside.... All my activities would have been restricted with and around you, Radha."

"And it didn't concern you what happened to me in all these years? You betrayed me... left me... never to return back...."

"But where was I able to go away from you? Had I gone away, I would have definitely returned. I surrendered my being to you, Radhike. Even today, at this very moment I'm looking for that Krishna I left behind in Gokul... I have to take him back with me, Radhike, so please return that old Krishna to me...."

"But he isn't yours any more, he is mine. Didn't you just admit that you had left him behind in Gokul... I have preserved him, treasured him all these years and now just because you ask for him, should I return him to you? Go away... everything cannot always be on your terms, Kaanha..."

"My dear Radhike.... That's the only thing I ask of you," Krishna was pleading like a child to her. It was a replay of their childhood when young Radha would lure him with butter from distance and Krishna would run, determined to snatch the earthen pot from her hands.

"That's all I have now with me and if I give you away that, I have nothing to call my own," Radha implored him, feeling even more helpless than Krishna. Radha stubbornly held on to her memories of him like a child holds on to her favourite toy.

Now Krishna turned serious and began to make Radha see reason, "It's time for both of us to complete our circles. So far we have resided in a single circle and lived for each other. The Cosmos celebrated me as the complete man but you were the complete woman who contributed in making me so. It's difficult to determine my identity without you. Everything feminine, fragile and aesthetic within me is you, Radha. Everything that is pure, proper, in-depth and stable is all you. My entire structure survives on the foundation of your virtues residing in my heart. You are the moving force, the purpose of my existence. You are my mortal carnation, my inspiration to survive Nature. It's you who has preserved me as the untouched, eternal and pristine image for mankind."

"Kaanha, you have become a big man now, haven't you? That's why you deliver these profound lectures to me. I don't understand your complex thought process... I only understand matters of the heart."

"You are so right, Radha. I got so absorbed in the profound political matters that I have forgotten the pastoral paradise of Vrindavan.... But with your arrival, the fragrance returns as well. It feels as if I'm seated at the Yamuna river bank, holding your hand... the moonlight is creeping through the *kadamb* trees and spreading its light on you... and I'm watching this beautiful imagery..."

"Kaanha, come with me, let me take you away from all this intrigue back to Brajbhumi. Let's get lost once again in the beauty of that small village where hearts are as pure as the raindrops… let's return to the familiar sound of the mooing cows… to the fresh butter served at the hands of mother Yashoda. Come, come back with me, Kaanha…"

"Radhike, how can I come…? It's too late now…!"

"It's not…. Everyone is still waiting for you eagerly…. Everything is still the same there… we will play, dance and sing like old times… you can rob butter and get scolded… you can tease me and I will sulk… then you cajole me like you always did. We will celebrate festivities together with the other cowherds… you may take your cows for grazing… you are free to break as many milk pots as you desire and let the milkmaids complain to their heart's content to mother Yashoda…. Every moment is still alive and unchanged in Gokul…. Let's go back to it, Kaanha."

"Radhike, it's my destiny that I cannot return to the direction I have once departed from. I'm destined to begin from one root and spread like *dhaara* (stream)… but you are *radha*. You are like foliage. It's your nature to absorb everything from the Universe and return to the roots. You are fortunate… you bring colour to everyone's repressed yearnings…"

✦

[109]

Images conjured in Krishna's mind and got erased subsequently.... He recalled Gokul drenched in torrential rains... dewdrops shining on *kadamb* leaves... full blown red and white lotuses floating on the Yamuna water held by the large, miraculously dry leaves.... The peacock dance... the cow bells and their painted horns... the sound of butter churning in every courtyard... the eternally waiting eyes of mother Yashoda... her bright red *bindi* on the forehead resembling the blazing sun... his favourite peacock feather... the familiar loft in the courtyard where he was frequently tied up as punishment by his mother... everything today appeared so desolate... so forlorn....

The images formed and vanished quite like the expression on Krishna's face.

Draupadi and Rukmini scrutinised Krishna's changing expressions and understood. It was as if Krishna was lost in the joyous memories of Brajbhumi and relishing every moment. Little Krishna was harassing his mother and running helter-skelter. Now breaking the earthen pot of Radha and hiding on to the *kadamb* tree... now robbing butter from the milkmaids and polishing it off with all his friends... and now taking shelter with Sudama atop a tree and shivering in the rain...

◆

[110]

"Kaanha, tell me one thing."

"Ask me, my love."

"Would you say you were always truthful or did you also falter sometimes, with yourself and with others?"

"I have never cheated but this much I will admit that I haven't lived my life the way I would have wanted to. I was forever driven by my duty, my *karma*, while my heart desired something else. I have caused a lot of anguish to a lot of people... at times they must have even felt that I did them injustice... but whatever I did was never for vested interests."

"Do you have any idea how innocent, affectionate and uncomplicated you were...? All this politics, this abundant knowledge, your profound sermons of debit and credit, how did you get trapped in this maze of *karma*...?" questioned Radha.

"I have often wondered about this myself.... In those stressful moments during Kurukshetra, I would remember you in the midst of clanging weapons, trumpeting elephants, neighing horses and wrenching wails.... Every time I blew the conch it revived memories of my flute.... It happened so many times and yet coming back to you was not possible for me."

"I know," whispered Radha.

"You know, how...?" asked Krishna.

"If it was possible, you would have definitely returned. You didn't because the circumstances were not in your control. You were helpless.

If you could, there was no power in the Universe that would have prevented you from returning to me, Kaanha."

"But why didn't you ever come to visit me, Radhike? Didn't you ever want to find out how I was, whether I was happy?"

"You left Gokul and one amongst us had to remain here. You had your duty to adhere to and I had mine. How could we ever be together, Kaanha?"

"Radha, I don't know if you will believe me but there were so many times, I just longed to throw away everything and rush back to Gokul. I yearned to drop all my political and social responsibilities, my throne and all the complexities surrounding the crown and escape with you... I wanted only to be by your side... spend quiet moments... and then come back."

"I believe you, Kaanha, because on many occasions, when I was sitting all by myself at the river bank I have sensed you beside me, drawing patterns with your stick in the water. I have sensed someone beside me breathing heavily, expressing his anguish to me in silence. I trust you Kaanha that invisible one had to be you."

"Where else could I have gone, Radha? Whenever I felt myself wavering from truth, from conviction, I thought of you... your beautiful, vivacious eyes prevented me from getting disconnected with life.... I have accomplished all my responsibilities, completed all my duties on the strength of these two doe-like eyes." Then a bit hesitantly Krishna changed the topic.

"Radhike, is all well with you... your husband... your children... are you happy?"

"Kaanha, I don't know why but I feel I have been blessed to be happy... I have the knack of finding happiness at all times... under all circumstances."

✦

[111]

The sun was ready to set. The cold breeze coming from the river was blowing furiously. The sky had turned a beautiful orange and looked radiant as a flame was spreading its rays far away into the horizon. It had steadied itself in the middle of the sky… not far away from the river and not too close to the clouds.

"Radha, I feel relieved to know that you are happy," Krishna sensed an unfamiliar expression in Radha's eyes. He had always been able to read her face but today he sensed something intriguing that Krishna couldn't decipher and which made him restless.

"Don't go away so pained, Radhike… I'm truly concerned about your happiness."

"My happiness revolves around you, Kaanha. My husband and my son are my duties, not my joy. The memory of the time I spent with you is in the true sense my definition of love. You are the only one who knows my heart and the only other person is Shyama…"

"Shyama…?"

"Do I sense envy in your voice? Let me add that Shyama is my son Aryak's wife…"

"If anyone knows you so intimately, I'm bound to feel threatened, Radha… for nobody should reside in your heart except me…"

"How can you say this…? Everyone calls you God… how can you react like an ordinary mortal?"

"You are the only one, Radhike, with whom I'm myself, natural and ordinary. The layers wither away and gradually I revert to my old self. You are entitled to threaten me, scold me and fight with me. There's nobody besides you who can arouse all these emotions within me. I'm dependent on you, so don't ever take me out of your heart, Radha... even when I'm no more."

The tears Radha had been controlling for a long time, burst like a dam. She felt choked but disguised her tears into rage and said, "You've been meandering all this while, but now finally you come to the point.... So please tell me, where are you going?"

"Returning to where I came from... where else?"

"Where did you come from, from Gokul, right? Come on, let's return there. I have come to take you."

✦

[112]

Krishna roared with laughter. His eyes still shut and all his friends still around him. Draupadi, Arjuna, Rukmini or Daruk had never heard Krishna rock with laughter. Innocent as a child, it was the laughter of a person soaked in the joys of life. Everyone was amazed. Everyone understood who he was engaged in a dialogue with. Draupadi and Rukmini especially couldn't stop marvelling at Radha's good fortune. They were astonished that the Krishna they held in such high esteem should drop his inhibitions and laugh thus. This could only happen with his childhood sweetheart Radha.

✦

[113]

"So tell me, where have you come from, Kaanha?"

Krishna's voice resounded like the sound emanating from the five ingredient conch. Draupadi, Rukmini, Daruk, Arjuna and Jara got engrossed in the divine echo. Arjuna was reminded of his oratory on the Kurukshetra battleground. His eyes still closed, Krishna was saying…

"I don't come from the North.

…I don't come from the West.

…I have neither come from the East.

…Nor have I come from the South.

…I don't hail from the top.

…Nor do I emerge from below.

…I don't come from any direction.

…Actually, I don't come at all. I was always there and will continue to be there."

"Just stop it. I don't want to hear all this," Radha closed her ears.

"As you wish… but much before I arrived in Gokul, much before I arrived in the *karavaasa* (jail) in Mathura, before the stormy night on the eighth day of the Shravan month, even before I invaded into the womb of mother Devaki, wherever I was, I will have to return now…."

"So go… who's preventing you or like always, you will first tease me, trouble me, torment me and reduce me to tears before departing?" Her eyes brimmed with tears, "What joy do you find in frequently loving me and going away... you make me so angry that I want to chain you to this *peepal* tree..." Radha expressed.

"Haven't you chained me sufficiently, Radhike? How long do you want to bind me... free me, Radha so that I can leave in peace."

"Please leave... I'm not going to prevent you any longer."

"Do you promise me?"

"Kaanha... I'm warning you not to provoke me any more."

"I like to provoke you because you become all the more adorable when you are angry," teased Krishna.

"Adorable? That is why you leave me, don't you?"

"That's true. I leave you for that precise reason. If you continue to love me so intensely, I will not be able to go anywhere.... Do you have any idea how many eons I will have to remain chained to these human bondages?"

A perplexed Radha continued to stare at him wide eyed.

"I don't understand what you say..." she stated finally.

"Never mind..." Krishna said in resignation.

"Kaanha, I often don't understand what you speak...."

"Where do I fully understand what I speak, Radha...? That's why it's imperative for me to take this journey.... Do I have your leave now?"

"Please leave and don't ever come back," Radha turned her back on Krishna. In his mind, Krishna rose and stood beside her.

"Say it again..." Krishna spoke incoherently resting beneath the *peepal* tree.

"Yes... yes... go away and don't ever come back...."

Krishna's eyes brimmed with tears. He looked sorrowfully towards Radha standing with her back to him. Though his eyes were closed, he could clearly visualise Radha's torso. He felt as if he was standing just beside her and touching her. He raised his arm and thought of placing it on Radha's shoulder. Then for reasons best known to him, stood there for a few moments....

With his eyes closed, he was able to recreate the imagery before his eyes.

He felt as if Radha was far away and his arm would not be able to reach out to her. He let his raised arm remain where it was and uttered:

"*Tathastu*...!"

He felt choked and tears streamed down his closed eyes.... The more he cried the fainter became Radha's image.

The visual of Radha standing with her back to him was slowly fading away.... Radha for a moment thought of turning around to look at Krishna. Her eyes streaming with tears she told Krishna, "Go Kaanha go... and don't ever come back... I return to you all that you showered on me... I relieve you of all your bindings with me, for binding you is not my temperament. I didn't hold you back even then, so why now? Go away Kaanha... I grant you my consent...."

Then turning to move, she walked as if determined to travel somewhere far away...

✦

[114]

Krishna opened his eyes.

Draupadi, Arjuna, Daruk, Rukmini and Jara were seated surrounding him.

There was a strange tranquillity in the surroundings. Far away the sun was preparing to depart from the sky. Between the sky and the river was a splash of orange colour.

Krishna took a deep breath and closed his eyes.

Somewhere inside him he was in the process of disconnecting something very precious and substantial and leaving it behind... very softly, almost imploringly, he managed to say...

"Now there are no bindings, no yearnings, no expectations and no debts. There are no questions, no responsibilities, no conflict and no waiting for anyone. I feel stronger than earth, lighter than air, brighter than light, purer than water and bigger than the sky. I have determined my path. I'm finally adequate to embark on my journey. I can sense the flood lights eager to lead me to my destination."

It felt as if numerous *pundits* were performing a combined *yajna* and their chorus chanting reverberated in the surrounding...

Mamaivasho Jeevloke Jeevbhootah Sanatanah ।
Manah Shasthanindriyani Prakrutisthani Karshte ॥

"When I'm no more, the surviving part of me will prevail amongst the five ingredients of Nature. The sixth will be the heart of human beings... anyone who pulls me to himself and gives me space in his heart...."

He was breathing very slowly and with great difficulty. There was a glow on his face, a tranquillity that was unusual. Far away the sun had set into the sea. It was as if a part of a flame had dived into the river and transformed the water into golden.

Sri Krishna folded his hands and took a deep breath.

Those surrounding him once again witnessed the divine soul getting ready for his final journey...

All around them, they could hear just one sound reverberating...

Nainam Chhindanti Shastrani Nainam Dahti Pavakah ।
Na Cha Enam Kledayantyapah Na Shoshyati Marutah ॥
Achchhedyoayamadahyoayamakledyoashosha Eva Cha ।
Nityah Sarvagatah Sthanurachaloayam Sanatana ॥
Jateya Hi Dhruvo Mrutyudhruva Janma Mrutsya Cha ।
Tasmadpariharyadrathen Twa Shochitumarhasi ॥
Avyaktadin Bhutani Vyaktmadhyani Bharatah ।
Avyaktnighnanyev Tatra Ka Parivdeyanah ॥

Weapons cannot pierce through this soul and fire cannot burn it. Water cannot drench it and the wind cannot dry it.

The soul is eternal and therefore cannot be damaged, burnt, drowned. It is ageless, timeless and therefore eternal.

The one who is born has to die and the one who dies has to be reborn, so it's futile to mourn for something so transitory.

The soul has no image, no attachment. It is disconnected from the cycle of life and death, unlike the body. It watches the body embroil in the maze of desire and hope, fully aware that it is all futile and transitory.

✦

[115]

Krishna opened his eyes for the last time and smiled.

Weary, he folded his hands in a silent prayer and took a deep breath....

Rukmini, Draupadi, Arjuna, fearing the end, instantly stepped closer, but Krishna raised his arm and stopped them.

Far away the sun dived into the blue sea and the sky tuned a pale purple....

A stong breeze blew in the direction carrying with it a wave of peacock feathers soaked in sandalwood that formed a carpet below Krishna's feet.

Then very slowly, the *peepal* tree below which Krishna was seated began to shiver and drop innumerable leaves until they had formed a throne around his seat.

The sky, the sea and the woods had bidden their farewell but there was still something missing...

A signature tune befitting the occasion....

That's when a young cowherd accompanied by his grazing cows passed by... the sound of the cow bells mingled with the mesmeric flute... the time and setting was perfect...

It was the time to exit...

◆